ECHOES OF SILENCE

ECHOES OF SILENCE

A NOVEL OF NAZI GERMANY

Patrick W. O'Bryon

Brantôme Press
CAMERON PARK, CALIFORNIA

Cover Design by G. S. Prendergast

Book Layout ©2013 BookDesignTemplates.com

Echoes of Silence/Patrick W. O'Bryon. -- 1st ed.

ISBN978-0-9910782-9-5

To my wife Dani
and in memory of my father

As all historians know, the past is a great darkness, and filled with echoes.

—Margaret Atwood, from *The Handmaid's Tale*

THE GERMAN REICH

November 1941

Not to Scale and Partial View

© Patrick W. O'Bryon

Kiel

Hamburg

Bremen

NETHERLANDS

Die Weser

Die Elbe

Hanover

❖ BERLIN

Magdeburg

Köln

Kassel

Der Rhein

BELGIUM

Leipzig

Koblenz

Dresden

LUX.

Frankfurt/Main

Der Main

Prague

OCCUPIED

Nürnberg

BOHEMIA & MORAVIA

FRANCE

Baden

Ulm

Die Donau

Basel

München

Mauthausen

Zürich

Bregenz

OSTMARK

SWITZERLAND

Geneva

FASCIST ITALY

FOREWORD

The *Corridor of Darkness* trilogy spans a dozen tumultuous years in Germany from the Great Depression to the months before Pearl Harbor. In the course of the novels the brilliant but initially untested Ryan Lemmon commits himself to countering the Nazi menace. He moves through Europe as an American operative while struggling to outwit a brutal Gestapo nemesis.

Inspired by the journals of the author's late father, *Corridor of Darkness* tells of espionage, vengeance and love against the backdrop of the chaotic Third Reich. One related storyline remained untold. In *Echoes of Silence* that chapter from Ryan's 1931 past returns to haunt him on the streets of 1941 Berlin.

This tale can stand alone.

However, if you are new to the story, you may wish to start at the beginning of the trilogy to better appreciate the characters, intrigue and many twists and turns along the way. If not, enough of the backstory lies herein to encourage you to turn the page.

PROLOGUE

Berlin, Germany
September 1931

Pedestrians leaned into the brisk wind sweeping down the Spree River. A dray horse trudged wearily across the bridge as it struggled with a wagonload of heavy roofing tiles. The driver snapped his whip in encouragement. Frustrated by this plodding obstruction, a produce vendor scraped gears on his Ford and downshifted to pass. He flicked a cigar butt from the open window but paid scant attention to the official van parked at the quay. Already running late on deliveries, he knew it was always best to turn a blind eye to police business anyway.

The officers eased the body toward the bank. Floaters had become more frequent in recent times. Personal vengeance and political vendetta inspired the cruelest of murders and a rash of suicides reflected the nation's economic woes. The wash of the patrol boat rolled the swollen corpse to the side, exposing a breast and blanched arm with outstretched hand, its splayed fingers begging for attention. The neck ended in pale flesh, bone and sinew.

The men drew the remains to the edge of the channel, their hooks gingerly avoiding further damage. Unable to mask the quiver in his voice, a rookie shouted up to the sergeant at street-level. "Should we go back and look for the head?"

His superior understood the young man's revulsion but he himself felt nothing, having long before accepted the realities of the job. "You'd have to search the landfills," he called back. "The Kripos can take it from here."

The launch now bobbed against the concrete riverbank. They wrapped the corpse in oilcloth and hefted their bloated find into the arms of comrades above. The doors of the van stood open to receive the morning's find.

Traffic remained light on the steel span overlooking the recovery scene. Kriminalinspektor Brandt observed from the bridge, his drab overcoat blending with the weathered girders. The pipe clenched in his teeth had grown cold. He allowed the spent tobacco to fall to the sluggish waters below and returned the briar to his pocket. His eyes shifted to a facing tenement at eye level with his perch. Beyond the panes of the window he could see fingers clenching the curtains, ready to draw them shut at a moment's notice.

The observer in the apartment shuddered at the fate of the dead woman. She swallowed back the lump in her throat. As tears coursed down her cheeks, she made a silent vow to avenge the brutal slaughter of her friend. With luck her actions would also assure that a person dear to her would live on.

She released the curtains and stepped from the window, her hands shaking and jaw trembling. She had seen enough.

Her new life could now begin.

TEN YEARS LATER

CHAPTER ONE

Geneva, Switzerland
November 1941

E dward Lemmon wasted no time as he strode across the lobby of the Hôtel du Lac, a briefcase in one hand and his hat in the other. "Sorry, Ryan, but Berlin must wait," he whispered. Ryan Lemmon heard the regret in his older brother's voice. They had said their good-byes the previous evening over a nightcap, so Ed's reappearance meant a new and unwelcome irritant stood in the way of imminent departure. "Something important arrived in this morning's London pouch."

Both men worked for the Foreign Service with Ed assigned to the Geneva consulate. Ryan's task was more complex. He belonged officially to the State Department's Special War Problems Division. Covertly he was an operative for America's fledgling intelligence service, the Coordinator of Information Office under "Wild Bill" Donovan.

Ryan didn't try to mask his disappointment. His bill was settled and the taxi already waiting curbside. He'd been brooding over a final farewell with an on-again off-again lover of many years and knew the excitement of espionage work would brighten his mood. "So what do they want now?"

"We need someplace quiet." Ed led his brother into the back corner of the lounge they had frequented the previous evening. He ran a quick comb through his hair as they settled into the leather chairs. A waiter appeared to take orders but Ed waved him off with a gratuity and request that he cancel Ryan's ride. He kept his voice low as he handed Ryan a long envelope: "Seems a new guy is taking over all COI operations in Greater Germany. Name's Ellington, and you'll answer to him from now on as sole intermediary with David Bruce in London." Bruce was Donovan's point-man for all European operations.

"What about the orders from Donovan himself by way of Bruce?"

"On hold for the moment. According to what you have in there," he indicated the envelope Ryan had pocketed without a glance, "Ellington wants a face-to-face before you meet with your admiral again." Ryan had recently established a promising contact with the head of Reich military intelligence, Wilhelm Canaris. A joint covert operation revealed American and British corporations financially supporting the Reich, and Ryan had thereby proven his value as a conduit between the admiral and the Allies.

"So how long do I sit around before meeting with this Ellington?"

"Tomorrow afternoon. In Basel."

"At least it's soon." He patted his pocket. "So spare me from having to read this crap—what else should I know?"

"Not much in there, actually, but it does mean you're done with State. The documents office will take new photographs for your cover this afternoon, and from here on out you're free of the Foreign Service."

Ryan was disappointed. Having Ed to buffer his covert activities had been a bright spot, and belonging to the Special War Problems Division had permitted use of his real name and cover story. Just knowing someone trustworthy watched from the wings had been comforting. For the first time Ryan would go it alone. "So we're no longer a team?"

"That's my read." Ed fished out a cigarette and signaled the waiter for coffees. "With Ellington as your coach it's a whole new ballgame for you, brother."

"Any idea why?"

"I've got ideas, but I'll ask around at the consulate. They actually wanted COI to give you this news but I pulled strings to be here instead. After this Basel meet you'll know a hell of a lot more than I do. Word is the bigwigs no longer want Donovan to use State's facilities for intelligence-gathering. They claim it compromises their 'solely' diplomatic mission," a cloud of smoke billowed from his nostrils, "as if anyone truly believes that's all we do!"

Ryan knew full well that Foreign Service outposts usually had intelligence-gathering officers on staff. "Makes some sense, I suppose, keeping the two separate. But it does throw a wrench into our personal arrangement. Anything else?"

Ed smiled enigmatically and reached into his breast pocket. "Oh, almost forgot. Seems I do have something else here that may improve your mood." He produced a square envelope. "It brightened my day, I must admit."

Ryan removed the metal clip and slid out a stack of photographs that left him momentarily speechless. Stretched out on a coroner's table lay the pale corpse of Horst von Kredow. Even in death, the Gestapo officer appeared menacing, given Ryan's past torments at his hands. The images documented damage done by a killer's blade: stab wounds, at least seven in number and deep. But equally disturbing were track marks of countless hypodermic injections across arms, legs and buttocks. His nemesis had been a user, morphine or heroin. And recent slash marks and healed scars mapped the dead man's chest and lower body, evenly spaced, deliberately done and thus likely self-inflicted. There could be no doubt that it was truly von Kredow, for he saw at the throat the striations he himself had made with the man's own blade just months before in France. "My God, brother, where the devil did you get these?"

"Beneath my apartment door first thing this morning, with your name on the envelope and no note of explanation." He smiled. "Should be a bit of a relief if that's who I think it is."

Ryan nodded, acceptance beginning to settle in. "Von Kredow, dead at last." His cruel adversary of seven years finally put to rest. He stopped abruptly at one particular picture and moved it under the lamp for a better look. His tormentor appeared to have circumcised himself and botched the job, a particularly odd act from a man who despised all Jews. Perhaps he'd hoped in his madness to bring his enemy closer at a most personal level. Ryan could only shake his head at a thoroughly unbalanced mind. "You look at all of them?"

"Yes, and once was enough."

Ryan returned the photos to the envelope and handed it back with the observation: "And this man had free rein to maim and torture under Germany's great Führer."

Ed wisely kept silent, allowing his brother to digest this new information.

Ryan felt again the sear of glowing metal on his body, the stench of his own burning flesh as he struggled against his bonds. The man's relentless pursuit of his friends and the covert manipulation of Ryan's own fate had distorted his reality for years, robbing him of all peace. But the horrors inflicted by von Kredow had hardened him, as well, taught him to be cruel and efficient where needed. Were those days of constant dread truly over?

"Thank you for this, Ed. It frees me to do my job in Berlin without constantly looking over my shoulder."

"Thank your friend Canaris when you see him next. The admiral clearly wants your focus on what you do best."

After brief discussion, Ed decided to accompany him as far as Basel. He could catch up on paperwork along the way. Having spent some time in the ancient city where Germany, France and Switzerland converge at the Rhine, Ed volunteered to be his brother's guide to the sights. Bumming around the Old Town seemed a pleasant enough diversion before they went their separate ways. The plan was to have a fine meal, down some good Basler beer, then overnight in an inn close to the train station before Ryan entered the Reich and Ed returned to Geneva.

The following morning they met for a quick breakfast before boarding the 6:35 express. Their first-class compartment was temporarily free of other travelers. Ed settled in to chain-smoke his way through his files and Ryan lapsed into silence. Doing nothing wasn't his style, and his mind focused on his recent past and the uncertainties of where he headed now under new and unfamiliar guise.

Sudden movement in the corridor caught his eye. A stylish blonde had stumbled while avoiding a passenger boarding from the opposite direction. She stooped to retrieve her fallen handbag as the train began to move. Righting herself, she momentarily pressed a hand against the window of their compartment. Ryan sprang to his feet to offer help but she'd already recovered her bag and was straightening the seams of her stockings. Ryan received a smile as she moved on. He followed her progress down the aisle. She entered the vestibule without glancing back.

"Quite the dish," he noted to his brother as he returned to the window seat.

Ed's face remained buried in a file. "Well stacked, that's for sure."

Ryan's smile broadened. "And what would your lovely Grace say to her minding the kids at home while your eye's over here roving?"

"Brother, you know full well my eye appreciates the aesthetic but never roves. And Grace knows it, too. It's one reason I remain in her good graces." Ryan moaned as Ed continued: "No, I've no interest in that lovely creature out there, but I do know your type." He plucked a shred of tobacco from his tongue and his banter turned cautious. "So how'd you leave it with Marita? The good-byes were difficult, I gather?"

"Tough as the devil, I'll admit." It was clear Ed had also seen something familiar in the passing blonde, a touch of Marita Lesney. Certainly not the hair color or even height—Marita was petite and brunette—but those shapely curves, yes. And something in the walk perhaps, self-assured, knowing her own attractiveness, or in that smile. "For the best though," Ryan confessed. "Let's face it: I'm not cut out for a relationship, at least for now. Who knows? Perhaps never." He checked his watch, figuring an hour to go before Basel. "Marita will find her footing in Palestine and end up running a night spot again. It's in her cards. She's a survivor. Maybe I'll visit if this world ever returns to normal." Ryan knew it was a lie. Ed gave a non-committal nod, lost again in his endless stack of files.

Ryan pressed his forehead to the window glass, the cold surface a relief in the overheated compartment. The slick surface fogged with each exhalation. He lowered the pane a bit to welcome frigid air on his face. The beauty of the snowbound countryside lifted his spirits. Edward took no notice of his surroundings, his attention devoted to a seemingly endless parade of documents emerging from the briefcase beside him. He absentmindedly brushed fallen ash from his vest.

Woods of birch and beech clipped by, spikes of color still clinging to tangled branches. A chill blue blanketed the hillsides, prelude to the blinding white to come with sunrise. From moment to moment the meadowlands parted to reveal an ice-rimmed lake or huddled village. He waved to schoolchildren waiting at a grade crossing.

Boyhood trips to Green Mountain Falls came to mind, pristine Colorado blanketed in winter snows. He thought of his parents, both so recently lost to age and disease. He'd lived away nearly as long as he'd lived in Kansas, yet home would always be home, right? The subject seldom arose between the brothers, perhaps because it seemed selfish to dwell on personal loss when the horrors of war destroyed the lives of so many. Or perhaps their silence meant there was little more to add. Firstborn Ed had always been their golden boy; his success in the parents' eyes a high hurdle for Ryan. Should he have written home more often, or telephoned more while still able? It was never enough.

Smoke curled from farmhouses squatting under snow-laden eaves. Dung steamed in the courtyards and firewood lined the walls in stacks so symmetrical the word "pile" insulted their perfection. With the sun finally breaching the hills, a farmer swung open the doors to his basement and his herd filed out toward the field beyond. The heavy bell of the lead cow rocked at her throat, and gossamer auras surrounded the animals as stable-warm hide met frigid air.

Ryan sat down again and closed his eyes. Switzerland. How odd it must feel to live in such tranquility while surrounded by tyranny and war! Ahead lay Germany and Berlin, nexus of Hitler's new Europe. To the west struggled poor France, torn in two by oppression and economic deprivation, ransacked by the Occupation to fuel an invincible war machine. To the south, Mussolini and his fascist thugs terrorized Italy, Greece and Africa. And now eastward, beyond a once proud Austria demoted to the "Ostmark," the mechanized hordes of Wehrmacht and Waffen-SS seemed destined to conquer Russia in weeks if not brief months.

How many families already annihilated? How much suffering and death for untethered ambition and hubris? Ryan felt the deep pangs of inadequacy and guilt, knowing he'd once held proof of a Nazi plan to annihilate European Jewry. Despite his best efforts, the warning had fallen on deaf ears, and now the demons were devastating the continent. *Let it go*, he told himself, *let it go*. Focus on what comes next.

He shook off depressing realities and settled on a far more mundane issue—his growing hunger. Breakfast had been quick at the Place de Cornavin rail station: bread rolls with butter, strawberry jam, and several cups of real coffee, not the ersatz brew of malted grain Berliners christened *Muckefuck*, their witty interpretation of *mocca faux*. He smiled. Right now he could go for another cup of the genuine article. In truth, he could handle another thickly-buttered roll. "Damn it, Ed, I'm already famished," he said. "What I wouldn't give for a couple of fried eggs, sunny side up." A passing memory of Mother and Maggie the cook, warm biscuits emerging from the oven, bacon sizzling in the iron skillet. Now that was breakfast!

Edward stubbed out his cigarette butt and cleared his throat. "How about shutting that icebox door first?" Ryan obliged by closing the window. "We'll reach Basel by ten-eighteen. Let's grab a quick bite at the station, then you handle your Ellington business and we meet for something more substantial right after."

"Works for me." Ryan filled his pipe with the Latakia blend Ed had chased down in Geneva while his brother tore the foil from a new pack of Chesterfields. He put one to his lips in time to share Ryan's light. "I'm still wrapping my head around losing the Special War Problems cover," Ryan admitted. "It was a nice safety net." He found his seat again. "There's something to be said for being with State, official, credentialed." He felt fully exposed for the first time heading into the Reich under an alias. "You pick up anything new on this Ellington business I'm walking into?"

"A three-way tug-of-war, as suspected. Washington bureaucracy meets dueling agencies. COI operations are spreading like wildfire, and we'll jump into this war sooner or later, even if some in Washington don't want it to happen." He set aside the file. "Donovan knows his intelligence operations will be key to eventual victory, but first he must convince Congress to loosen its purse strings, and that means tighter controls over all expenditures, including covert missions. It's like moving from freelance to corporate: you always face greater oversight and accountability. Meanwhile, State wants to keep its hands as clean as possible, while your guys sure as hell don't want us claiming any credit for your successes." Ed tapped ash into the armrest tray. "That's Donovan's bread and butter now, and your man's hungry. So welcome to the ways of my world."

Ed had been with the Foreign Service for over a decade and Ryan knew his distaste for interference and carping from higher-ups. An independent streak ran deep in the Lemmon family. Their mother had done charity work in the Cherokee settlements near Lawrence, much to the bewilderment of the other well-born matrons of eastern Kansas. She had viewed it as a bit more than simply benevolence—she was also thumbing her nose at high-society snobbery. Their dental surgeon father had refused to give credence to so-called "safety concerns" when pioneering the new X-ray technology and he'd paid the price with an untimely death from cancer. And Ryan had been chewed out more than once for what he preferred to call "personal initiative" rather than "ignoring the rules." Only Ed had been a play-by-the book guy growing up, turning him into an ideal State functionary. But now, in working behind the scenes with Ryan, even stable Ed had become more daring, more willing to rattle a cage or two.

"I do wonder how Admiral Canaris will take to my new situation. He's a traditionalist, from all I know. He might have preferred my official cover with State in our dealings."

"He's a savvy type, your white-haired Berlin buddy, and you've shown what you're capable of." Ed chuckled at his casual reference to such a powerful figure in the Reich. "He'll be delighted to see you again no matter what mask you're wearing."

"I get the impression he's odd man out when it comes to Himmler and his cronies, an old-school whale in the Nazi seas, and the sharks around him will draw blood at the first sign of weakness."

"You're the one to know, Ryan. You've been through the mill with those Gestapo guys." Ed stubbed out his half-smoked cigarette and examined his fingernails, impeccably groomed but yellowed by his nicotine addiction. "Take it easy this time and stay out of trouble." He gave his brother an appreciative glance.

"I'll do my best, but things will get worse before they get better. Canaris loves his country but hates its government, so he walks a fine line. His opponents surely have him in their sights." Ryan ran a finger over the bend in his nose. Having almost lost his life to the machinations of von Kredow, he knew the value in pursuing a relationship with the enigmatic Canaris. The Abwehr chief was likely the only force in the Reich's hierarchy capable of thwarting Himmler's goons.

Ed looked his brother in the eye. "Just keep your wits about you and you'll come through fine, as always. Canaris obviously likes you."

"Let's hope you're right." Ryan leaned his head against the wood-paneled wall, sensing the rhythmic pulse of the train as it barreled along. He shut his eyes and sighed. Donovan's spy agency had offered him the opportunity to avenge wrongs done to his friends. Now he was heading back on his own, his enemies lurking in shadow, often unseen and unfelt, until perhaps they lured him down some blind alley. He shuddered, remembering that stranger's neck wrenched in the crook of his arm. He felt again the muffled snap of bone, the limp burden eased to the stones of that fog-shrouded Berlin passageway.

An express shrieked past, the thwack-thwack-thwack of the coaches startling him from his memories. The parade of windows offered momentary glimpses into the lives of others—dozing passengers, a child's face pressed to the glass, newspapers spread wide with the latest news of war. All fleeting, relentless, like the months just past and the years come and gone. Suddenly he felt tired, emotionally and physically. He massaged his temples and willed away the melancholy threatening to imprison him. Return to Berlin and set the wheels in motion, he told himself. Keep your wits about you, as Ed said.

Canaris would surely help.

CHAPTER TWO

Basel, Switzerland
November 1941

B asel teemed with spies so any public meeting was out of the question. Swiss authorities turned a blind eye as long as foreign agents remained discreet, but expulsion was swift should espionage operations threaten the Helvetic Confederation's vaunted neutrality. Consulting a city plan he'd purchased at the station, Ryan quickly located the address for the Ellington meet. Situated in the desirable St. Alban neighborhood, the elegant, somewhat stuffy flat belonged to a renowned Swiss internist. As pre-arranged, the physician had left for his practice early that brisk morning while his wife was off shopping in Zürich. Ed would occupy himself in a nearby café with the International Herald Tribune and copious cups of real coffee.

Ryan found the front door ajar and entered quietly, setting the lock behind him. He made his way through the apartment in search of a study overlooking the river. The doctor may have married an American socialite half his age, but the flat lacked any signs of a young woman's touch. Foyer and parlor were heavy with dark wood, thick drapes and fussy moldings. The memory of cigar smoke hung in the air, and faded wallpaper sucked any liveliness from pastoral landscapes and commendations in overwrought frames.

The door to the study was open and his eye slipped past leather fauteuils and a heavy mahogany desk to the brilliant scene outside. A dusting of overnight snow brightened rooftops where tendrils of smoke wafted from myriad chimneys. Inside, coal briquettes glowed behind an iron fireplace screen. The room was a pleasant relief after all the gloom. His new boss stood at the cased windows, seemingly unaware of his presence.

Ryan was intrigued by this summons, coming as it did on the heels of recent orders directing him back to Berlin and his Canaris contact. Ed had shared what little he knew about this recent high-level recruit by David Bruce, head of COI's European operations. Dash Ellington was reputed to be a brilliant business strategist who had served under Donovan in the Great War before returning to his family enterprise providing rubber products to the world. Ellington's gaze remained fixed on the red-tiled roofs and the wide and churning Rhine. He only turned from the window after Ryan cleared his throat to inquire: "Mr. Ellington?"

Shorter than Ryan by an inch, the man stood with an officer's correctness, shoulders back, chest out, chin slightly elevated. White thatch at the temples framed the steel gray of a receding hairline and his deep-set eyes held a piercing glare. A gold chain linked the waistcoat pockets of a bespoke herringbone suit. Ryan spotted the dangling Phi Beta Kappa key, kin to the one he himself had left behind in Kansas. His new boss was about ten years his senior, a Yale man.

The voice carried no warmth, just calculating efficiency: "Ryan Lemmon, I presume?" Ellington casually gestured toward a dossier lying open on the corner of the desk. Ryan's photo was stapled to the cover sheet.

"At your service, sir," The man's handshake was firm but perfunctory. According to Ed, Ellington was said to be difficult at times but also subject to flattery. Ryan removed his overcoat, took the offered leather armchair and crossed his legs. His new boss remained standing, dossier now in hand, as Ryan continued to speak into the uncomfortable silence: "A pleasure to meet you, sir. My brother Edward Lemmon says State speaks highly of you."

Ellington still said nothing, perhaps gauging the sincerity of the complement. His gaze remained steady and Ryan felt ill-disguised animosity but refused to look away. This was not to be a pleasant meeting and he had no idea why.

Ellington removed a sheet from the file and handed it to Ryan. "Before we begin, you will sign this."

Ryan glanced at the document. It was only a few paragraphs long, a work contract between the Government of the United States and the agent with $350 to be deposited monthly in an American bank on behalf of the operative. The employee was to "subscribe freely and without reservation to any oath of office prescribed by the employer," keep forever secret his employment and all information obtained in exercising his duties, and concur that the arrangement was entered into without duress and solely voluntarily on the part of the agent. Ryan chuckled, took out his fountain pen and signed on the line. He handed the page back to Ellington. "Anything else, sir?"

"Take a seat, Lemmon." The new director bent over the desk, spun the sheet, and affixed his own name to the document. "I've spent hours reviewing your dossier and those of other operators currently working within the Reich." Ellington finally took the chair behind the desk. Ryan was forced to look up to meet his eyes. "I must tell you from the start—things are about to change around here."

Ryan frowned and leaned forward. "In what way, sir?"

"I realize you've grown used to your independence, an unfortunate result of laxity exercised by our superiors in the haphazard setup of German operations. But times are rapidly changing, and we need men who understand the meaning of following orders."

"I gather you've found things in my performance evaluations," Ryan motioned to the file, "which suggest my work has been less than satisfactory?" He drew a deep breath to calm his vexation, recalling a similar conversation when fist recruited to COI.

Ellington stroked his mustache before responding: "Here's what I've gleaned from the file—you, Mr. Lemmon, are head-strong and averse to management. In essence, a renegade, and that's a recipe for disaster in our new COI. Those traits may have sufficed back when President Roosevelt had his cronies gather intelligence, no matter how dubious its value, but times have changed." He squared the loose papers in Ryan's file. "And you clearly have not."

Ryan chuckled at the absurdity of the dressing down. "May we stick to perceived faults in the intelligence I've brought in, not my personal character and aptitudes?"

Ellington did not share Ryan's amusement. Elbows propped on the desk, he steepled his fingers and fixed Ryan with a penetrating gaze. "Granted, you gathered some strategic information in western France, but you simultaneously went off on some personal quest which might have compromised your mission…our country's mission. And most recently, and without guidance from us, you somehow managed to link up with the head of Reich military intelligence." He spit out the name: "Admiral Wilhelm Canaris."

Already fed up with the overbearing attitude of his new boss, Ryan saw his future in the COI on the line. He held his tongue. He had no wish to return to a university chalkboard so he would play along, at least for now. "As instructed by General Donovan himself, I was to make myself at home with the Germans."

Ellington's gaze held steady. "Frankly, Lemmon, I don't trust you. Word back in Washington is you played footsie with the Gestapo back in '38. You may have even worked for those sons of bitches, or so rumor has it."

"That's absurd!" His cheeks reddened as Ellington plowed on.

"In fact, how are we to know you haven't been turned, that you're not some Canaris plant intent on wreaking havoc with our intelligence operations?"

Ryan took a deep breath. He recalled a final meeting with his State Department boss back in '38 when he'd nearly throttled the fellow for destroying vital intelligence gained at a dear price. Later he'd learned that the very same bastard had been a Gestapo mole working on behalf of von Kredow. A few months had now passed since he last encountered the man during negotiations in Paris between the Reich and the Special War Problems Division. Could Ellington himself be a double agent? For now he calmed both thoughts and voice, saying simply: "Proceed…sir."

Ellington was on a roll: "It strikes me as patently absurd that you suddenly find yourself holding hands with Canaris, so much so that he rewards you with some Parisian floozy who'd caught your eye."

Ryan refused to let the man goad him. He dug his nails into the flesh of his palms but steadied his voice. "That woman is a dear friend almost destroyed by the Nazis. And you, sir, are now well out of bounds."

Ellington appeared unfazed. He rose from his chair to address the glistening roofs of the city. "No matter— fact is, you climbed into the arms of one of the most powerful intelligence operatives in Europe, a man we'll face on a wartime footing soon enough, and the man played you for a fool." He turned back to Ryan. "Your romantic inclinations got the best of you with that woman. Perhaps she was herself a plant to entrap you, and who knows what compromising information you've already shared with her or with your Canaris." He returned to his chair. "Either accidently...or on purpose?" His eyes burned into Ryan's, obviously frustrated at failing to get the younger man's goat.

Ryan sat back and crossed his legs. Without requesting permission he took out his pipe and slowly filled the bowl. "May I remind you that I just delivered, with the aid of Canaris, damning information about American and British complicity in support of the Nazi war effort?"

"What dilettantes you take us for, Lemmon! Complicity be damned! Coolidge got it right, so I'll paraphrase and you should drum this lesson into that idealistic skull of yours: 'the business of America is business, and will forever remain business.'" He picked up his fountain pen and tapped it repeatedly on the desktop, an unconscious distraction. "Had you done your homework, you'd know that President Roosevelt's old law firm represents several of the major corporations you hoped to 'expose' with your little Reichsbank revelation. Do you really think the White House isn't aware of, and doesn't value, the political and economic advantages in keeping all sides in this conflict happy?"

Ryan spoke without obvious rancor: "So Allied soldiers die to improve our corporate bottom lines." He tamped the tobacco and struck a match. "What a pretty picture you paint." He tossed the spent match into the ashtray and released a cloud of aromatic smoke, recalling Ellington's own involvement in producing vehicle tires and other rubber products for a worldwide market. The revelations in the purloined intelligence must have struck close to home. "So now our business is promoting death for profit."

"Don't be so naïve, Lemmon. You work for the big boys now, so forget your Midwestern 'ethics.' Either you're on board, or you're not. Life is never straightforward, never black and white. In case you've yet to realize it, our enterprise, like any powerful and successful business, is founded on subterfuge and deception."

"So we make no moral judgements, no ethical decisions in the course of our work?" Ryan took another puff.

"That's exactly your problem, Lemmon. You think like an idealist in a world crafted for the manipulative. How far do you think that will get you in this business?" Ryan left the question hanging, drawing out the silence. Ellington shook his head in obvious disgust. "Either you work with the team or I bench you, but I'll warn you upfront—with me calling the plays you won't get an opportunity to embarrass the COI."

He dropped Ryan's dossier into his briefcase, marking the end of the interview. "So listen carefully: I'm allowing your return to Berlin. Go hold hands with Canaris again—kiss his ass, for all I care. Find out what you can about his intelligence operations, as you rightfully should. But I'll be watching your every move, and don't think for a moment you're a lone operator." Ryan stood and took his overcoat and hat from the back of the chair while Ellington remained behind the desk. "And as for that brother of yours, he's off your case. No more liaising through State. He's not handling you, I am, and believe you me, I'm not some pushover impressed by your ability to blend in with the Krauts. That's a given for members of my team. I shall work you as hard as I can, and if I see you stumble, I'll be the first to take you out of the game, understood?"

"Clear as a bell." Ryan took a deliberate draw on his pipe and knocked the remaining embers into the ashtray.

"Then get the hell back to Berlin." Ellington, obviously pissed at having revealed his anger, retrieved a manila envelope from his case and tossed it to Ryan. "You'll find identity papers, coded contact instructions, and three thousand Reichsmarks." He pushed a paper in front of Ryan. "Sign here to acknowledge receipt." Ryan obliged. "Now go find a room close to the center of the city. No more life of luxury at the Hotel Adlon for you. Make contact with your little admiral, then sit tight for further direction from me."

Ryan shoved the unopened envelope into his coat pocket. "*Zu Befehl*...sir." At your orders.

Ellington grimaced at the impertinence. "And mark my words—you'll follow those orders to the letter or be back teaching in Podunk in a New York minute. Now get out of my sight." He stepped to the window, calling out over his shoulder as Ryan left the room: "And leave that front door ajar. You're not the only one on my list today."

Ellington had just revealed he had others coming by that morning. That odd breach of protocol weighed on Ryan's mind as he descended to the street. Agents were never supposed to know the identity of fellow operatives unless vital to a mission. Nothing would prevent Ryan's sticking around to catch a glimpse of other COI personnel had he so wished. Yes, he had left his new boss rattled. Not necessarily a good thing.

A minute or so passed. Dash Ellington continued to stare out at the city but nothing held his interest. He had intended to demonstrate just who was now fully in charge. Instead, that damned Lemmon had managed to unsettle him with his accursed Midwestern morality. Without turning he became aware of Robertson standing at the threshold. "And?" he said.

"Gone, sir." His subordinate remained at the door, awaiting further orders. "How'd it go?"

Ellington knew full well his assistant had overheard every word from the adjoining room. The fool probably had his ear glued to the connecting door, for God's sake! What's a man to do when surrounded by incompetence and insubordination?

"This Lemmon is a disaster waiting to happen, Robertson." Ellington returned to the desk. "My guess is he'll step on his own prick and we'll be rid of him soon enough, but in the meantime, I wouldn't trust him to toe the line."

"As intractable as you anticipated, sir?"

"The man's a school teacher, not a spy. Has a touch of luck along the way and thinks he qualifies for the big leagues. But what else can one expect from such a type?" He retrieved Lemmon's dossier from the briefcase and jotted down a few notes."

"Anything else, sir?"

"Put someone reliable on his tail, then let Lemmon sit on his hands in Berlin for a few weeks. Given a bit of rope, this one may well hang himself out to dry." He straightened the contents and closed the dossier, silently fuming over his own loss of composure. "And if he doesn't compromise our operations before we're rid of him, we'll all be the better for it."

Ed speared another chunk of his meat patty and dipped it in the dark, onion-flecked gravy. "Sounds like one unpleasant son-of-a-bitch, brother." He corralled pan-roasted potatoes with his fork. "So, what comes next?"

Ryan's grin carried no trace of warmth. "Just let the bastard try to take me down." He ignored his schnitzel, having only taken a few absent-minded bites. His beer glass sat empty. He had a thirst for payback no amount of brew could sate. "At a time and place of my choosing, I'll make a fool of that pompous idiot. Then maybe I can bring you back into the works."

"Buck up, Ryan." Ed drained his glass. "It's not as if we didn't know our arrangement was doomed. Covert and diplomatic never merge easily." He held up his thumb and forefinger to signal the waiter for two fresh glasses of pilsner. "Always a matter of time before State kicked us out of the joint espionage business, so perhaps it's for the best, right?"

Ryan gave it a few moments thought. "Not necessarily, Ed. I'm wary of putting my COI career entirely in the hands of that man. What say we keep in close touch, but covertly?"

"Risky," said Ed, then added with his usual husky chuckle, "but I'm nothing if not game. What's on your mind?"

"Newspaper classifieds. You need to reach me—you hear anything at State I can use—just advertise a room to let in the *Morgenpost*. Berlin West. Have someone on the consular staff place it for you and use our old Lawrence telephone number. I'll check daily. I spot your message, I contact you immediately by message left at their switchboard."

"Understood."

"Now, about your landlady. From what you've said she can be trusted?"

"She can. Thoroughly vetted."

"In that case, should I need to reach you in a real hurry—an actual emergency—I'll use her number, calling later in the evening when you're likely to be in. Otherwise, we use only public callboxes, and, of course, all discretion."

"I'll need your Berlin address. How are you going to get me that discretely?"

Ryan took a moment to consider. He reached for a paper napkin and his fountain pen. "Once settled in, I'll send a postcard to your apartment in Geneva, somehow working my new address into the text." He began to sketch something.

Ed nodded, chewing again as he used a bread crust on the last of the gravy.

"So here's the deal: for the name of the street I mention some fictional person I met, a 'Herr Potsdamer" or a 'Fräulein Thüringer."

"Got it." Ed scanned for their waiter and signaled again for the beers. He turned his attention to the image Ryan was generating on the napkin.

"On the face of the card I draw a simple Prussian landscape, something I claim to have admired. Let's say a farmyard. The birds, pigs, chickens or cows mark positions on an imaginary clock." He drew a rudimentary cow at the three o'clock position."

"Piece of cake: the number three."

"Correct."

"And the sequence for the numbers?"

"The count of like animals in any grouping reveals the sequence. So three crows at two o'clock—" he added three m-shaped strokes to the sky of his sketch, "—mean the third number in the sequence will be a two."

"And the three-o'clock cow stands all alone, so she's the number three and first in line. Clever, my brother."

Ryan shredded the napkin. "Push comes to shove, you're my fallback. Ellington's made clear he expects me to land on my ass, so I wouldn't be surprised if I end up needing your help."

The waiter delivered the beer and Ed offered curt thanks, miffed at the delay. He pointed to untouched potatoes on Ryan's plate. "You done with those?"

Ryan pushed the plate across to his brother. "All yours." He laid claim to one of the tall glasses and drained the beer by half, then poured some onto the napkin remnants and mashed them into a sodden ball.

"Appears your thirst is alive and well." Ed reached over to clink glasses.

"Yeah, but this Ellington business stole my appetite."

"A rarity for you, brother." His fork speared some untouched *Rösti*. "But as for your plan, count me in. Let's show Ellington what Kansas boys can do."

CHAPTER THREE

En Route to Frankfurt, Germany
November 1941

Wheels squealed on icy rails as his train rolled over the Rhine bridge. The Swiss authorities had just walked the train doing a perfunctory inspection of travelers' documents, but the German gauntlet at Weil am Rhein was sure to be more thorough. Ryan wasn't getting comfortable. Not yet. In a matter of minutes his train would enter Germany.

Despite Ed's hope for a relaxing break, Ryan was glad to be done with Basel. He'd made little attempt to hide his impatience at the delay, unable to mask his anger over the morning's Ellington interview. After lunch the brothers wandered through the cobbled streets and down along the river. Scudding clouds hinted at a change in weather and a brisk wind from the north forced them to turn up coat collars and seat hats more tightly. The conversation became desultory, almost forced. Ed attempted to lighten the mood with reminiscences of boyhood pranks, but Ryan made clear that no amount of forced joviality could distract him. Over mid-afternoon cake and coffee Ed finally surrendered to the inevitable. He suggested Ryan catch the overnight rather than wait till morning. Ryan had leapt at the proposal. They found their way back to the Centralbahnhof where Ryan reserved a first-class sleeper compartment to himself. With what lay ahead, this was likely the last luxury he would experience in the foreseeable future. He intended to arrive in Berlin as refreshed as possible.

Over dinner he'd surrendered for safekeeping the last personal items linking him to his true identity: his passport, the gold ring with hidden compartment that once concealed a suicide pill, and his leather-bound daily journal. Pressed between the pages lay the dried flower Leo had given him, a token remembrance of his young son, now in London with his adoptive parents. "Don't worry: they're in safe hands," Ed assured him. His brother meant the personal items, of course, but Ryan thought only of the friends with whom he'd shared so much excitement and terror in the previous summer. At the station he'd waved good-bye to his brother, wondering under what circumstances they would next meet.

The brisk weather of the waning day had yielded to a strong cold front pressing down from the north. The moon hid behind heavy clouds and brittle sleet descended with a fury. But once the express left central Basel, his spirits began to lift despite the weather. He yearned for a clean break from the trials that had plagued his loved ones over the past months.

He was returning to the fray, to the Reich's many dangers, but he was on his own at last. The risks were his alone, not shared with others. His forehead pressed to the window, he sensed more than heard the tick-tick-tick of ice crystals assaulting the pane. Such a relief to know von Kredow was no longer a threat. Despite a conscious effort to resist the memory, he relived the brutality of torture, the relentless pursuit, the nearness of imminent death. And then he was back in that same dark alley, crouching in wait before taking a man's life. That act would once have seemed reprehensible, but now he felt more alive than ever in the face of such ruthless enemies. As long as he risked all on a daily basis, no one should care enough to worry about his fortunes.

He consciously released the tension in his neck and focused on the darkness beyond the train window. Pinpoints of light pierced the shroud of snow and gradually coalesced into lamp fixtures. Ice crystals whipped around like so many desperate insects as trackside buildings and canopies slid into view. The express shuddered to a halt alongside armed troopers in winter coats lining the platform.

He knew the customs inspectors would walk the length of the train searching the occasional bag, followed closely by border police examining travel documents and identity papers. But oddly, only border police officers entered the lead carriage. They moved along swiftly, ordering all passengers to gather up luggage, detrain immediately, and enter the customs shed. Something was amiss. Or someone special being sought.

Ryan joined the growing queue of passengers on the platform, moving through the bitter cold like so many herded sheep. Fiercely-barked orders directed them toward the building entrance. Bundled in overcoats and mufflers, those without hand baggage flapped their arms to ward off the chill or warmed hands in armpits as the line moved forward. Every expelled breath glowed bluish under dim light. The corrugated iron of the building creaked under the onslaught of brittle cold as they entered. Inside, the customs inspectors, not immune to the discomfort, appeared resigned to their unusual assignment. They moved the new arrivals from post to post with only the occasional stumble or delay.

An official invited Ryan to open his calfskin valise. Pushing aside clothing and toiletries, the inspector rooted around in the recesses. He fruitlessly sought to lift the bottom panel. With nothing found to further pique his interest, he waved Ryan on and shifted his attention to the next in line.

Now a border policeman demanded his papers. Ryan had memorized his new cover story: a representative for Monarch Rubber Goods of Peoria, he traveled to Berlin to peddle synthetic rubber tires to both Wehrmacht and industrial concerns. "A nation at war is only as strong as the tread on its tires," or so read the

German-language brochures he carried. A newly-minted but suitably-weathered passport listed him as Lewis Graf, age thirty-five. His entry visa, ostensibly stamped by the German embassy in Bern, displayed the required photo. Ryan regretted the demotion from Special War Problems official to Midwestern sales rep. Ellington's ploy in choosing this alias underscored Ryan's precarious status within the COI. He returned the papers to his inside jacket pocket. The thought of the heated compartment waiting across the platform already warmed him.

A man in leather overcoat and black fedora stepped into his path and raised a hand. "Those papers again, please." Accustomed to the process, Ryan complied without hesitation. Remain calm; volunteer nothing; stay friendly. Nerve-testing, but endurable. The man perused Ryan's documents and compared the photos to the traveler standing before him. "Remain here." He gave a subtle nod to a Brownshirt standing barely a meter away. The Gestapo agent disappeared with Ryan's papers into an office beyond the inspection counter. The SA man moved closer, one hand resting lightly on a holstered Mauser 9mm.

A forger's error? It happened, though rarely. An intentional move by Ellington? Could the new boss be that duplicitous, blatantly trying to undermine him fresh out of the chute? Equally unlikely. *Don't get paranoid, Ryan.* He dug for his briar, filled the bowl and struck a match. The tobacco soothed his nerves and the curling smoke warmed his cheeks.

Vexing minutes passed before the agent reappeared, now accompanied by a uniformed SS officer far removed in stature from Himmler's ideal. Multiple chins overlapped the collar of his uniform, the silver runes competing for attention with the sagging folds of flesh. The man's paramilitary rank was equivalent to that of a Wehrmacht major.

"Here's our boy," the Gestapo agent said to the Sturmbannführer.

The stout officer requested Ryan remove his hat and held a flyer up to Ryan's face. He caught only a glimpse of the artist's sketch, so there was no telling how closely the features matched his own. The travelers to his rear had come to a halt but no one complained, at least within earshot. The Brownshirt directed them to form a new queue ahead. All eyes forward; not a single glance back.

"Is there a problem here, sir?" Ryan inquired, peppering his voice with righteous annoyance. "I'm an American pursuing legitimate business with the Reich."

The SS officer nodded, chins bobbing. "An American, you say, yet your German is flawless." He grinned at the Gestapo man. "I'd say Prussian, wouldn't you?" The secret policeman's crease of a smile remained unchanged. The SS officer thumbed through the passport a second time. "And your surname is certainly German...*Herr* Graf."

"My grandparents came to Pennsylvania in '87 with kids in tow. From Potsdam." Ryan was well prepared to recount the cover story. "We spoke German at home to keep tradition alive."

"No doubt," the SS officer said, dismissive, having clearly moved on from discussing Ryan's heritage, "but we've been watching for someone who looks remarkably like you. Our man also speaks excellent German, and he recently robbed an important Berlin bank."

Ryan, all senses on alert, played the indignant innocent. "Do I look like a bank robber to you, sir?"

"Indeed you do, *mein Herr*..." He compared Ryan's face to the artist's sketch one last time before folding the sheet. "Indeed you do. Please follow me and allow your fellow travelers to be on their way. We'll have further questions for you and definitely need a closer look at these papers."

Ryan's eyes swept the building. Another train had just arrived, a new cluster of cold, irritated passengers already clogging the entrance to the customs barn. The door at the far end was the only option. His identity somehow compromised during the Reichsbank incursion, there was no time to wonder how, only to seek escape.

The officer spotted his hesitation. "Now, now, sir, do come along. Just a formality, you understand. If you've nothing to hide you'll soon be on your way. Don't worry about missing your train. They arrive with boring regularity." The man waddled toward the office.

The Gestapo agent had already turned his attention to some new suspect up the line. The SA trooper with the Mauser fell into place behind Ryan. There would be no running.

At that moment a woman hurried toward them. "Major, a word please?" She threaded past the others, pushy, almost rude, her heeled boots clacking on the damp concrete. It was the same woman spotted in the aisle of the Basel-bound train, the one who'd brought to mind Marita. Close up, she was taller, more voluptuous, with shapely calves and full breasts barely constrained by her gray trench coat. Dimpled cheeks reddened by the cold, plaited blond hair beneath a green hat with feather, and deep blue eyes under long lashes. Definitely his type, but then, he had many. Elsewhere he would have made an effort to introduce himself, but those eyes favored only the portly SS man. She placed a hand on the officer's arm and gave it a light squeeze. "A moment of your time, sir?"

The major couldn't mask his pleasure at being her sole focus. He grew taller in his uniform, losing a chin in the process. Having momentarily forgotten his bank robber suspect, he stepped closer still with a slight bow of the head. "How may I be of service to you, *gnädige Frau*—" squinting in appreciation, "or is it perhaps *Fräulein*?"

"*Fräulein* it is." She showed him a flirtatious grin. "A private word, if we might?" With raised brows and a tilt of the head she gestured toward the privacy of his office.

He found the invitation irresistible. "Of course, Miss." He took her proffered arm. His voice turned gruff and authoritative as he tasked the trooper to "Hold him here!" The Brownshirt clicked his heels with a snappy salute and drew Ryan off to the side. The officer gallantly guided the woman away.

The unexpected intrusion opened new options. The Gestapo man was off targeting newly-arrived travelers, and incapacitating a young Stormtrooper was well within Ryan's training. A forceful blow between nose and upper lip or across the Adam's apple would quickly put him down for the count. Then grab the pistol and make a run for the door. Others were already filing out the far end of the shed, their visit to this frozen purgatory over. His actions would raise an instant alarm, but he would be armed.

Yet, where to flee once out in the cold? An empty freight car to hide in, or would the doors be locked or frozen shut? Seek refuge in a nearby building perhaps, or enter a *Gasthaus* from a service entrance out back? But how to find an inn on a night such as this? The thought of hunkering down in the frigid darkness awaiting the baying dogs held no appeal. A run remained ill-advised. He glanced around but no one met his gaze. In the other travelers' minds he no longer existed. He was now property of the Reich.

The woman emerged from the office. She led the way, the fleshy officer tagging at her heels. Her eyes twinkled and a smile played on her lips, but now her full attention was directed at Ryan. Remarkably, the SS major's demeanor had also changed. He appeared anxious to settle matters. Returning Ryan's documents, he told him to grab his valise before directing the trooper to step aside. With a curt nod to the woman and a look of relief, he wished them both safe travels. She gave the officer a final commiserating smile before steering Ryan toward the exit and the platform.

The cold wind was bracing. The express idled, steam hissing loudly from the Reichsbahn locomotive, its brake pump throbbing. As the two emerged from the shed, the trainman raised a whistle to his lips and waved his red paddle. The locomotive responded with a quick chirp and took up the slack of the cars with an ever diminishing clunk of metal on metal.

Ryan assisted her up the steps and into the last railcar. "My God, *Fräulein*, what the devil happened back there?" He pulled the carriage door shut behind them. "How'd you pull that off?"

"We'll talk later." Now she gave his arm a squeeze, her smile infectious. "Room in your compartment for one more?"

Ryan laughed, exhilarated by his unexpected salvation. Who would deny that request? "Allow me," he said, guiding her down the corridor. As they entered the cabin, she hung the small *Nicht Stören* placard outside and drew the privacy curtains closed. "Enough nuisance for one night, wouldn't you agree? And the coach steward surely deserves some rest."

Ryan removed his hat and shook off the clinging sleet. "I have to agree—enough disturbances for one night." He shoved his gloves into the pocket of his coat.

Her face, now relaxed, was even more appealing—the smile warm, genuine. "First off, friendly greetings from our mutual friend in Berlin." She extended her hand. "Please call me Klara."

Admiral Canaris, of course. "How on earth did you...did he...know I'd be here—that I'd run into trouble?"

She held his hand a fraction longer before releasing it. "Ah, yes, that..." She hung up her coat and handbag, then removed the chic hat. "First we settle in, then we chat."

The heat of the compartment was a relief after the bitter cold. He hung his overcoat and scarf on the hook opposite hers. With a sigh of relief, he took a seat at the window, expecting her to sit opposite him. Instead she drew the window curtains closed and sat down beside him. The warmth of her hip was disconcerting. She leaned in, conspiracy in her husky voice. "You asked how we knew you might run into difficulties. That was simple enough—I've been following you and your brother since Geneva." Her finger traced the line of his jaw before lightly tapping the tip of his nose. "And that wanted poster almost does you justice, but misses the strength of your chin." She settled back against him. "You Americans really have to stay on your toes if you're to play this game well." Her perfume was subtle.

He shook his head at his own stupidity. Switzerland had seemed so safe, so far removed from the intrigues of Greater Germany. He'd let down his guard and almost paid dearly for it. "So it's Klara, is it?" Certainly a *nom de guerre*. "I'm Lewis—Lewis Graf." He shook her hand again, as if meeting her for the first time.

"Sure you are," she said, eyes sparkling. "For the moment, at least."

His laugh easy now, tension waning in the company of an interesting woman. He leaned back and shut his eyes, the pressure of her thigh an increasing distraction. "So how did you convince them to release me?"

"We keep track of the other security services, alert for weaknesses that might prove useful. Basel control is especially active, so gets special attention." She pressed even closer against his leg and he felt himself rising to the occasion. "So many spies around, you know?" she whispered theatrically in his ear.

He opened his eyes again and grinned at her. "Hard to trust anyone, right?"

Harsh sleet tapped at the window panes beyond the curtains. She took a lipstick from the handbag, applying it before she spoke again. "In this case, our portly friend back there has some less than admirable tendencies." His eyes remained riveted on her full lips, and he shifted a bit in his seat, relieving the pressure on his trousers. She blotted with a tissue before trading the lipstick for a silver flask. "Brandy? I find it soothes the nerves after such excitement." Ryan gratefully accepted. The woman took a quick nip for herself and tightened the cap. "That fellow back there likes to shake down travelers for 'contraband' and occasionally overlooks 'transgressions' in exchange for—shall we say—favors?" She attempted a demure smile but couldn't quite pull it off. She dropped down beside him again, set aside the flask and pulled off her boots.

Ryan felt a silk-stockinged toe explore his ankle. "Disgusting behavior on his part, but good news for me, right?" He gave her knee a grateful squeeze. "I sincerely thank you, Klara, for keeping me out of his clutches!"

"Happy to oblige. But to be honest, he's more interested in clutching a woman like me."

"Well, at least he shows good taste."

She flashed those intriguing dimples. "So getting him into the office was easy. Once there, I made clear what might happen if he didn't cooperate. The man's wife is quite the socialite—some local *von*-this or *zu*-that—and her wealth enables his career in both SS and the local Party." She drew closer and pressed a breast against him. "All the better for us, the dear woman holds a very low opinion of married men who fool around." She smiled innocently, but the pressure against his thigh was anything but. "So tell me—what do you think of a man who would do such a thing, Herr…'Graf,' was it?"

"Yes, Lewis Graf…" he replied, voice deeper than usual, "in the rubber business."

"Rubber, you say?" Her smile grew more mischievous. "So you're an expert in *Gummis*?" The same double meaning in both German and English.

Ryan flashed his broadest grin. "Quite well versed, Klara."

She took another sip from the flask before tossing it toward the far seat and rising to her feet. "Then I believe it's time we celebrate your rescue."

She gave his obvious erection a squeeze, then found her balance with the rocking of the train and stepped out of her skirt. Her garter belt was black lace, the sheer panties confirming a natural blonde. Bracing a leg to either side of his, she bent forward and encouraged him to undo her blouse. He freed her breasts from the bra, then tasted the brandy on her lips as she worked his trouser buttons to set him free. "Now," her voice becoming huskier still, "where is that *Gummi* of yours, or must I provide my own?"

"A gentleman never makes a lady wait," He fumbled in his vest pocket and tore open the white cellophane, setting things right. She giggled as she pulled aside the crotch of her panties and slowly eased him in.

"Welcome back to the Reich." Her voice was barely a whisper as she gave her ass a saucy shake.

Ellington stood as usual at the study window observing the flow of the Rhine, but his mood was particularly foul. Robertson watched intently for some signal that his boss was ready to hear the rest of his report. The gray river appeared more sluggish than just a day before. Damn, Ellington thought, what he wouldn't give for a Scotch. His watch confirmed a long afternoon still before him. Running a major corporation was child's play compared to whipping these COI operatives into shape. Washington was supposed to send him new agents, effective and highly-trained people, but so far the results had been mixed. His assignment was to expedite and improve the many operations already running across the border, but now he would have to report to Bruce in London that he'd lost track of the one spy he'd most like to forget. He surrendered to the inevitable and turned away from the frigid scene. "So where'd Harris lose him?"

"At the border station, sir. They made everyone detrain." Robertson reported. "Harris was only steps behind Lemmon in the same queue. The Gestapo nabbed our guy within minutes of entering the customs shed."

"That arrogant fool! So sure of himself yet he can't even make it to Berlin."

"No, sir."

"So then what?"

"Harris couldn't stick around without blowing his cover so had to move on. Lemmon was already being questioned by an SS major. A Gestapo agent had singled him out first, and an armed Brownshirt stood by, as well." Robertson sounded pleased to be so well informed. "The SS man was waving around a police flyer. Looks like they nabbed him for that Reichsbank job; at least Harris is certain of it."

"In Gestapo grips by now." Ellington shook his head in disgust. "That know-it-all won't last more than an hour before he spills his guts."

"Hundred-percent right, sir."

Ellington despised sycophants, but Robertson was dutiful. Useful until someone better came along. "So we know they have him now, and we know he'll fold when they bring out the blades and bludgeons. Luckily, Lemmon's been out of the loop under that War Problems cover, mostly running some private show in France. He can't compromise any of our current operations. And Himmler's men will already know what I'm here for, so there's little risk in Lemmon's divulging that."

"Correct, sir." Robertson appeared not to realize his boss was voicing considerations for his own clarity of thought, not to share them with a lackey.

Ellington leaned forward, bracing his chin on his fist. "Well, serves Lemmon right. I told him he'd land on his face given half a chance. Nothing for it, so we leave him to their ministrations." He picked up his chromed lighter and flicked the wheel, observing the tight flame. "And they'll have his new identity to work with, so any communications we get from him, phone calls to the cut-outs, anything at all," he lit a cigarette, "we ignore them all. Total blackout on our end, understood."

"Yes, sir, I'll pass the word down the line."

"And make a call to the Geneva consul. I don't want him trying a work-around with his brother. Nothing gets through to that fellow either. Word is he's too involved in our business anyway. Understood?

"Yes, sir. Clear as a bell."

"What of Harris?"

"Passed through the unusual inspection without a hitch, caught a local north to Freiburg, then doubled back here without incident. Ready for his next assignment."

"Excellent. Just as it should be. Wish I had more of his ilk."

"Don't we all, sir." A statement, not a question.

"As for Lemmon, no loss there. One loose cannon we won't have to deal with now. That Canaris nonsense was going nowhere anyway. I'm convinced the old man of the Abwehr was playing us for fools."

"Indeed, sir."

Ellington pulled open a desk drawer and reached for a bottle of Dewar's and two crystal glasses. He poured his own a double, a single for Robertson. "Now let's lift one to dearly departed Ryan Lemmon." He grimaced at an errant thought. "I'm no monster, you understand. I hope they finish him off quickly. Our cruel friends over there are true masters of intel extraction."

He toasted and drained his glass and Robertson dutifully followed suit.

CHAPTER FOUR

Frankfurt, Germany
November 1941

He jolted upright in the sleeper, his head brushing the compartment ceiling. That same recurrent dream, disorienting and dulling his senses: the Berlin alley draped in darkness, the snap of the neck felt rather than heard, the weight of the limp body as they both hit the cobbles. An unknown life snuffed out. Had he heard a cry? A woman shout? He looked around in confusion. There had been no witness.

Ryan shook his head clear. He reached across the bunk to part the curtains. The sign out on the platform read Frankfurt am Main, the hands of the clock beneath the high arching roof approached four. Still nighttime in a nation at war, yet twilight reigning forever under the canopy of one of Europe's busiest rail terminals. Travelers rushed past below his window: a middle-aged man eyeing his wristwatch, a mother pausing to quickly bundle a toddler, a family burdened by suitcases. An unwieldy baggage cart frustrated a sleep-deprived porter.

He turned at a disturbance out in the corridor, luggage bumping against the wall, muted conversations, travelers detraining, but no one knocking at his door. Klara was gone. No green coat, no feathered hat. On his own again.

He came down from the bunk and pulled a clean shirt from his valise. His trousers lay crumpled on the opposite seat with no regard for the creases. Once dressed, he raised the drop-bed. Only then did he spot her note: *Thanks for making things interesting. Watch your back, and should you come this way again...?* A smudge of red lipstick her only signature. He could still feel the softness of those lips. Their second round had been slower, more pure fun than unbridled passion. Laughing co-conspirators, they had lowered the cantilevered bed for room to play. She'd hopped up, guiding his head to that pale triangle of blond. God, what a night! They both dozed for a while, and at some point she'd climbed over him, full breasts swaying as she hovered above, laughing softly as he arched his neck to reach her. She pressed a nipple to his lips, then whispered: "Must go wash up," before lowering herself to the floor. He moaned his disappointment. She gathered up her clothing and pulled on the boots. As the door closed behind her, he had yet to open his eyes again, still savoring the moment.

So much carelessness on his part, allowing himself to be tailed across Switzerland. It had felt good to be on neutral ground, to not view every stranger with suspicion. He'd relaxed his guard—a potentially fatal error—but how well it had paid off, to be pulled from the fire by a blonde bombshell! In relief over dodging arrest and imminent death, he had surrendered all too willingly to her charms. It could easily have been another snare.

But such laxity couldn't happen again. Who else might be tailing him? "Lewis Graf" was obviously compromised, and Ryan felt uneasy. He couldn't quite put a finger on it—perhaps just a gut feeling—but he wouldn't be caught with his pants down again. The pun intended. Was her note more than a warning? He had to break the chain of expectations. Others might be anticipating, even dictating his next moves. If Canaris knew exactly where he was—where he was headed—perhaps others did, as well. The Gestapo? They couldn't have been pleased that the major sent him on his way. And he even had concerns about Ellington. The man admitted he was waiting for Ryan to trip up. Could he be that duplicitous just to prove a point?

With sudden resolve, he packed up his valise, pulled on his coat and grabbed his hat. Down the aisle the sleepy-eyed porter wrestled a bulky suitcase into a compartment. The corridor to the right was empty. How much time before departure? He wouldn't wait to find out. He moved quickly toward the vestibule, passing two other compartments with the curtains still drawn. The WC beckoned, but his bladder would have to wait.

A shrill whistle blew. Doors slammed the length of the train as it shuddered in preparation for departure. A Reichsbahn worker's shout of *"Vorsicht!"* drove him back as the door closed in his face. Ryan waited until the last moment, the train already easing out from beneath the massive canopy. Lifting the handle, he leapt onto the platform.

Only then did he spot the commotion on the opposing platform. Dour agents hustled Klara along in search of their prey. They must have snatched her as she left the terminal. In their haste to arrest Ryan, they were allowing her to lead them astray by targeting the wrong train. She was buying him time to escape. Klara looked quickly in his direction and gave the subtlest of nods. They both knew that any action he took would only further compromise her, and Canaris knew how to look after his own. Only the admiral could save her now.

He still felt like shit.

The massive locomotive showered him in cinders and steam as it backed from the terminal. He squatted in the cover of a waiting baggage cart, one more traveler taking inventory of his belongings. A suitcase would only slow him down. He stuffed his pockets with identity papers, cash, ration cards and pocket knife, then added his valise to the pile on the cart. The disturbance on the opposing platform had drawn away other police controls and he joined without incident the now sparse crowd moving toward the exits.

It wouldn't take long for the Gestapo to know they'd been had and focus on his just-departed train. They'd likely target its next stop rather than search the station, but Ryan couldn't trust in luck. He needed speed and a plan. He would somehow make his way to Berlin, avoiding police controls if possible, then telephone Ellington's cut-out. Until he learned who or what had compromised the bank intrusion, he would take nothing for granted. Canaris' own people may have been turned. He ran through his options. Without good papers, he risked arrest at any juncture. No way to simply buy a new ticket for Berlin. The Gestapo now had that artist's rendition of his face and knew the clothes he wore. They might or might not already know his intended destination. He needed a disguise.

He spotted a hallway off the concourse leading to double doors marked *Eintritt Verboten*. They would likely be unsecured, since solid Reich citizens would never enter a forbidden space. Glancing right and left, he tested the handle and met no resistance. He slipped into a baggage storage hall beyond. Should he encounter someone he would claim to be lost and count on a winning smile and embarrassed excuses, but be prepared to disable as needed. The vast space was unheated and beastly cold. Light fixtures ran the length of the ceiling with a burned-out wartime bulb scattered here and there. The room appeared momentarily unoccupied, but that could change in a flash so time was pressing.

Crates, boxes, and suitcases rose from the concrete amidst a jumble of hand-trucks and wheeled carts. A broad bank of shelves along the far wall stored unclaimed property under a fine layer of dust. He pulled out his penknife and exposed the blade. Honed to razor sharpness, it was his weapon of last resort. Shoving aside bulky and leather-sided suitcases, he slit open a fabric valise and found only items of women's wear. His next target, a bag bound by cracked belting, revealed a jacket befitting a clerk, a faded blue shirt, and a worker's cap. These would work.

A rattle at the entrance caught his attention and he dropped to the dusty floor. Beyond the doors someone hesitated long enough to return a colleague's greeting. A draft followed the man in. Hunkered down to peer past the ranks of luggage, Ryan watched a baggage handler compare the number of a cart with a notation on a clipboard, then release the wheel brake and back the carriage out into the main hall.

Once the doors closed he hurriedly slit open a few more bags until he had shoes of loose but passable fit, a neck scarf, and woolen gloves to offer some protection from the cold. None of the trousers came close to fitting, but his overcoat of fine quality was the real problem. There had to be something more suited to the average man. He hastily broke into several more cases before acknowledging that a traveler in inclement weather would be wearing his overcoat, not packing it in luggage.

He called it quits, pulling the rumpled shirt over his own and wrapping the scarf around his neck. He transferred his valuables to the pockets of the jacket and the knife to his pants pocket. The well-worn footwear replaced new shoes purchased in Geneva and he slipped on the tired gloves. Once his hair was mussed for an unkempt look, he pulled the laborer's cap low on his forehead. His tailored woolen trousers, badly in need of a pressing, would have to do.

As he reached for the handle, the metal bar fell away from his grasp. He hugged the wall behind the door as a porter propped it with a brace, grabbed the clipboard off its hook, and moved quickly down the center aisle. The man hummed as he checked cart numbers against his list. Taking advantage of the man's inattention, Ryan already had one foot through the open passage when the worker abruptly reversed direction. Ryan moved back into hiding behind the door and pressed himself to the wall. He held his breath. The porter hesitated at the first cart, ticked off something with a pencil and re-hung the clipboard. He released the wheel brake on the heavily-burdened truck and backed it out, still humming some indistinct tune.

Alone again, he exhaled and became aware of softness at his back. Outerwear left by workers lined the wall. He would get to Berlin without freezing. He chose a worn tweed overcoat of coarse wool. It smelled of moth balls but beggars couldn't be choosers. He left his own fine coat in its place, sure to be a pleasant surprise for its unwitting new owner.

The lack of identity papers was worrisome. Any fit man not in uniform carried proof of exemption for some critical labor on the home front. Ryan had nothing. Just months before he'd ridden a flatcar through Occupied France, hiding beneath canvas with a lovely partisan, their backs to a motorized field weapon. He knew that railway men were always in short supply and often excused from picking up a rifle. Better yet, he knew the possibility of finding a sympathetic ear increased among rail crews, the last hotbed of trade union resistance before Hitler did his damnedest to obliterate them. Now the only "unions" were shams, Party-run monopolies.

With his full bladder killing him, he released a stream into a far corner and sighed with relief. Thirst and hunger would have to wait. For now, high time to make his way out into the freight yards and play his new role for all it was worth.

He stooped to mimic a much older man and headed out toward the administrative area. An abandoned baggage cart hugged one wall, a box of rusty hand tools resting on its splintered planking. He gave the cart a test and found a wobbly wheel rubbed the axle with every revolution. Borrowing a hammer from the tool box, he began his journey. From time to time he stopped to pound the stubborn wheel into submission. Reichsbahn personnel twice demanded his business as he trudged along, bent over, cursing his cumbersome burden. Twice he explained in Hessian dialect his orders to get the cart to the machine shop for repairs. Happily, the terminal was too vast and the staff too large for the tight camaraderie among workers that might hamper his chances in a smaller locale.

Once into the blacked-out railyards, he abandoned the cart and headed toward a distant freight terminal. The storm had hit with lesser fury here in Hesse. Only a light layer of snow covered the graveled yard. Dampness seeped into his worn shoes but he made steady progress. Despite the darkness and an instinctive urge for stealth, he now moved purposefully as a man on an important mission would. Why else cross an unlit railyard without lantern or flashlight? He took in the wide sweep of the ranging tracks, halting periodically to allow a train to rumble past in a cloud of smoke and cinders. At last he spotted a goods train stationed alongside a long shed, its massive locomotive idling with a periodic release of pent-up steam. The transport appeared to be pointed north, and anything moving that direction would bring him closer to Berlin.

An engineer labored beneath a kerosene lantern suspended from the catwalk of the engine boiler. The man worked with an experienced touch, rapping each high wheel with a hammer as he listened for the dull sound of metal fatigue or a serious crack. Years of exposure to soot and outdoor work had turned his face to burnished leather. Coal black seemed to exaggerate every crease and wrinkle, giving the look of someone decades older than middle age.

Ryan called out while still meters away to avoid undue surprise: "Hello, there!"

"Hello, comrade. What brings you out at this ungodly hour?" The man greeted him with a friendly wave of his hammer and the dark tracks at the man's eyes suggested someone used to smiling.

Ryan's father had put himself through college as a part-time brakeman on the Santa Fe and loved to share stories of those days. Ryan had learned enough as a youth to discuss the basics in a pinch. "I work Magdeburg and points west—brakeman—but should've slowed myself down last night. Too much beer and schnapps, too much trust in the local dames." Ryan massaged his temples. "God, my head's killing me."

The engineer gave a knowing grin. "Age-old story. Sorry for your suffering." He squatted to pick up an oil can. "Plenty of traffic heading north in the next few hours, so get yourself over to the passenger terminal and catch a hop." He gestured in the direction Ryan had just come. "Excuse me, but I've no time to chat; we're out of here in fifteen."

Ryan idly scuffed gravel as if hesitant to reveal the truth. "Yes, you see, there's a catch. My footloose brother's on leave here before heading out to the eastern front. I came down to help him enjoy a night on the town. We won a few hands at cards, romanced a couple of lovelies, then got rolled on our way back to his room." Ryan explored the back of his head as if feeling for a lump. "Likely done in by the fellows we bested at cards. Never saw them coming." He gingerly adjusted his cap. "Woke a few hours ago with a splitting headache and double vision and thought it best I head home."

"That'd be the schnapps!"

"And now I stand before you with no papers, no cash, no ration cards." Ryan held up his hands in surrender. "They got it all." He shook his head. "My woman will have my hide for this."

"Not the first time for a visitor here, my friend. Sorry things turned sour for you."

Two men at the far end of the train had spotted them and one called out. The engineer waved them back. Ryan knew to give his story some time to sink in. He stood silent while the man lubricated the running gear, the wait marked by the throb of the air compressor feeding the brake lines. Finally the driver spoke again, his words punctuated by the repetitive squeaks from the oilcan. "So, I take it you're wanting either a hop north or for me to spot you some cash?"

"A ride home will do just fine."

The trainman hefted his lantern and took a good long look at Ryan, then rehung it with an enigmatic smile. "That first boxcar there—" he directed Ryan's gaze toward the freight car coupled behind the locomotive tender, "it and its mates run empty as far as Mag-

deburg. Door's unlocked, so go settle in." The man returned to squirting oil. "And better luck with the cards,
comrade. Consider losing now and then so no one feels
obliged to get even."

Ryan thanked him profusely and strode back toward the car, only to have the engineer call out: "And
consider yourself lucky they didn't steal those fancy
pants of yours!" Before Ryan could respond, the man
had returned to his labors. By the light of the lantern he
could see a grin.

He slid back the door and climbed aboard, rolling
it shut behind him. Hunkering down in the rear, he prepared for an uncomfortable and brutally cold stretch
ahead. The worn planks reeked of oil and fertilizer, a
biting stench in the darkness. At least the smell should
improve with the constant rush of frigid air. As his eyes
adjusted to the darkness, phantom images drifted about
and his mind began to wander. He sensed slight nausea,
either from the acrid smell or from an empty stomach.
It would be dawn soon enough, but he would face
many hours before finding food or drink.

Abruptly, the iron-framed door creaked on its roll-
ers and stopped with a resounding clang as it met the
catch. Ryan was already on his feet, opening the blade
of his penknife. He spotted the engineer in the glow of
the upraised lantern. The man climbed up into the car
and gestured for Ryan to retake his seat. He carried a
rolled bundle beneath one arm and a paper sack. "It'll

be damned cold once we get moving, and I suspect food will help."

Ryan returned the knife to his pocket but left the blade extended. The bundle was a thin woolen blanket cinched with a cord. Inside the bag he felt a bottle and the soft give of bread or a sandwich. He set the items down quickly, keeping his eyes on the train man. "Most considerate of you, sir."

"Name's Gunther." He reached out and shook Ryan's hand.

Ryan started to offer an alias, but the man made a dismissive gesture. "Don't reckon we'll meet again, so why bother. Gave mine by force of habit." He ran his fingers through his hair and replaced his cap. "Don't know as how I believe your story, but you haven't the look of a criminal, you're lacking the arrogance of someone trying to trip me up, and you're a bit too polished for a brakeman on any crew I've worked." His smile seemed genuine enough.

Ryan grinned and started to speak, but Gunther interrupted: "No—better for me I know nothing—" He lit two cigarettes and offered one to Ryan before crushing the spent match underfoot.

"Much obliged, and the blanket's a lifesaver."

"What's in the sack will help with hunger and thirst. We get in late afternoon, so prepare for a long haul. And—my apologies—not going to be a comfortable ride."

"How can I thank you enough?" He took a drag on the cigarette, grateful for the warmth.

"Believe me, nothing to thank. Just doing a man a favor, right?" Gunther swung down with practiced skill. He grabbed his lantern and rolled the door shut behind him. Ryan rose to his feet and opened the opposing door a crack, ready to jump and run at the first sign he'd been conned. Instead, he heard the engineer shout up to the fireman in the locomotive that he'd be back in a moment before heading toward the rear of the train.

Something about the encounter gnawed at Ryan's gut. Had the engineer played along with his yarn a bit too easily? His friendliness had seemed forced, his curiosity too limited when encountering a stranger in the darkness of the yard. Perhaps it was Ryan's wariness on the heels of Klara's arrest and his renewed commitment to take nothing at face value. *Watch your back.*

He waited moments for the man to move beyond earshot before pocketing the sandwich and beer. Easing the door open a fraction, he stuck his head out to sight the length of the train. A glance forward assured that the fireman was nowhere to be seen. The engineer stood conferring by lantern light with some men at the far end of the shed. He had said the train would depart in mere minutes, so shouldn't he be up in the locomotive by now? A flashlight emerged from beyond the building to join the group for a brief discussion. That man disappeared briefly from Ryan's sightline before abruptly reappearing in the company of another man who appeared to hold something on a rope. Darkness and snow flurries made trusting his vision a challenge, so he sensed rather than saw a large dog pass beneath the lantern's glow.

The building only meters away offered a long wall with no doors or windows. No escape route. Edging out sideways, he lowered himself to the cinder bed. With another quick glance in either direction, he dropped to the cinders and crawled beneath the railcar. The sharp odor of grease and oil bit at his nostrils. Crouching on the track, he moved forward and eased beneath the thick axle to emerge between buffers flanking the brake lines and the coupler. Standing atop one pneumatic buffer shaft, he used a vertical handrail as his next step. Reaching high, he braced his other foot on a metal upright and pulled himself atop the boxcar.

The roof curved gently away from the center line. Lying prone on the slippery ridge he hoped to remain unseen. He had a real chance as long as no one scanned the roof with a flashlight. He felt the snow beneath him begin to melt and saturate his trousers as he waited on his high perch. Moments later the careful crunch of boots on cinders announced men approaching from both sides. They trod cautiously enough, but he had been alert for the sound. He lifted his head just enough to spot a man wielding a metal bar. Likely there were pistols drawn. He plastered his cheek to the cold surface and held his breath.

Abruptly coarse shouts rose to either side of his boxcar. *"Raus, raus! Hände hoch!"* Both doors slid open simultaneously and a chorus of voices competed with a baying dog. Someone loosed the excited animal within the confines of the carriage and it ran from one end to the other, seeking prey and barking excitedly in frustration.

Ryan recognized the voice of the engineer: "He's gone!"

"Look for tracks!" The command carried the authority of someone used to being obeyed. "Can't have gone far."

A flashlight threw shadows along the shed wall. "Snow's already a mess," a new voice shouted off to his left.

"Same here," the response from the other side of the car.

"You bucket-brained fool, you must have tipped him off!" The authoritative voice was now damning as it turned on the engineer. "You tipped him off."

"No way! The man didn't have a clue. I made him right at home!"

"Sure you did. Now search the other cars, one by one."

The engineer had clearly had his fill. "I did my duty and blew the whistle on the guy. You can't fault me on that, so the rest is on you. And if I don't get this consist out of here—and now—there'll be all hell to pay."

"Don't even think of using that tone with me!"

"You really want to delay us further? For God's sake, he was likely exactly what he said he was—down on his luck. Just didn't want to spend his day riding in this shitty icebox!"

The engineer wouldn't have dared talk to Gestapo that way, so the response surely came from a railyard policeman: "I'll have your stinking hide for this!"

"You can kiss my ass for all I care! Right now, my hide is worth twice yours, unless you know how to drive this train north, and right now! We're a good quarter hour late already. So you and your man get the hell out of our way or you'll be the one explaining the shot schedule to the Transport Ministry!"

A muted curse. A shouted command to retrieve the frustrated dog from the boxcar. Doors slamming shut and voices fading until only the steady thump of the compressor marred the silence. Ryan took several deep breaths. Crouching low, he worked his way back toward the leading edge of the boxcar. A look to either side showed he was in the clear. In one fluid movement he eased over the lip, his foot sought out the vertical rail and he dropped to the buffer shaft. Perched there, he scanned once more the length of the train in both directions, then slipped around the corner to enter the darkness of the boxcar. There would be little or no sleep coming but he knew they were unlikely to search again.

As he calmed his nerves, he noted the stench of dog feces had joined the previous odors. *Oh well, sure as hell beats a Gestapo interrogation.* He felt with his foot along the rear of the car, hoping to avoid the source of the sour odor, and found what he sought. The rolled blanket was still where he'd left it.

A whistle shrilled, the engine drew out the slack and the cars creaked and moaned in protest as they eased from the yard. Ryan remained by the barely parted door until the train reached the outskirts of the city and began to gain speed. He then settled back, grateful for the modest warmth of the blanket, and contemplated his next steps.

First and foremost, he must determine who had blown his cover on the Reichsbank job. He relived his tense charade as an auditor just six weeks past. The guards had paid him little notice, the same for the receptionists. Johannah, secretary to the vice president of Hitler's bank, secretly worked for Canaris. She had made it possible for Ryan to obtain proof that Allied industries were helping finance Hitler's war. Her aid stemmed from outright hatred of the Nazis and the terror they had wrought, so only the worst torture could force her to talk. And yet the secret police had very effective means to loosen lips. And then there was that mysterious courier, the one without a name. Had he been coerced into revealing Ryan's likeness, perhaps even Johannah's role in the undertaking?

Surely the admiral knew where things had gone wrong and how he'd been exposed. After all, Canaris sent Klara to shadow him in Switzerland and the bank incursion was the admiral's own operation in play. But the fact that the Gestapo had arrested her showed a bold new confidence on their part, a willingness to directly challenge the strongest intelligence operator of the Reich. The Sicherheitsdienst, Himmler's state security apparatus, had long fought covertly to undermine Canaris' military intelligence operation. Now they had taken a bold, open step. The balance of power between Abwehr and SD may have shifted.

Equally troubling was his compromised new persona. The Gestapo agent in the customs shed recognized him from the flyer and delivered his fake papers to the portly major. It seemed probable they'd immediately reported to Berlin the discovery of a likely suspect for the Reichsbank intrusion. After Klara's intervention, the major would have worked overtime to convince the Gestapo that they'd been mistaken. His standing in the Party and the SS depended on it. But Klara's arrest clearly showed that the secret police weren't buying that story.

Ryan was a man without viable identity now trapped in a totalitarian state. He would need to avoid police checkpoints until new papers could be arranged. Another clandestine meeting with the admiral would be necessary to learn how he was compromised at the Reichsbank and what became of Klara. The number Johannah had given him to memorize was a cut-out contact, for sure, but that was his sole link to Canaris. He would contact Ellington for a new identity before going underground until COI sorted it all out.

CHAPTER FIVE

En Route to Berlin, Germany
November 1941

The long hours dragged on, the tedium punctuated by seemingly endless delays in ranging yards as new rail cars joined the train and others were left behind, destined for parts unknown. Wrapped in the threadbare blanket and chilled to the bone, Ryan dozed as best he could and recalled his weeks in Geneva severing ties with Marita Lesney. Their on-again, off-again dance had finally come to an end. For a dozen years Ryan had drifted in and out of her life, her letters pursuing him on the road while he kept his emotional distance. Yet she remained a special friend through it all, never wavering in her personal support. On some level he always knew that such a time would come, but staring it in the face he felt deep sadness over the self-inflicted loss.

He pictured her in her Parisian milieu, so full of spirit, so proud of her night club off rue Pigalle. With hips swaying to the rhythm of the small orchestra, she had chided him for his inability to commit to any one woman. But that mental image surrendered quickly to reliving their reunion only a few weeks past: the shorn hair, the fragility in the eyes, the barely-healed chemical burns on her hands and arms. An undeniable beauty still radiated from within, but deprivation and vile treatment at Nazi hands had rendered sassy Marita a wisp of her former self. The hotel's beautician had done her best and his brother had seen she had new clothes before staging the surprise reunion with Ryan, but Marita's old verve appeared gone.

For two days he listened to her narrative of abuse, emerging in fits and starts before expanding into a vivid account of torments in Gestapo captivity, a French prison, and finally the German munitions plant. He comforted and commiserated as best he could. Impossible for him to picture the strength she had shown, yet she seemed to take it all as a matter of course. For her it felt like fitting punishment for failing to perish with her family on the road out of Paris.

She knew the fate of her last lover, the Abwehr agent known as Argent. Again she felt a deep responsibility. Her eyes brimmed with tears in recounting his death on a dark square, shouting out her name before falling to the rifles of her guards.

Ryan felt there was something he must reveal: "He loved you, you know. He told me so."

She acknowledged the fact with silence and a nod.

"Was it mutual?" Ryan found himself asking.

Her eyes carried silent recrimination. "Such a fool you are, Ryan Lemmon. Brilliant in so many ways, yet so blind. You really don't know what I was doing with him all along? How callously I treated him?"

He hedged, suspecting the truth: "What do you mean?"

She looked away. It was on the second day as they sat below the Hôtel du Lac veranda, occupying the same bench where Edward had orchestrated their reunion. Another frigid morning but without the bitter wind, and she leaned into his shoulder. A swan ambled up in anticipation of crumbs, then wandered off when they ignored its pleading look. A steamer chugged by, gulls squawking in its chilly wake. Marita stared out at the disturbed waters. He kept silent, wondering just how much of herself she intended to reveal.

Her eyes met his again. "I fell for Argent when I couldn't hold on to you. Surely you saw the resemblance—handsome, each debonair in his own right, and yet both gentle at heart. How could I not turn to him when I realized you wouldn't—couldn't—share your life with me?"

He searched for words but none came.

"*Non*," she said, "allow me to finish so you know there's no blame." Her eyes sought something distant, out of reach in the blue sky above. "You've always chased some unknown dream, *mon Cher*." She kissed his cheek. "You know, you're much like that cloud up there." She singled out a solitary puff of white. "You always have been. Remember long ago when you first saw me dance? I was barely eighteen, and you wanted me for my body, my looks? I let you pursue me, though I'd sworn to avoid stage-door Johnnies. Why? Because I thought you might actually be all I'd hoped for in a man." She touched his lips with a gloved finger to still his interruption and continued: "I knew deep inside I could eventually win your love as well as your desire."

"You succeeded at that, you know."

"Oh, I know." She rearranged the crimson shawl at her neck. "You've proved that." She took his hand in hers. "But I didn't really understand you then…and now I finally do. Yes, you're forever my shining cloud, Ryan. You drift into my life and I find you so bright and wonderful in a barren sky. But then you wander off again, some new wind drawing you away." He started to speak but she hushed him. "You know, I used to fantasize about receiving a cable asking me to join you in your golden America, but our timing has never been quite right, has it? And you're always on the move, always shy of settling down. There's simply too much you want to experience, and your destiny isn't tied to any one woman—" she lightly stroked his cheek, "to any one love."

He had only himself to blame for her regrets. She read him right, knew him too well, better perhaps than he knew himself. In truth he had already moved on, by personal choice his future too uncertain. Some part of him craved the excitement he still faced, and he couldn't imagine settling down now. If ever. "You know, Marita..." His words again found nowhere to go.

"No explanations, darling. We have now what we've always had—companionship, tenderness, and support where needed. At some point that must suffice." Another kiss to his cheek, a friend's kiss. "And I will always treasure it." He had drawn her closer and felt guilty.

On the second evening a soft knock had pulled him from his bed. He thought first of Edward, some news out of London or Washington demanding immediate attention. But Marita stood there, lovely in red lipstick and new crimson boots of Spanish leather. "We both deserve this much," she whispered, opening her overcoat to reveal she wore nothing beneath. Now wide awake, he cast a quick glance down the hotel corridor, then pulled her in and hastily locked the door. Shrugging her coat to the floor, she tugged off his bathrobe.

A knowing smile played on her lips as she slipped a hand into his pajamas and led him to the bed. She teasingly pushed him onto his back and straddled his hips. Catching his breath at her heat, he still noticed how fragile she had become, yet the caress of her tongue and the fluid rhythm of her dancer's hips had not changed. It was only their past she sought to relive in that moment of passion, memories of times shared before her old life went to ruin. In the throes of their desire he knew it, and knew she recognized it, too. Afterwards, deep in the crook of his arm, her breasts pressed to his chest and her hand protectively cupping him, she said her first farewell. He held her close until she appeared to sleep, fully aware of the dull ache in his heart, then rose to stand at the window and stare out at the frigid lake.

They remained together through that night and the days that followed, planning for her future during long walks, often reminiscing about Paris before the Nazi conquest. They met Ed several times to help arrange her new life. She graciously rejected his offer of a temporary stay with his wife and the young boys in Virginia. "They'll find you as delightful as I do," Ed assured her, "and I'm sure the connections of my parents-in-law will find something fulfilling for you in no time."

"What use has American society for a former Parisian nightclub owner?" she chided with a hint of her old smile. Instead she accepted his suggestion to find refuge in Palestine. With support from the American consul she received an immediate invitation from an agency resettling Jews driven from Europe. The pay would be modest; her needs would be, too. "After all," she said, "anything's better than slave labor in a munitions plant, *n'est-ce pas?*"

Ed's associates expedited her new identity papers and a visa. She would fly to Marseille at Ryan's expense. From there an American-flagged freighter would bring her to Palestine. Had her family survived their exodus from Paris, their entry into their new life would have benefitted from people like her, and this charitable work would return some meaning to her life.

A lake steamer had carried them to the walled town of Yvoire for a final dinner by candlelight. They returned to the city well after dark. On the following morning a car brought them to the airfield. No words came, only tears and a last peck on the cheek. She did not look back as she boarded. As the plane taxied across the airfield he had finally accepted all that he was surrendering. The hurt had been real and deep, but he was not prepared to change the direction his life was taking him.

The sudden approach of another train, its whistle screeching as it rumbled past, distracted him from such memories. His body had suffered from long hours in the jolting boxcar and his mind felt equally numb. Once his freight car rested on a siding in the Magdeburg yards and the shuttle locomotive ambled off, he slid open the door. With no personnel in sight, he bundled the blanket and moved quickly from one string of cars to the next, crawling over buffers and couplers to get distance from that accursed boxcar. At last he spotted a scalable fence and reached a service road fronting a noisy machine shop, a foundry blasting heat, a storage yard for heavy road-repair equipment and several nondescript buildings. He finally caught sight of the high roof of the passenger station in the distance. His first stop was a restroom where he made himself as presentable as possible. The mirror convinced him he needed rest before tackling the final leg into the center of Berlin.

Over coffee and a sandwich at the canteen he considered where to catch up on sleep. Along the service road he had spotted a particularly decrepit storage shed. With a box of crackers and two bottles of mineral water, he retraced his steps and confirmed the building was abandoned. The only dry spot was under the eaves in back, well-shielded from public view by long-idled refuse containers. Cocooned in the blanket, he finally slept. He awoke too late to beat the Berlin curfew, so he settled in with restless thoughts to waste the long hours till dawn.

At first light the station facilities allowed him to wash up and slick back his hair. He could do nothing for the two days' growth of dark stubble. A razor or barber could wait until he was housed in the city, and for now his grizzled appearance suited his attire. After consulting a schedule board, he joined the queue and purchased a one-way third-class ticket on a local to Berlin-Pankow leaving within the hour. From there he blended with the morning crowds, transferring from the elevated S-Bahn to the underground U-Bahn for the final stretch. No police checkpoints interrupted his back-route journey.

He joined the other subterranean commuters emerging like so many ants onto the broad square of Alexanderplatz. The expanse already swarmed with laborers and businessmen, shoppers and merchants, cabbies and street vendors. Sharply-tailored uniforms of yellow, brown and black were everywhere. Vehicle horns and bells fought for attention and yellow trams shrieked against their rails under sprays of blue sparks. Cars, trucks and double-decker buses lurched to and fro, navigating the busy intersections.

Placards in the windows of the huge department stores warned that much on display was unavailable for purchase, but cafes, delicatessens and bakeries fared better, serving foodstuffs, wine and liquor plundered from Occupied France. He passed cigar stores, apothecaries, travel agencies, milliners and clothiers. Waiters scurried about in the beer gardens preparing for lunchtime patrons.

There were few signs of wartime footing. A bomb had pocked a nearby street, but otherwise damage near the Alex seemed negligible. Forced laborers carted stone and sand to fill a crater facing the famed statue of Berolina, the goddess herself standing proud atop her tall pedestal. Air raids over the city had recently tapered off dramatically. The nocturnal sirens still wailed on occasion, but usually to announce a rain of propaganda flyers falling from the skies. No one knew a reason for the respite, at least no one amongst the Berliner citizenry. Some speculated with hope in their eyes that the British were running low on airplanes or materiel.

In the warren of tight, walk-up offices just east from the main square, import/export firms worked their trades, cut-rate dentists improved the much-neglected mouths of Berliners, and doctors of every specialty consulted on latest afflictions. Behind the scenes, insurance vendors issued dubious policies, fortune tellers fleeced believers, and print shops churned out flyers and advertising posters and—if the money was right and security tight—false ID's and forged ration cards. Up the side streets, bars, sex clubs and strip joints dozed, ready to awaken once the urban day would again fade to black.

This shady neighborhood had long been a center of Berlin's crime world, rife with gangsters, forgers, swindlers, pimps, and prostitutes. Despite the Criminal Police headquartered alongside the high arch of the rail station, the entrepreneurial spirit of the city's underworld lived on. After all, the locals reasoned, if big-league criminals and thugs could rule your nation, why should they have all the fun? Ryan counted on this laxity to shield him for a few days longer.

Despite his long hours of sleep, exhaustion began to slow his step and he couldn't quite shake a gnawing headache. Tobacco would help. He missed his pipe, overlooked in his haste to abandon his jacket back at the Frankfurt station. A sense of guilt was his other heavy burden. Had Klara gained her own release as expeditiously as she had handled his? No doubt Canaris had already raised a major stink at Gestapo intervention, or so Ryan hoped.

He caught his reflection in a shop window and paused. The disheveled clothing passed fine but his features appeared drawn. Since the luxury of a Hotel Adlon was off the table, he hoped for a simple room where he would await new identity papers from Ellington. And once he had lodging, he would dial the contact for Canaris. In the meantime, carrying no identity papers was one nerve-wracking problem he intended to remedy quickly.

He joined the pedestrian flow and quickly came upon a small tobacco shop likely to cater to locals. Tobacconists tended to be free with neighborhood gossip. The rich aroma hit him like a welcome friend. Though tempted to buy a new pipe, he would stick to his plan: first room and board, then perhaps a smoke. True relaxation could only come later once he again had papers in hand. The tobacconist appeared friendly enough, his broad brush of a mustache harboring mustard from some morning snack. Ryan had noted a pretzel vendor's cart outside and wished he'd made a purchase of his own.

He waited while a legless customer completed his transaction. Clearly identified by his threadbare tunic and medals from the Great War, the veteran reluctantly reached up a ration card and the shopkeeper used his scissors. The old man clutched the tobacco can to his chest and scooted toward the door on his roller board. Ryan opened for him and wished him a good day. The man grunted a reply.

"May I be of help, sir?" the shopkeeper called over to Ryan, a forefinger smoothing down his mustache. He noted the mustard residue in the process, laughed at his discovery, and dabbed his upper lip with a handkerchief. "Never a bad time to finish breakfast, right?"

"Indeed." Ryan ignored the tempting display of pipes. "A moment of your time, sir? I'm looking for an inexpensive room to rent. Have you heard of anything?"

The shopkeeper eyed Ryan's shadow beard and rumpled clothing but still deemed him worthy of consideration. "See the widow Küpfermann. She's just off Dircksenstrasse—ten minutes by foot at most. Lost her man a couple of weeks back—done in by a Grosser Mercedes in a big hurry. Sad story...our proud men in black had no time to stop for a look, just left him untended on the square." Ryan nodded in commiseration. "A goner before the ambulance even arrived and that with the Police Presidium just around the corner. My friend Erik out there—excellent pretzels, by the way— saw it all as he shut up his cart for the night." The tobacconist shook his head in disgust. "Anyway, Anton Küpfermann used to come in here weekly, nice fellow, another veteran of the last one."

Ryan expressed his sympathy before inquiring: "And his widow has a room to let?"

"Little choice, from what she tells me." The shopkeeper snipped the tip of a cigar and fired up. "Anton had only been working part-time. His knees had been acting up again. His pension is *Scheisse*—wasn't a lot there to begin with, judging by what little he spent in here, and the poor woman barely gets enough from the state to get by. She was in here just last week wanting me to buy back what little tobacco he'd left behind. Sad story. The flat is all she's got left." Ryan let the man ramble on. "Inheritance you know, but upkeep and city taxes will get her in the end. All that being said, however, her sad plight might help you both out. She tells me she's just put out a sign."

Ryan placed a coin on the counter. "Much appreciated."

The man slid it back. "Save it for Frau Küpfermann." He tore a corner from the morning paper, jotted down an address and laid it alongside the rejected tip. "Take a left out the door, head around the square past the S-Bahn overpass, then steer right and you're on Dircksenstrasse. Then watch for the street signs. Look for Emmengasse and the *'Zimmer'* card in a window. Half a block down on your right. Can't miss it."

"Most helpful, sir. My thanks for your time and information." Ryan turned to leave and had a second thought. Funds weren't a problem, but dressed as he was he should appear frugal. "Don't happen to have a bargain on a pipe, do you? Stem straight or curved, doesn't matter. Needn't be pretty, just draw well."

The man smiled and reached under the counter. He removed a crushed box with a jagged tear on the lid. "This one suffered a bit in transit, but place your thumb in the right place and you'll hardly notice the scratch on the bowl."

Ryan smiled. "How much?"

"How does four sound? And I'll toss in a little tobacco, if you're not particular."

"Done." Ryan added a couple of two-mark notes to the coin still resting on the counter. "I've been missing the one I lost."

CHAPTER SIX

Berlin, Germany
November 1941

Ryan eased his sore feet onto the hassock and sighed with relief. He would drain a few blisters before the day was done. In a while he would lay out his possessions and take stock, then make his way to the nearest shop to pick up razor and blades, shaving soap, and small adhesive plasters for his heels. For the moment it was enough to relax while breaking in his pipe.

His attic room looked down into a narrow street, the window modestly shielded by a lace curtain. Opposite the bed was a chest of drawers topped by a wash bowl and mirror. Ryan sat in the only chair, an ornate monstrosity in worn red velvet, likely some inheritance that no one else would touch. His footstool in faded embroidery had also seen better days. The WC with bathtub was two flights down.

The rail traffic on the Stadtbahn tracks, elevated almost to his floor level, reverberated down the Emmengasse with great regularity. Perhaps the rumbling of the electrified cars and the huffing of the small freight engines would become less noticeable deeper in the night. He had no intention of remaining long in this cubbyhole, anyway.

Mrs. Küpfermann was a frail woman in her late sixties or early seventies. Her life must have been harsh and demanding, and the wear and tear showed in her demeanor and gait. She kept her gray hair pinned beneath a dust cap and her house coat clean despite its fraying cuffs. She'd clearly made numerous attempts to hem them before surrendering to the inevitable. Her pale skin and red-rimmed eyes went beyond recent grief to suggest some debilitating disease, and Ryan felt for her in her suffering.

Her legs could no longer navigate the shallow treads and uneven risers, so he had taken the steep staircase alone to view the room. How the heavy chair had made it up was a mystery. He came back down with effusive praise for its cleanliness and suitability, which seemed to please her despite her sorrows.

She accepted his condolences graciously, and his payment of two month's rent in advance even more so. His intention was to move on long before that. Regulations required her to register with the police any household guest who remained beyond three days, but he sensed a lack of interest in observing legal formalities, at least for the moment. She had not asked for his identity papers once she had seen his cash, and accepted his story of a bag left in an S-Bahn locker to be fetched once he got his bearings in the city. She even offered to provide a daily cup or two of *Muckefuck* and a bread roll with margarine in exchange for ration coupons. That would be every morning except Sundays, and he would have to join her in the kitchen by nine.

A decent night's sleep did wonders. The radiator had banged and clanged for hours, even after he'd turned the handle till it swiveled to no effect. At least the racket had kept his mind off the rail traffic up the street. He'd ultimately surrendered to total and mindless exhaustion and awakened refreshed. He sponged down with a washcloth and water warmed in a bowl set atop the radiator, then lightly dampened his trousers to help smooth out the worst of the wrinkles before hanging them up to dry. He would have to find better shoes before the day was over. Removing two days' growth of beard helped as well. The considerate Mrs. Küpfermann had supplied a few adhesive strips for his feet, and even offered a half-empty bottle of aftershave from her departed husband's shaving kit. Faced with her barely concealed tears, he felt obliged to accept. Now he splashed the citrusy 4711 on both cheeks and a bit under his arms in lieu of deodorant. Feeling renewed, he headed down to breakfast.

"How are you set for menswear?" she asked, setting a cup of ersatz before him. "You're much the same size as my Anton was, bless his soul—" she blew her nose and slipped the handkerchief back in her pocket, "and his clothes won't do me any good hanging in the closet."

Ryan was pleased by the chance offer, but his expectations were low. "Happy to take a quick look."

She returned with her hands full. "You can have these for a song, seeing as how he'd be pleased to have them put to good use." She sniffed again.

Most of what she brought out was of no interest, but Ryan was happy to pay twenty marks for his Sunday suit. Though the jacket was a fraction short in the sleeves, the overall fit appeared good. "We buried him in his other, but that was his favorite. He outgrew the waist in recent years, but you do it proud." She threw in two passable shirts, a tie, a woolen scarf, and some undergarments. Ryan insisted on paying an additional ten marks. "Sorry, but the accident left his overcoat in tatters." Her voice broke with emotion.

An hour later he reappeared, decked out in her husband's best wardrobe. Her eyes again brimmed with tears and she asked him to wait, returning moments later with a serviceable pair of leather gloves. "No charge. Now you'll look as dashing as my Anton in his prime."

His highest priority was losing the compromised Lewis Graf identity. No telling how long it would take for a substitute cover once Ellington's cut-out contact passed along word of his distress. He mentioned needing photos for a new work permit and Frau Küpfermann recalled a photography studio less than a ten-minute walk away. He was surprised but pleased at her

lack of curiosity. Was she naïve or simply too dis-
traught over her recent loss to care? Perhaps she was so
anxious for his rent that she preferred ignorance.

Dircksenstrasse was abuzz with freight deliveries.
High-wheeled wagons butted up to the open archways
beneath the elevated rail line. The double-teams of dray
horses stood placidly in the traces, their manure added
an earthy smell to the bright morning air of the city.
Drivers unloaded wooden crates onto hand trucks and
hustled them into the subterranean storerooms. The inclement weather of several days had moved on, leaving
behind a glassy sky with scattered clouds reflected in
the canopy of the rail station. A chill wind sent errant
newspapers and advertising flyers tumbling across the
cobbles. Ryan dodged a sputtering motorcycle as he
stepped into the street and almost lost his footing on the
slick pavement.

Egged on by a lack of legitimate identification, he
spent several minutes placing calls from a pay telephone fronting the station. Loitering in any public
space without proper papers was an invitation to trouble. Any fit male had best be doing productive labor for
the Fatherland. He reached a female voice on the COI
cut-out number, gave his Lewis Graf identity, and
briefly explained his urgent need to speak with someone. She told him to call back the following day. He
phoned the consulate in Geneva and left a message for
Ed to check his mail. Finally, to move things along, he
dialed the number for Canaris' cut-out and found it dis-

connected. He had the operator give a second try with the same result.

Next came a quick visit to a stationary shop at the head of Dircksenstrasse. With a few blank postcards and some postage, he quickly sketched out a farm scene revealing the location of his new lodgings. On the backside he penned a note which described the farmyard and alluded to its owner, a charming "Frau Emmen." Ed would now know how to locate him. He would send an update should his stay at the new address be cut as short as he hoped and fully expected. He dropped the postcard in the box on the front wall of the police presidium.

With his cap pulled low and collar up, he turned right at the tower anchoring the rail station and headed into the labyrinth of lesser streets leading east of the square. These backstreets of Berlin Mitte were quiet compared to the constant hubbub out on the Alex. A street sweeper whisked rhythmically at the stones, the stub of his cigarette bobbing with every whoosh and scrape of the rush broom. Two women chatted amiably over the shards of a clay pot knocked from a window sill. A few geranium stalks, long deceased, rested in a clump at their feet. A few steps farther along he came upon a second-hand clothing shop and acquired a passable pair of shoes at an attractive price, since his old ones were taken in partial trade.

His spirits were now surprisingly high, given the improbable task of quickly finding someone to forge a passable new identity. He would start with a photographer and then, offering sufficient cash inducement, seek out a forger's atelier. He understood little of counterfeiting but suspected skilled players could take the compromised documents and, with the help of new photographs, manufacture a persona not listed on any Gestapo watch list. If anyone should know how to contact a forger, a photographic studio seemed a reasonable place to start.

The shop entrance was little more than an inset doorway beside an angled display window. Up front hung a family vignette in sleek frame; next came a portrait of a serviceman forever at attention, and then an older fireman in uniform staring intensely at the camera, his waxed mustache drawing the viewer's gaze toward his sunken cheeks. In stark contrast to that formality was the last portrait, a young couple in a woodland setting with a picnic spread out before them. Ryan finally spotted a sign advertising professional headshots for any civil or business need. Quick delivery—four marks for an equal number of standard-sized prints.

He entered the anteroom and the bell above the door rang to a standstill. An unmanned reception desk overwhelmed the tight space. He found himself surrounded by countless portraits in heavy frames, some old-fashioned and gilded, others sleek and linear in black and silver. Among all the forced smiles and sullen glares he noted endeavors in architectural photography, here capturing a gothic gargoyle exposing his backside to the world, there the crisp lines of some modern structural columns and an unadorned pediment.

When no one appeared, Ryan reached up to tap the bell by hand. At last a muffled voice sounded from well beyond a curtain: *"Moment mal...komme gleich."* Ryan took a seat on the caned chair at the desk and idly thumbed through a photo album. Two minutes passed before a man with a decided limp shuffled out from the hidden recesses. The photographer wore a black apron of rubberized fabric shielding him from collar to mid-calf and smelling of vinegar. He had a bald pate, a massive goiter at his neck, and a bottom-heavy build. Ryan's uncharitable thought was of a bruised eggplant. The man's eyes were moist and inflamed, and he dabbed at them with a handkerchief, sniffing as he spoke. "My apologies, sir. A bit of an accident mixing chemicals and you witness the price for my carelessness. Were my wife in the shop this morning, I'd catch all hell for neglecting the goggles."

"No apologies needed, and sorry for your misfortune." Ryan rose to shake the man's offered hand. "Shouldn't you flush them with water?"

"Indeed I should. And have. Gave it a lengthy go at the tap already." He snorted into the handkerchief. "Not the first time I've been this clumsy." He chuckled, embarrassed. "For the time being, we'll let nature take her course." He stuffed the soiled cloth into his apron pocket and, with one eye nearly closed, attempted a smile. "Now, how may I be of service?"

"I need a few photos for passport purposes."

"Right up my alley. Come into the studio, I'll work my magic, and they'll be ready by closing." He parted the curtain to reveal a larger room, temporarily unlit. Floods and spotlights climbed tall metal standards. A box camera with a bellows occupied a tripod facing several background screens suspended from the ceiling. Before the front panel, a neutral pastiche of grays and browns, sat a four-legged stool. Other chairs, props for group shots, hugged the far wall.

An open door in the back revealed a darkroom, its red safelight still burning. A heavy porcelain sink occupied the nearest corner. Drying prints and lengths of processed film dangled from a cord disappearing into the darkness. A row of large trays ranged atop the counter. Ryan made out the contours of a tall photographic enlarger, its shiny metal trim glowing rose-colored, its matte-black surfaces dissolving in the gloom. The chemical smells were more intense that close to the darkroom.

"Please be seated." The man gestured to the stool. Ryan obliged, assuming the disinterested air most common on official documents of identity. The photographer snapped a film cartridge onto the back of the apparatus, turned on a few lights and adjusted a reflecting screen to remove shadows from Ryan's face. He clicked off a dozen shots as he rolled the film through the case. "That should do it, sir." He dabbed at his left eye, then switched off the lamps, leaving the room in semi-darkness. "Four marks. Rush orders an extra two. Close of business today. Otherwise, noon tomorrow, if that works for you."

"And if I need them sooner, say by early afternoon?"

The man held his watch up to catch the light from the front, then glanced toward the darkroom to gauge his work load. Ryan guessed it wasn't that pressing. The phone had remained silent and no new customers had entered the shop. "Two hours, but I'll have to move a few orders around. Cost you double."

"Not a problem," Ryan said, reaching for his wallet. "And perhaps you could help a bit further with a little information?" The man's grin faded. "I'll gladly pay," Ryan added.

The shopkeeper sensed murkier waters. "What type of information?" He wiped his hands on the front of his apron, a gesture both nervous and futile given its slick surface.

"Just a name, sir. A local printer, someone who does quality work, and can fill an order quickly." Ryan knew the risks but wouldn't hold back now. He casually pulled out a twenty-mark note and laid it on the stool. "Someone who doesn't ask a lot of questions." The photographer rubbed his temples before running both hands over his bald head. Clearly deliberating the risk involved, he glanced repeatedly toward the curtain shielding the front of the shop. Ryan could read his thoughts: could this stranger be setting a trap; a policeman or a snitch?

The man spoke at last: "I run an honest studio here, no funny business."

"And all I need is a name. You aren't involved in any way, just sharing a bit of information." He set down a second twenty.

Another silence, then a determined answer: "There may be someone. I don't know him personally but people do talk. Come back at two for your photographs…and a name."

"And a way to reach this someone?"

"Phone number is the best I might do." The man stepped closer to the stool, protectively hovering over the cash, certainly far more than he earned on the best of days.

Ryan added another five marks and put on his cap, anxious to escape the chemical fumes. He left the man in the back room, fidgeting with his hands, eyes blinking rapidly, tearing up.

"Bis später," he said, "till later."

At a quarter past two Ryan again entered the photo studio. He felt somewhat tense and prepared for quick action, knowing that—should the photographer have betrayed him to the police—this was the moment when they would close in. He'd spent the last hour in the shadows of an alleyway facing the studio, smoking his pipe and discretely watching for activity. Nothing extraordinary had caught his eye, just typical neighborhood comings and goings: a bicycle messenger with a package for the studio, two elderly women strolling past while deep in conversation, a postwoman making her rounds, and a young man lighting a cigarette while looking into the display window and then ambling off again. Ryan had spotted the photographer at the front desk, dabbing periodically at his eyes, eating something from a paper sack and drinking from a thermos, perhaps waiting for Ryan's photographs to dry.

This time the bell above the door had barely announced his arrival when the photographer emerged from beyond the dark curtain. His eyes were still blood-rimmed, but he appeared more relaxed than before. He stepped onto the sidewalk and glanced up and down the street, then returned to withdraw a dun-colored envelope from the desk drawer. Ryan slid out the pictures, professionally-done and trimmed to size for any official document. "Very nice work." Ryan returned them to the sleeve and checked the cover for any notation. "And the name and number of that 'someone?'"

The man wiped his face with both hands. He picked up a pencil and pad and handed them over. "You write while I dictate." He bit at his lower lip. "Better not to be too involved, right?" He gave the information from memory. Ryan recorded the name and a phone number. He slipped the envelope into his breast pocket and left an additional eight marks on the desk, wishing the shopkeeper a good day. The door jingled noisily behind him. Step one accomplished.

The telephone rang repeatedly. At last a gruff voice picked up and identified the locale as *Schultheiss Taverne*. Muffled noise at the bar made hearing difficult, and the man on the line interrupted repeated efforts to make himself understood. "Becker!" Ryan shouted into the mouthpiece for a third time, drawing the attention of a woman beneath the canopy who clearly waited for that particular pay phone. He ignored her and gave it another try: "I'm trying to reach a Stefan Becker!"

"One moment, please." The background sounds diminished, and Ryan pictured the barkeep shutting a door to escape the clamor of boisterous customers. The voice returned to the line, still something less than friendly: "What d'ya want with Becker? He ain't here."

"I was given this number. I need an emergency print job."

Silence.

"Did you catch that?"

"A print job, you say."

"Correct. I'll make it worth his while."

"Say I can track him down, how does he reach you?"

Ryan read off the number on the dial. "How long will it take? The phone's public."

"Stay put." The line went dead.

Ryan kept the receiver to his ear, feigning further conversation. The impatient woman finally moved on with a look of disgust. She picked up at a newly-vacated telephone closer to the station entrance. He clicked off but held down the lever, unconsciously tapping his foot on the concrete as he awaited the call-back.

A full three minutes passed before the phone jingled. *"Guten Tag,"* Ryan said, not giving a name.

"You the gent that needs a quick print job?"

"You got him. This Herr Becker?"

"Works as good as any. You got money?"

"More than enough."

"Just what I want to hear. Where you at now?"

"Alex S-Bahn station." Ryan preferred meeting in a less public spot. "But I can come to you."

"Better we meet there. Waiting hall. Thirty minutes. What are you like?"

"Mid-thirties. On the taller side, slender build, dark hair, blue eyes. Billed cap and tweed overcoat. I'll smoke a pipe. How about you?"

The man ignored Ryan's question: "I'll find you. If you're late, I'm outa there, got it?"

"Got it," Ryan replied to the buzz of an empty line.

Twenty-five minutes later he found an unoccupied bench against the far wall of the waiting room. As usual, a constant swarm of passengers came and went. He needed a spot that offered some privacy, but men huddling in too a quiet a corner might arouse official suspicion. He wanted to observe each passer-by for any sign of interest but knew that wasn't wise. It made better sense to pretend to read, so he'd stopped briefly at the newsstand. His first inclination had been the latest edition of the *Völkischer Beobachter*. Blatantly displaying that rag, rife with anti-Semitic propaganda, might lessen the curiosity of a suspicious policeman. But a man making a living forging documents would be wary of approaching a fervent Nazi, so he chose instead the relatively neutral *Abendblatt* at the news stand. He sat down and lit up.

Precisely ten minutes later a man in his mid-twenties took a seat on Ryan's bench. A brown fedora concealed most of the cropped blond hair matching a sparse mustache. The fellow—slight with a sunken chest and hunched shoulders—removed a watch from his wrist, and, squinting at the station clock high on the opposite wall, carefully set the time and wound the stem. He wore thick lenses. Casually, he turned his head toward Ryan to inquire: "You finished with the *Abendblatt*?"

"Yes, of course." Ryan refolded the paper and handed it over.

"Thank you. Most considerate." The man turned to the back pages and ran his fingertip down the columns of classifieds. Ryan feigned disinterest. A minute or two passed before the man commented quietly: "Never can find a good print shop when you need one, right?"

Ryan nodded. "Herr Becker?"

"Sure. Why not?" The man lit a cigarette and released a cloud through his nostrils, then hacked from deep in his lungs. "What's your pleasure?"

"An embarrassing situation, actually—I've misplaced my identity papers. Likely stolen."

"No shortage of thieves around, right? And so tedious to replace them through official channels, don't you know? Always a bucket load of questions." He chuckled. "Suspicions and accusations."

"My thoughts exactly." Ryan re-lit his neglected pipe and shook out the match. "So what would you need from me?"

"What are you looking for, exactly?"

"The typical, I suppose."

"Well then, an identity card and some sort of work permit. Or if not a permit, at least a letter excusing you from duty?"

"That should do just fine. Would it help if I could get ahold of, say, outdated papers? Ones your capable hands could improve upon?"

The man smiled ever so slightly, considering the proposition before slowly shaking his head. "No, I prefer working from scratch. Artist's prerogative, you understand."

Ryan didn't, but nodded anyway. "So, what do you think?"

"I think three days, and a couple of passport photographs. Two hundred marks now, another two on delivery." The man's eyes never left Ryan's, clearly gauging his ability to pay.

Casually observing the comings and goings of the station, Ryan removed several large bills from his jacket pocket and slipped the cash into the photographer's envelope. He set it down between them. "You'll find photos inside."

The man coolly slid the thin bundle between the folds of the newspaper. "Anybody special in mind, or should I get creative?"

"Military exemption is a must. I'm thinking a civil engineer with the Todt Organization would be just the ticket." Ryan knew the massive construction firm received a blank check from Hitler in building both the new Berlin and the Reich's defenses. "Use the name 'Ernst Mahler.' Born 21 July 1906 in Frankfurt an der Oder."Ryan released a puff of smoke. "Got all that?"

"Memory like a vault. 'Ernst Mahler.' Got it. I specialize in detail work."

"Then that should do nicely. Other than that, a letter from the Todt people explaining my temporary stay here would be a nice touch."

"Not a problem. You'd be surprised to learn how many official documents come my way. That pickpocket problem, you see."

"Excellent." Ryan gave up on his pipe, tapping the bowl against the edge of the ashtray stand to loosen the smoldering tobacco. "Anything else you need from me?"

"This will do. Meet me in three days, same time of day."

"Where?" Standard protocol for illicit dealing was never to meet someone twice in the same locale. Was this guy an amateur? "Here again?"

The forger touched the brim of his hat with his forefinger and casually picked up the folded newspaper concealing the cash. "No way." He glanced toward the exit. "Wertheim's. Men's room on the mezzanine. Wait till we're alone." He slipped the paper beneath his arm, crushed what remained of his cigarette underfoot and ambled off without a glance back.

Ryan knew he might have seen the last of both the two hundred and his photos, but his options were limited. He waited five minutes before purchasing a ticket and boarding the next train that pulled in. He paid no attention to its destination, only to the people who boarded after him. Half an hour later he returned by underground to find afternoon foot traffic beginning to build on the Alex. He joined a group of shoppers at the main entrance to the Hertie department store, took the elevator up two floors, then rapidly descended by the back staircase and exited a side door. He had not been shadowed.

Now there was little to do but wait. The sooner he was rid of "Lewis Graf," the better. Those incriminating documents would disappear the minute he had Becker's replacements in hand. Assuming he got them. It certainly couldn't hurt to have a secondary identity even should Ellington come through in the meantime.

On the way to his room he stopped to dial the number for Canaris one more time. Out of service. He couldn't count on another Klara should he step in it again.

CHAPTER SEVEN

Berlin, Germany
December 1941

At precisely ten to six Kriminalrat Gregor Brandt rolled to the side of the bed and slowly lowered his legs to the floor. He took a moment to stare out the murky window and shuddered. Not from the cold, but from memories equally dark. Always ten minutes to six. Always the same troubled dreams, the same memories upon awakening. He switched on the lamp and fastened his watch. No need to check the time. He knew.

His alarm clock had given up the ghost the previous spring, the winding mechanism sprung after a long life. Finding a replacement even in the wartime economy would not have been difficult for a man with his connections, legal and otherwise. But the demise of the old silver and brass timepiece had not disrupted his routine. He left the hands standing at eight past three. Years of punctuality had created a mental clock that set the limit for his night's rest, and it was unfailing in its accuracy.

His sense of passing time, awake or asleep, had always impressed Gisela. He lifted her framed photograph from the bedside table—the smiling bride, Heidelberg's castle in the distance, a bouquet in her hands—and greeted her with a *"Guten Morgen, Liebling,"* just as he had for years, just as he had when she was still with him and would rise from bed without a complaint to prepare his breakfast. Fresh bread rolls, delivered warm to the stoop just minutes before by Helmut, the baker's boy with the withered arm and unfailing smile. And that unmatched Edamer cheese wrapped in waxed paper, the one that only Frau Helke sold in her little milk store up the street. Butter. A single soft-boiled egg. And, of course, coffee. Those were the days when breakfast still meant something to him.

Gisela had been by nature a late riser, so when given a choice on Sunday mornings she would stay in bed until he brought her a cup of coffee. But ever a diligent wife and companion, she had accepted the late hours and unpredictable absences of a police inspector. Brandt was thankful that she had not lived to see what had become of her beloved country, of once high-spirited Berlin, of him. "Too old for this," he said aloud. Glancing again at the photograph, he repeated the complaint to her lovely face frozen in time, and added another "my love."

Arthritis kept him on the edge of the bed as he flexed his legs and massaged away the pain in his knees as best he could. At last he shook his head with resignation and allowed his bare feet to feel for the felt slippers which somehow always wandered just beyond reach. At least, at sixty-three, he could still make it through the night without rising to pee.

He stood, allowing gravity to settle his joints. He entered the bathroom to stand before the mirror and let frigid water run from the tap. Gisela used to bring him up a pot heated on the stove, but since her passing he made do with cold. He splashed his face and stared into the mirror, disgusted by his tired looks. How unkind the years had been. He sometimes wondered if the hateful things he'd seen, all the cruel suffering and wasted lives, the bloodied bodies and tortured souls, had somehow left their indelible print on his own features.

In his youth his intellect and deductive powers shone in school, putting his comrades to shame and him near the head of his class. He had done well at his Abitur exams and even been offered a scholarship, and his parents surely wanted him to be the first in the family to go on to university. But Gregor had grown up on the streets of Berlin and witnessed from an early age the broad spectrum of humanity and inhumanity. He intended to further his understanding of all that made the inner city tick rather than head off to study with the wealthy elite.

For several years he shuffled papers for an export firm, earning little money but a great deal of criticism from family who felt he was wasting his God-given talents. Finally, tiring of their disapproval and ready for a new challenge, he accepted a job offer from a local constable and former captain in Bismarck's army who drank beer nightly with his father. Hands-on police training began in his early twenties under the man's guidance. He quickly gained respect from his colleagues for solving difficult cases and developed a broad understanding of and with powerful figures of the Berlin underworld. By the time the Great War rolled around he was already approaching forty and considered indispensable to the Kriminalpolizei.

In recent decades the young up-and-comers in the Kripo learned the arts of criminal investigation in a civil police training school. They tended to look down their noses at old-timers using old-time methods. Even more troublesome, his lack of advanced education put him at a disadvantage in the eyes of those colleagues and superiors who placed high value on their academic degrees. Yet Brandt felt that his kinship with the lesser denizens of his city allowed him to think as they did, feel their wants and needs, and better understand what drove them to do sometimes unspeakable acts against their fellow Berliners.

The great irony was that those in charge of the new German state who directed and oversaw his everyday existence at the police presidium were now often far worse criminals than the many he sought to bring to justice. The Nazi big boys committed their crimes for self-aggrandizement, raw power, or financial gain, and used brutality on a whim. More thuggish than most of the small-time lawbreakers he tracked down, they literally got away with murder and seemed to enjoy their unfettered cruelty all the more because they carried it out in the name of "protecting the Reich."

He desperately needed his first morning coffee. Although ground who-knew-when and certainly a bit stale, his was the genuine beverage, an advantage of commerce with both legal authority and the underworld. What Reichsmarks and ration coupons could not obtain, influence usually could. He drew a wet comb through his thinning hair, then lathered up his face and neck, stropped his razor, and carefully worked his way past the deep grooves in his cheeks and around a mustache which artfully hid the scar from an assailant's blade during his first year with the Criminal Police. The morning ritual nearly complete, he oiled his drying hair to keep it in place and headed down to the kitchen.

He knew why he delayed as long as he could. It was still difficult to face the reality that Gisela would not be waiting there at the stove or sink, her hair pinned up to offer her lovely neck for a morning nuzzle. It was a full decade since she had left him, the cancer too much to withstand. The memory tugged at his heart.

Forcing himself to move on, he set the coffee pot on the gas burner, then picked up the telephone and placed a call to the office. He knew Sergeant Schönheim would already have reviewed Brandt's instructions from the previous evening. The young man always arrived at the most ungodly hour.

Emil picked up immediately, clearly awaiting the call. "Schönheim here. Good morning, sir."

The inspector had never understood the young sergeant's chipper demeanor, especially at the break of dawn. Had he himself ever been so obnoxiously upbeat? Emil looked fit as a fiddle, but his induction physical found a debilitating weakness in his lungs that allowed him to remain on the Kripo roster rather than risk his life in Africa or on the Russian Front. Even more surprising, the young man had dared to share in private several liberal views in a department well represented by fervent admirers of Hitler.

It had not always been that way. Early in the '30's, when political mayhem still shook the city, Brandt had several compatriots on the force who shared his belief in the open exchange of ideas, a Berlin tradition for generations. This certainly came from growing up in a milieu of small shopkeepers, minor and sometimes major hoodlums, and working class stiffs like much of his extended family. Brandt had been a Social Democrat. Many colleagues, though affiliated with the more conservative Nationalists, still maintained a certain respect for democratic ideals, and he had often lifted mugs of beer with the Communists occupying the other end of the spectrum. With the ascendancy of the National Socialists and the elimination of competing parties Brandt became perhaps the last of his breed in his precinct to honor the concept of rational justice. Yet, despite occasional harassment from superiors who already wore the swastika pin, he was left to do his job, even while politely declining to join the Party. He might well have been ousted from both office and duties had his successful investigations not put the department in such a positive light. It also didn't hurt that his special connection with a certain powerful underworld figure contributed to the financial well-being of a few well-situated overlords.

In those early days, and especially in the working class district of Wedding and the eastern reaches of Mitte, petty criminals and police officers had established an easy truce, and the judicial system knew how to react judicially. More limited punishment was meted out for minor crimes and the harsher measures reserved for those who did serious bodily injury or upset the complacency of the very wealthy and powerful. This was a comfortable arrangement, leaving the cops free from wasting time on trivial peccadillos to pursue the heinous criminals harbored by any large city.

Pity the poor fools in the current climate who ran astray of the Gestapo. The secret police stuck their noses into the most mundane of local criminal matters, determined to make life a literal hell for anyone transgressing against the strict laws regarding race and loyalty. No one wished to be deemed "unreliable," a stigma which could and often did put families and friends in basements for cruel beatings and torture, or sent off to the prison camps, rarely to return. Brandt had learned to be excessively discreet in all his dealings, no longer confident that superiors would look away and let him do his job as he saw fit.

"Listen carefully, Sergeant. Time to reel in my American fish."

"Yes, sir. DT will be in by seven. I briefed them last night."

"Perfect." DT stood for *delirium tremens,* the department's nickname for Diedrich and Tannenfeld. The men were booze hounds of brute strength, limited intelligence, and easy confusion, but dependable for any simple arrest where intimidation sufficed. "Tell them he's to walk in on his own two feet, understood?"

"Perfectly, sir."

"I want the suspect in my office by ten, ready for interrogation and a bit subdued. But make it perfectly clear: no really rough stuff, and no mention of my name."

"May I ask what you have in mind with this one, sir?"

"I'm playing this close to my vest for the moment. Don't want to compromise you should things go sideways. I'll clue you in once it's clear I'll have success, but best you avoid the office this morning when they bring this one in."

"Avoid the office, sir?"

"Yes, take the rest of the morning off once the DT boys come in. You deserve it. But first put DT to work.

It's important that the man's caught off-guard and pliable, but not damaged."

"Understood, sir. Pliable."

"That's all, Sergeant. Tell the office I'll be in by eight."

Brandt set the receiver in its cradle. This should prove an interesting day. He poured himself a cup of the scalding coffee and unwrapped a chunk of cheese. *A bit on the green side, but what's the risk, right?* He made a passable sandwich from stale bread, planning to grab something fresher on his way to the subway.

He knew it was approaching seven so placed a second call. The phone rang four times, then five, and a familiar woman's voice answered with the surname "Friedrich."

"It's on for today," the detective said. "Can you start tomorrow?"

"As ready as I'll ever be." She sounded strained.

"Tomorrow then. This looks to be the break we've been waiting for."

"Won't be any easier for me, though." She hung up without further comment.

❖

Each morning Ryan placed a call to the cut-out number, always from a different public phone. Each time he received the same terse reply from that unknown woman: "Stay put. Call tomorrow, same time." Three weeks had passed since meeting the forger in the train station, and he was thankful for the fictitious identity of "Ernst Mahler" that now allowed him to relax a bit as he moved about. Becker had done an excellent job. The new papers had passed their first control check on his second day in that guise. Ellington appeared to be stonewalling him, or perhaps his messages were going astray. Was the new boss purposefully trying to box him in, render him ineffective, willing to waste him as an asset? Without so much as a reply, he could do nothing but wait.

The silence from Canaris spoke volumes, as well. Ryan's calls to the admiral's cut-out had all proved fruitless. The number remained disconnected. Clearly, nothing would come from German military intelligence as long as wanted posters might link the admiral's Abwehr to Ryan's Reichsbank caper. Was the conflict between German military intelligence and Himmler's security services coming to a head? Ryan would have to depend on Ellington and the COI.

Extending the stay at his current lodging added to the pressure. Every housing block in the vast city had a warden, and every warden was duty-bound to report suspicious talk or behavior. A casual conversation with Frau Küpfermann revealed that the timing of his arrival on Emmengasse had been fortunate, for Herr Richter, the local block supervisor, was out in a ward at Beelitz-Heilstätten recovering from a near-fatal heart attack. Yet he might return to his eagle-eyed duties at any moment and report the stranger rooming above the widow. Ryan was prepared to vacate at a moment's notice of Richter's return.

In the same second-hand shop where he'd earlier replaced his shoes he had found a decent snap-brim fedora to better mask his features when on the street. He passed hours hiding behind the local papers in crowded cafes. Whenever possible he stretched his legs during the busiest times of day, usually during the morning commute. Evenings he holed up in his cramped quarters and read whatever he could put his hands on. On occasion he joined his landlady sitting before the radio, listening to music over a glass of the sherry he provided. Mostly he simply "stayed put," as ordered by the cut-out.

On this particular morning he headed out toward the Alex for a brisk walk. He quickly spotted something out of the ordinary, a large man in a wrinkled suit leaning against a building at the intersection of Dircksenstrasse and the square. The stranger shielded his face behind a newspaper and ignored his busy surroundings. There were far better places to catch up on the morning's news. Heading across the boulevard toward the shops, Ryan casually glanced in a display window and spotted the man trailing him only a few meters back. He slowed his pace and noted the follower adjusting his steps as well. The man appeared quite inept at tailing a mark. Ryan decided to test his theory by stepping into the shop of the mustachioed tobacconist. Would the stranger proceed down the street, loiter outside near the pretzel vendor's cart, or enter the shop as another customer?

Shutting the door behind him, Ryan greeted the friendly shopkeeper while listening for the bell to announce someone on his heels. It rang a second time, and the tobacconist's smile faded instantly, his eyes darting rapidly left then right. Just as quickly two powerful men gripped Ryan by the arms. He instinctively lurched down and away to break free but his struggle proved futile. He could smell booze on the one, Bay Rum on the other. The trembling shopkeeper sought refuge behind the counter, sweat beading on his forehead.

"*Kriminalpolizei*," Bay Rum hissed in his ear. "Easy, buddy, you'll come with us now." Ryan tried a lunge to the left, desperate to throw them off-balance. Instead a fist drove the air from his lungs. He doubled over, gasping, and they patted him down, confiscating his papers and penknife and snapping on handcuffs. "Nice try, asshole." Bay Rum pulled up sharply on the chain and Ryan felt a jolt of pain in his shoulders.

A black sedan idled at the curb. Bay Rum took the driver's seat while the other cop forced Ryan into the rear. He hunched over to ease the pain in his gut and lessen the pressure on his wrists. "What's this all about?" he demanded, knowing full well it was for the Reichsbank intrusion. Nothing else made sense. "What the devil's going on?"

Bay Rum concentrated on his driving. His partner, now seated beside Ryan, laughed. "Yours to find out soon enough, buddy boy." The man's breath reeked of alcohol.

Ryan's old State Department identity would have meant a single phone call to Pariserplatz and swift release from custody. Although the American ambassador had left Berlin after Kristallnacht in '38, the Chargé d'Affaires who maintained the embassy would have intervened on his behalf. But now he could divulge nothing. Instead, he played the offended innocent: "Where are you're taking me? I've done nothing wrong. My papers are in order—just have a look."

"You can shove your papers. Just shut your trap or you'll get another good pasting." A jab in the ribs made the boozy cop's point. The driver's eyes remained on the traffic as they negotiated several turns before merging into the ebb and flow of the Alex. The massive stone façade of Kripo headquarters quickly loomed overhead. They pulled to the curb at the very spot he had passed a quarter hour earlier on foot. A short trip. A dangerous trip. Pain and misery waited inside.

The long, bland corridors swam in a bilious shade of pale green. The arresting cops spoke briefly with the officer at the reception desk before hustling Ryan up the staircase. Offices lined the aisle, some with doors shut, others revealing industrious occupants behind metal desks. Men and women worked through stacks of dossiers or busied themselves with typewriters, ringing telephones, and filing cabinets. For the moment he'd landed with the criminal police and he was pleased to be upstairs. With the Gestapo he would be down in some basement cell awaiting a particularly cruel interrogation. Here he couldn't expect niceties or coddling but would likely survive. He'd heard the Berlin Kripo maintained some semblance of respect for legalities. That meant a fighting chance if he saw an opening, but for now he had no cards to play.

The cops shoved him into the anteroom of a larger office where a colorful wall calendar offered stark contrast to the drabness of the surroundings. On the opposite wall hung a large plan of the city, a smaller map of the Mitte district, and a corkboard burdened by numerous wanted notices. A matron wearing gray herringbone and an equally gray hair bun worked a typewriter, glasses perched low on her nose as she alternately consulted a dossier, then returned her gaze to the keys to enter notations on some official form. She paid no attention to the new arrivals.

An open door beyond her desk revealed the chambers of a detective. Ryan started when he read the name on the brass plate: "Kriminalrat Gregor Brandt." A first glimpse through the doorway confirmed it. Despite a decade of wear on the man's face, Ryan recognized the same detective he'd last seen back in '31. This same inspector had shown up unexpectedly at the von Haldheim villa to investigate Isabel Starr's disappearance. He'd suggested Ryan back away from any personal search for his missing girlfriend. Ryan had long suspected that Brandt had been the source of a newspaper clipping arriving in his mail shortly thereafter. It reported the body of a woman found in the Spree River.

The two oafs shoved him into the inner office. The inspector remained behind his desk. Bay Rum made a show of laying out Ryan's confiscated wallet, knife and papers. His partner stood beside their prisoner, one hand pulling up on the cuffs to force a subservient bow before the detective. Brandt thumbed through the identity documents, a vague smile playing beneath his mustache. He read through the bogus letter from the Tod Organization and counted out Ryan's cash and coin, making separate stacks for each. Finally, he slid everything aside and gave Ryan a studied glance with no hint of recognition. He addressed himself to Bay Rum: "Any difficulties?"

"No, sir, like a walk in the park. Nabbed him entering a tobacco shop, pretty as you please."

"Good work, the both of you. Now remove the cuffs and leave us alone."

"Yes, sir." The cop nodded to his partner, who unlocked the restraints with obvious regret. They shuffled out to wait for further instruction in the antechamber.

"You may have a seat, Herr—" he again consulted the forged documents, "Herr Makler, is it?"

Ryan knew the inspector was toying with him. "Mahler," he corrected, rubbing his wrists, steadying himself. "You will find everything there in best order, Herr Kriminalrat."

"Without a doubt." Brandt made no attempt to mask his sarcasm. He called out to the cops to shut the door. "Now, then—" he reached for a small leather notebook resting on the desk and absent-mindedly rubbed a thumbnail over blemishes on its cover, "tell me all about yourself—" his brief smile revealing a smoker's teeth, "Herr Lemmon."

Hearing his name still came as a shock although he'd half-expected it. Ten years was not that long a stretch and he himself had easily recognized the inspector. All the same, the game was changing in real time, the rules unknown, and his new cover fully blown. No point in feigning ignorance. "You and I have met before, Herr Kriminalrat, some years back."

"Ten years, to be precise. You were looking for a young woman gone missing after a brawl and fire in Wedding and you'd made quite a nuisance of yourself around town. I recall it all well." He set the notebook down on the desk, his index finger now resting on its surface. "You see, Herr Lemmon, I'm blessed with an excellent memory," he chuckled softly, "as well as a drawer full of little booklets just like this." His finger beat a quick percussive note on the leather. "Years of investigations, years of questions. Some answered, many not." He pulled open a drawer and dropped the notebook inside. "But now I have a bigger riddle to solve, and perhaps you can help shed some light. Why does an American live unregistered and under false identity in the Emmengasse?" He removed a pipe from his jacket pocket and began to fill the bowl. "You'll understand my curiosity, I'm sure."

"I know this looks suspicious, sir." He eyed the tobacco. "You may recall I'm a journalist. I'm now writing for an American magazine—Colliers. You've heard of it?"

Brandt nodded. He slid pouch and matchbox across the desk and encouraged Ryan to light up. "Sorry my men interrupted before you could make a purchase. We've noted you share my love of a good pipe."

Ryan, wishing he knew the detective's angle, took advantage of the offer while further spinning his tale: "Well, you see, my editor asked me to spend a few weeks as an average citizen in the heart of wartime Berlin. You know, getting an insider's feel for the New Germany."

"And the false identity? You must know you break the law in pursuit of a 'story.' Forgery is a serious crime, and we can't have foreigners pretending to be upright citizens of the Reich, now can we?"

Ryan shrugged as Brandt toyed with him. "It seemed the easiest way to go undercover for a week or two." He lit his pipe and returned the matches and pouch.

"So tell me—what have you learned about us, Herr Lemmon? What will you share with your readers once you're home again?" He struck a match and drew on the pipe.

"Well, let's see. First off, everyone appears to have employment, so no beggars on the streets." He drew on knowledge gleaned weeks before while staying at the Hotel Adlon. "And big changes are underway, what with the elimination of vast stretches of housing along the East-West and North-South Axes. Word is your Führer is building a grand metropolis to rival ancient Rome. So urban renewal is well underway, and the face of the city changing." He had run out of any observations he dared voice.

"And our citizens, our Berliners? Are they happy with all this change?" Brandt's eyes bored into Ryan, daring him to drop his gaze.

Ryan, following a hunch, decided on marginal candor. "They seem subdued, sir, likely worried about their loved ones off fighting the war. And that cynical old Berliner wit has all but disappeared." Ryan thought he might have gone too far but soldiered on. "Yet with a strong economy, Wehrmacht success on all fronts, and adequate foodstuffs—and given the wartime footing—it appears your citizens are doing just fine."

Brandt leaned back in his chair, its springs creaking in protest. Ryan knew what followed would determine his fate. A full minute passed before the detective appeared to arrive at a decision. He chuckled and released a cloud of smoke. "You must know I have you dead to rights."

Now Ryan nodded. "You do."

"I could throw you in a detention cell and have you interrogated by the likes of the men out there harassing my secretary. Worse still, I could send you down to our basement, where truly troublesome cases are resolved by our SS colleagues, sometimes in messy but often very productive manner. Or, were I in a particularly foul mood, I could—and probably should—have you transferred to Prinz-Albrecht-Strasse and turn you over to the Gestapo. Your story ambles right up their alley."

Ryan suppressed a shudder. The scars on his own flesh attested to the horrors awaiting any prisoner of the Gestapo. He pressed on with his story. "I'm well aware of the dangers, sir, but hope you'll show some leniency. America deserves to know of your National Socialist successes."

Brandt idly stroked his mustache. "Here's what I'll do for you—" he set his pipe in the ashtray and picked up Ryan's documents, "you may walk out of here with these phony papers. You may spend a few more days exploring our fair city, researching that magazine story of yours. But should you run afoul of the Gestapo, you're on your own. Should you manage to keep your head down, however, you return to America and write your Collier's story. Clear?"

"Clear." Ryan was hesitant to speak further. "Most generous and understanding of you."

"Good. You have one week to wrap up your observations, then you leave my city, understood?"

"Of course, and thank you for being so accommodating." Brandt offered only the wisp of a smile. "Then I'm free to go?"

The inspector slid Ryan's possessions across the desk. "We'll pretend I never laid eyes on these. Just stay out of trouble." He chuckled. "A few among us still value freedom of the press." Ryan saw something more in the detective's final look. This wasn't a free pass, but the reason for his release remained a mystery.

Once outside the police presidium he headed for a café on the Alex. A headache was coming on, his bruised belly hurt, and he was inordinately thirsty. Someone had him in his sights and knew his every move.

Brandt leaned back in his chair, reminding himself to have someone oil the springs. This man Lemmon appeared much the same after a decade—still decent looking, the hair a bit thinner on top perhaps, blue eyes as piercing as ever. He wished his own appearance hadn't suffered quite so much in the interim. He withdrew from his file the Gestapo flyer on the Reichsbank affair and positioned the artist's rendering before him. The notice had crossed his desk weeks before and awakened a remarkable memory. One of his little note-books had refreshed the full history. And then his relia-ble snitch, the forger known as Becker, had given him all he needed to track the man down.

A nice thing about growing up in proletarian Ber-lin: one learned that all men were basically alike. Some chose honest means to make a living; others chose more dubious and likely more lucrative paths. So it had always been, so it would always be, despite the mis-guided belief of many that force and intimidation would create an ideal society. Establishing social equi-librium was what he was all about, and having a gifted forger on his team served many purposes. Live and let live, he thought, as long as it leads to an appropriate goal, right?

But what was Lemmon really up to, hiding under false flag? What had he done to cause such uproar on Prinz-Albrecht-Strasse, and why hadn't the man quit the country after his bank job? Any theft of monetary funds or negotiable securities would have been a case for his criminal police, not the Gestapo, and the Reichsbank wasn't your everyday target. It was the Führer's personal operation dealing only with the high-est level of governmental finance and investment. In-volvement by Himmler's secret police meant espionage of some sort, so this man Lemmon was clearly a for-eign agent. With America's economic support propping up the Allies, the United States was an adversary of the Reich, if not yet a declared enemy. Hitler would surely target America eventually, but that battle would keep until after the Russian surrender. Germany didn't need another front until the vast eastern resources were won.

But for now, Brandt needed to know where Lemmon's allegiances lay. The American might just be the godsend needed to bring his plan to fruition, and Frau Friedrich was ready to do her part.

CHAPTER EIGHT

Berlin, Germany
December 1941

It had happened in a cut-rate Berlin hotel room back in 1929. Shaving at the sink, Ryan heard a feminine voice, soft yet demanding as it whispered his name. He'd scanned the reflection in the mirror, expecting to see a maid behind him there to straighten the room. Or perhaps to offer a more personal service, as had occurred the previous summer in Dublin. But this time the room was empty and the worn floorboards should have creaked at anyone's approach. Baffled, he attributed the aural haunting to a hangover and returned to rinsing the blade under the tap.

Two years later he found himself on the terrace of a French inn. That was in late spring, the Cher Valley aglow under a disappearing sun, the twilight heavy with lilac. His breath caught as he spotted a white-gowned woman falling into a pond at the far edge of the property. He vaulted the balustrade and sprinted across the broad lawn, only to find the placid surface disturbed by nothing more than a few curious waterfowl. No trace of the woman in white. Was that specter also a trick of the mind, his imagination writing stories in a moment of distraction?

These days Ryan had no time for apparitions with reality enough of a burden. He preferred his dead truly dead, the gone permanently gone. Yet the spectral vision just spotted from his tram left him stunned. The woman's features were identical: the curve of the neck, the full lips and dimpled cheeks, the shapely body once known intimately. Her crimson beret stood out in a sea of drab grays and browns. He lunged to the window, but she had already disappeared in the sea of pedestrians.

An American woman lost to Nazi atrocity a decade earlier was crossing Alexanderplatz!

They'd both been reporters in those violent early '30s when the Weimar Republic teetered on its last legs, but ravishing Isabel had been much more than just another journalist. She'd challenged him to explore the dangerous underbelly of Berlin. Journalistic excellence did not lie in dispassionate observation for this woman; her stance was total immersion in the historical moment, reporting as a participant looking out.

Together they'd snuck into a communist gathering in Wedding to get a good story, only to barely escape with their lives when a Nazi group staged a surprise assault. Days later Isabel had suggested infiltrating a closed meeting of those same Nazis. Still nursing a severely bruised belly from confronting the attackers, Ryan found the challenge too daunting and rejected the proposal. A furious Isabel had slammed down the telephone, going on without him and disappearing without a trace. Weeks later a headless body turned up in the Spree, a known calling card from Nazis discouraging investigation into Party secrets.

Racked by self-recrimination, Ryan had often wondered what might have happened had he only agreed to her hare-brained scheme. Might he have spared her that horrible death? His guilt still surfaced with disturbing regularity, eliciting a vivid mental picture of the horrors she surely endured. Now that same woman, clearly still alive, mocked that memory and left him bewildered. Though he feared a trick of the mind, he had to see if his eyes had deceived him.

His streetcar rolled on toward its next stop. Forcing his way past offended passengers, Ryan jumped off the rear step as the tram slowed. Pedestrians gave way begrudgingly, but his opportunity was quickly passing. She was lost in the crowd. He scanned the many businesses fronting the square and narrowed the choices. Entering an office building he took note of the tenants—physicians, dentists, lawyers, notaries. Where might she have gone? The concierge hemmed and hawed and finally accepted Ryan's tip, only to concede he had seen no woman in a red beret. The next lobby was equally unproductive, and each shop along the way—florist, tobacconist, millinery—gained him nothing once the sales clerks learned he had no interest in their depleted stock.

In frustration, he found a café overlooking the square and took a window table on the second floor. The long minutes ticked by as he smoked mechanically and observed the pedestrians below. To help pass time he eavesdropped on those around him. Two surprisingly fashionable women chatted about children, the weather, and the quality of the cakes. Bored businessmen smoked over beer glasses, casting the occasional glance at fellow customers. Two SS officers conferred in the corner, a bottle of schnapps between them. And an ill-tempered dachshund yipped each time the waiter approached his mistress's table. Once he would have overheard spirited political debates, the sharp Berlin wit taking down even the highest political figure a peg or two. Now Berliners were content to while away their leisure with bland small talk. No mention of war or of any deprivations. Ryan understood that little personal danger lay in shallow conversation. The waiter clipped another ration coupon and a fresh cup of ersatz coffee appeared before him. Ryan added a splash of cream and a little sugar to blunt the bite of burnt grain.

A Strauss fanfare interrupted the quiet radio concerto and another waiter dialed up the volume. A special report proclaimed new Wehrmacht successes in the North African campaign. Always a "campaign," never "war." Who needed a reminder of the humiliation of the Great One, of casualties and brutal deaths, of subjugation to the whims of the conquering powers? Ryan ignored the inflated count of that week's English captives, knowing well that Dr. Goebbels' incessant propaganda thrived on hyperbole. The news report shifted next to the massive Wehrmacht assault in the east, where the towers of the Russian capital were already in Reich gunsights. In the months since Hitler had broken his pact with Stalin the Wehrmacht had covered thousands of kilometers to put the screws to Moscow. Certain and uncompromising victory was the only acceptable outcome, and no one doubted it was coming.

As the radio report closed with martial music Ryan abruptly sprang to his feet. The phantom Isabel was again crossing the square to board a streetcar! Leaving a few coins on the table, he forced his way downstairs and onto the sidewalk, hurdling that same boisterous dachshund and ignoring the protests of the matron holding his leash. His full focus was on the departing tram. The streetcar rolled past him only a stone's throw distant but he'd seen enough to be certain. He pushed on, determined to reach the tram at its next stop, but a double-decker bus swerved to the curb, blocking his view and slowing his advance. Once around the obstruction he saw only indistinguishable streetcars in the distance.

Verdammt nochmal! How the hell to find her now?

Tamping down his fury, he returned to the café for his hat and pipe. He would get to the bottom of this deception, but suppressing his anger was a struggle. What the devil was she doing here now, alive and well in Berlin? Why had she disappeared on him and what the hell had she done since? Not one word in over ten years! If COI couldn't be bothered getting back to him, solving the mystery of Isabel's reappearance offered a new challenge. He would tackle this puzzle with or without Ellington's approval.

For the next two days he passed the noon hour in the same café overlooking the Alex, arriving before the lunchtime crowd to claim his table at the window. A one-time errand might have brought her to the square, but he was willing to endure a long wait on the off chance she might return. After all, what else to do but sit on his hands and wait for Ellington's contact? On day three he spotted her again, this time emerging from that very building where the concierge had pocketed his tip. She wore a bold red scarf at her neck and her chestnut hair partially hidden beneath the same crimson beret that had first caught his attention. Painful memories flooded back and for moments the long-standing grief gave way to anger and accusation.

He joined the pedestrian flow, hugging the storefronts, his collar up and his hat brim low. She was heading toward the tram stop of days earlier. Slowly she glanced back in his direction, as if aware of being observed. He pivoted toward a shop window and brought his handkerchief to his nose, just one more Berliner suffering from a head cold.

He was still uncertain how to approach her. *Hello, Isabel, long time no see.* Not a chance. *Well, Darling, didn't you get my calls?* Ridiculous. Nothing suited the hell storm of grief and worry she had put him through, no light banter could ease the gravity of her dismissal and loss. They had shared so much, yet her actions had been so callous, and he was determined to learn why.

Unusually heavy rains had surrendered to an early December chill. A stark wind raked the streets, pelting pedestrians with sleet and promising snow by evening. She claimed a seat at the front of the two-car tram, just as on the previous sighting. Isabel a creature of habit now? Not the woman he remembered. He boarded the second car, the overheated air soured by damp wool and unwashed bodies. He loosened the scarf at his collar and picked up an abandoned *Morgenpost* to shield his face. Sighting between the newspaper and the snap-brim of his fedora, his eyes never left her.

They moved northward. Scheduled stops came and went, sometimes smooth and marked by the squeal of brakes, other times in fitful lurches when ice on the rails refused traction. Ten minutes passed, then fifteen more as they moved farther out into Wedding. He occasionally lost sight of her as passengers moved on and off, but each time a quick look reassured him. Another quarter hour was gone before the ticket taker announced the end station.

She was barely out on the platform and he was already on her tail. He hid behind a man in a bowler waddling between SS officers. She headed toward the suburban railcar on the adjoining tracks. The men shielding him hastened to make the same connection, the destination Oranienburg, home to the notorious Sachsenhausen concentration camp. Being so damned close to that prison awakened a heart-rending memory: his dear friends the von Haldheims had disappeared into its depths years before.

He entered the rear carriage as the train eased from the station and found a seat among SS officers, businessmen in drab overcoats, and housewives returning from shopping in the city. The women sat quietly chatting, their headscarves obscuring their faces and mesh bags of groceries resting at their feet. Isabel's red beret was visible midway ahead in the leading railcar. Did she live in the village, or was she actually prison-bound? The hair at the nape of his neck tingled. For the first time in weeks he again felt truly alive. He barely noticed the suburban dwellings and fallow vegetable plots flashing by.

A military bus rumbled and smoked curbside at the Oranienburg S-Bahn station, vapor whipping from its exhaust. The sign above the driver's window read Sachsenhausen. He dared go no farther. At the bus Isabel greeted the two SS men who clearly knew and liked her. The officers introduced the portly man in the bowler. She shook hands all around, and even from afar he recognized her laughter. Baffling! He waited behind an iron pillar as the bus took on a half-dozen additional passengers, then left the station in a billowing cloud of exhaust.

The policeman at the entrance to the terminal nursed an inflamed tooth. A folded handkerchief pressed to his jaw did nothing to hide the pained expression on his face. He waved Ryan and the few others through with only a glance. It seemed obvious that a person dangerous to the Reich would unlikely spend an afternoon so close to a notorious prison. Ryan purchased the afternoon papers and took a seat on the hard bench to pass time scanning classifieds for a covert signal from Ed. No sign of the agreed-upon telephone number, so as of yet, no news forthcoming. He would stick to his private mission until directed otherwise, no matter where it led.

Shortly after seven that evening he was back in the heart of the city. He had followed her to a moderately prosperous housing block a short walk beyond Unter den Linden. He watched as she entered the building through a curtain of sleet, then waited for the closing of blackout drapes to reveal her flat on the second floor. He delayed a moment before approaching the stoop. The name on the call board read "I. Friedrich." The register identified the lower apartment to the right as the domicile of a *Hausportier*. Such concierges often functioned as apartment house snitches, earning credits with the Gestapo by noting unusual comings and goings. A sliver of light shone at one edge of the drapes shielding the concierge's window, an imprecise seal sure to draw the ire of any civil defense warden. Ryan decided to wait until the doorkeeper turned in for the night. By now the sidewalk was more suited to ice skating than walking, and the street itself had turned to a morass of slush after evening traffic. With no secure spot to wait, he took shelter from the biting cold in the deep shadows of a facing alleyway. Tightening his scarf and securing his hat from the wind, he settled in for the long wait.

Over an hour passed before luck glanced his way. The stray fissure of light blinked out. A minute later an elderly gent with a noticeable limp worked his way down the steps, one hand firmly gripping the metal railing, the other a cane. Another disabled veteran off to toast fading memories with comrades? He hobbled up the block and disappeared into the darkness. Ryan crossed the street, slush saturating his shoes and trouser cuffs. His toes felt numb. He rang her flat, got no response, then pressed a second time and did not let up. In the long hours at the Oranienburg station he had decided not to overthink his approach. Enough was enough.

"Hallo! Wer ist da, bitte?" A voice he thought never to hear again requested his identity.

Ryan sensed worry and hesitation, but who welcomed an unexpected nighttime visitor in Nazi Germany? He braced himself and lowered his voice: "Ryan Lemmon."

A gasp. *"Ach Du lieber Gott!"* Barely a whisper.

Ryan pictured her at the speaker box, perhaps as stunned as he had been upon discovering she lived. He spoke quickly: "Isabel. Open up. We must talk."

Only the low-frequency hum of the speaker rose beneath the patter of ice crystals pelting his hat and shoulders. She was not ringing him up, and his anger mounted. At last she spoke again, now in English: "I'll be right down."

Whatever might happen now, too much water had passed beneath the bridge to make up for all he had suffered at her expense. He sensed rather than heard her hesitant footsteps just beyond the door, followed by the clunk of the lock as she cracked the door. *My God, as beautiful as ever!* Isabel held a finger to her lips, her eyes wide, her face drained of color. She pulled him inside, then removed his hat to expose his face to the dim bulb and gave his cheek a gentle caress. Her hand trembled as she guided him upstairs to the first landing. The open door to her living room fed its warmth into the dark hall. She hurried him in and threw the bolt into place. Ryan started to speak, but she again raised a finger to her lips and led him deeper into the room. The radio was pre-set to a government broadcast. She turned up the volume, filling the room with music.

Only then did she dare speak, keeping her distance now, wary: "Oh my God, Ryan, what on earth are you doing here?" She shrugged off the coat draped over her shoulders, removing a pistol from the pocket and placing it on the table alongside the radio. "I heard you'd returned to the States, so what are you doing here? Damn but you're still handsome! Do you still write for Kansas papers?" Her words came without a break, as if questioning him would postpone having to explain where she had gone, what she had done, who she had become. "How on earth did you find me after all these years?"

"It's what I do now," he said, ignoring the serendipity which had brought him here. It was up to her to offer clarification, to somehow justify her cruel vanishing. He sensed deception in her response to his sudden reappearance, and she was clearly involved with the SS, which made everything she said suspect. He had seen the interaction with the officers at Oranienburg— almost a flirtation—so the danger was very real. But despite himself, he still felt attraction after all those years. He kept his voice hard. "I thought you were dead. There was a body in the Spree." He left the unspoken accusation hanging in the air.

She turned to the radio, as if drawn to the overly loud music, her eyes downcast. "I know. It was unfair of me, cruel even...but necessary." She smoothed her skirt. Her fingers fiddled with the top button of her blouse. It bore some crest. He realized her outfit was official, something appropriate for a government worker.

"Why didn't you contact me? I was in Marburg for years, and you had my parents' address in Kansas." He fought to keep his voice from cracking. "What the hell happened back then?" He held his fists clenched, the hurt ingrained and his anger surfacing. "I grieved for you, and yet you stand here very much alive. I deserve an explanation."

"You do." She dropped to the sofa and patted the seat beside her. "It won't be easy, but I owe you that, and more. But first—something I must know: how did you find me? At the risk of sounding melodramatic, lives do depend on it!"

He forced himself calm but remained standing. "Pure chance. I spotted you on the Alex."

She thought for a moment before speaking, her tone firm, now all business. "And you saw where I went from there? Where I work?"

His brow creased as he nodded. "The camp."

"Does anyone else know you're here?" Urgency in her voice. "Were you followed?"

"I'm too good for that." He thought of Klara and knew it was a lie. Had he been careful enough this time?

Her features relaxed a bit. He saw a gleam in her eyes. "You always were good, especially with that tongue of yours." When he failed to respond to the tease she became more earnest. "Honestly, Ryan, how often I've thought of those days and nights and wondered about the choices I made." She looked at him imploringly. "But made is made, done is done, and now so much depends on your understanding, your silence."

Ryan resisted the temptation. He wasn't about to let her off easily, and the SS connection was deeply disturbing. "I don't bring you trouble, but you do owe me clarity. What the hell happened?"

"A long story…" She glanced toward the front door, as if fearing someone might come bursting in. "And difficult to tell."

"It damned well better be a good one." She blanched at the sharpness of his tone, but the long-held pain lay too near the surface for him to surrender easily to a tale from their shared past.

Isabel was undeterred. "You're positive no one saw you come here? What about the concierge?"

"Out for the evening. Let it go—I know what I'm doing."

"Then here's my story—please don't hate me for it—and afterwards you must leave for now and go as invisibly as you came."

"The radio?" He gestured toward the wireless as he finally took a place on the sofa. "I'm a fan of Mozart, but perhaps a bit quieter while I hear what you have to say?"

"Of course." She rose to lower the volume, then returned to the couch and tucked her legs beneath her. Drawing a deep breath, she began to recall that night in '31 when she had hung up in a huff, determined to attend the Nazi meeting without him, undercover and in disguise.

CHAPTER NINE

Berlin, Germany
February 1931

"Come on, Doro! You know you want to." Isabel switched the receiver to her other ear. She needed a companion for the night's adventure, and the tight space of the Kranzlerecke newsroom was annoyingly loud. Chuck Brady, fellow correspondent for the Daily News, sat next to her, shouting at full volume to get his story across a scratchy line to Chicago. Isabel's dirty look went unnoticed.

After several exasperating attempts she'd finally reached Doro. Her Communist friend simply *had* to help her infiltrate the meeting. She looked forward to showing Ryan how two women could put one over on those same Nazis after Ryan got cold feet. She knew the close call the previous week had rattled his nerves and left him bruised, but she still bit her lip in frustration over the man. The political underground was no place for the lily-livered. Who knew, perhaps Ryan would still come to recognize his lost opportunity and screw up his courage.

What a story to wire home to her editor father! He would shit his pants when he read what she'd pulled off. Serves him right—so much for believing a woman should only report on society shindigs and gossip! But first, she had to get Doro onboard for the evening's adventure. "It'll be a simple in-and-out. You'll be my extra eyes and ears; we slip in unnoticed and get the scoop. Afterwards we down a beer or two and laugh ourselves silly over the fascist idiots, and then I file the greatest story yet."

She excused herself for a moment to shout at Brady: "Put a sock in it, Chuck! I'm trying to work here!" Her colleague swiveled away from her and extended a middle finger. She put a foot to his chair and sent him rolling into the narrow aisle. "Doro, trust me—it'll be a piece of cake."

"You lead a charmed life with all your risk-taking, Izz, but it sounds like we could both choke on this particular 'piece of cake.'"

"Risk just adds to the fun, darling. Tell me— why'd you join the Bolshies if you can't handle danger?" The silence on the line told Isabel she'd pushed too far.

Doro was determined to give women societal power equal to any man's. Political muscle would be the first step toward changing stubborn attitudes. Isabel's friend had flirted with joining the Social Democrats, but found most Sozis more talk than fight, their traditionalist members clinging to an old-fashioned attitude toward the woman's role in their political struggle. The Reichsbanner troops of the SPD were the exception, but this paramilitary organization still didn't want women fighting alongside them in street battles. Berlin's Communists, however, welcomed anyone willing to fight for the proletariat, no matter the gender, and the Reds weren't afraid to draw blood. Let the Nazis use violence and intimidation. Doro and her comrades would give tit for tat.

Isabel knew a change of tack was needed. She summoned her impossible-to-say-no-to voice: "Be a peach, Doro—it's a lark you'll never forget!"

Doro played along with the obvious manipulation. "So who told you about this meeting? They don't advertise the closed ones."

"Believe it or not, it was the detective investigating our run-in with these bastards. This guy seems as interested in keeping the peace as the Nazis are of messing it up. Says he wants me to spread the word on what Hitler's boys are up to these days."

Doro was clearly incredulous. "A Kripo inspector?"

"Struck me as a bit odd, too, but some bulls must bend to the left." Chuck, now off the line, sat facing her and eavesdropping with a supercilious grin. She shoved him away again, her foot coming perilously close to his groin. "The cops can't all be frigging fascists, can they?"

"What makes you think they won't recognize us from the other night? You bruised a few balls with that wicked knee of yours, and even I managed to dent a head or two."

Isabel chuckled. "Disguises, of course! It's all handled. We'll just blend into a large crowd and keep our heads down."

"So where's that dashing American of yours? Word is he gave as good as he got last week, so why not get him to go with you."

"Honestly, Ryan's a lot of things: charming as hell and plenty smart, and damned good in the sack, too, but the fellow needs more backbone to keep up with me." Isabel sensed the depth of her own disappointment. "Let's just say I've taught him all I can, but he's not ready to get down and dirty for my kind of reporting."

She and Ryan had done exciting work at street rallies and some of the city's shadier dives, yet she doubted he could ever lose that Harvard Business self-image. Despite her coaching he remained a neophyte at all this. Enthusiastic, yes, but a dabbler. His reportage was more observational, hers confrontational, and timidity had no place in the gritty underworld of Berlin.

Doro's reluctance was no surprise, though. Her watery-eyed boyfriend was still nursing a smashed ankle and a brutal gash at the throat. The Brownshirt's knife had narrowly missed the jugular, but happily Jürgen's larynx remained intact. Only that wooly beard had saved him during the memorable brawl and he would soon be on his feet again, preaching the manifesto on crutches.

"I don't know if I'm up for it either, Isabel. Shouldn't you invite a few others to join in?"

"Only room for the two of us tonight, friend." Isabel had no intention of taking another "no" for an answer. Time was short and she'd made some newsroom boasts she intended to back up. Come hell or high water, she was going to be there and needed someone to watch her back. "Any bigger numbers and we wouldn't get past the door. These Brownshirts think a woman's only place is in the home, ready to spread her legs for Fatherland and Führer. Tonight we're going to show how strong women take action."

Doro sighed. "Okay, so spill it—what's this grand plan of yours and how does my going help the cause?"

Isabel exhaled, her friend hooked at last. "Details later, but you'll love it! Just the two of us tonight, agreed?"

She heard the surrender in Doro's voice: "Fine. Who can ever say no to you? Where and when?"

Isabel glanced at the clock on the far wall. "It's a quarter past noon now. Meet me at two at the Marquardt Café, Parisergasse 2. We'll grab a bite, then see if Toni is out of bed."

"Toni?"

"Just be there. The Marquardt, and don't be late." She dropped the phone in its cradle, just in case Doro was tempted to change her mind. What a story to wire home tomorrow!

A working-class upbringing in difficult times made some people openly envious of those better off, others bitter or all-out angry. It had made Doro compassionate. From an early age she committed herself to improving the lives of the underpaid and overworked. Many of her friends had turned complacent in the face of economic suppression, but the plight of her long-suffering proletarian parents was painful to watch. Mistreated on a daily basis by a machine shop foreman who ignored overtime and deducted expenses for the slightest infraction, her father had weakened physically and mentally month by month, year by year. He now looked and acted twice his age. Her mother helped feed the four siblings by taking in laundry and sewing. Eventually she had become a skilled dressmaker, but as often as not, the wealthy patrons found some nit to pick in her custom-fitted orders—anything to justify ruthlessly reducing the promised payment.

For two years Doro had lined up at the soup kitchens, trading places every few hours with her mother, hoping to get enough to feed the family. She witnessed the squalor of homeless encampments and wondered how long before her family lost its modest apartment to the greedy landlord. Finally, at eighteen and working alongside her mother sewing for the oppressor and oppressed alike, she knew she must take a political stand.

The Communist Party had welcomed her with open arms, as had the sweet if verbose Jürgen.

While she knew her own borough well enough, the rest of Berlin remained a mystery. The vast wheel of boulevards stretched out to places she would likely never visit. Arrogant, well-to-do exploiters claimed the center of the city or the wooded lake land to the west of the city, many keeping luxurious villas and townhomes she glimpsed only from tram or bus. Meanwhile, the poor drudges she knew so well occupied the neglected outer neighborhoods of the metropolis or piled, one family upon the other, in squalid tenements at the edges of the bustling commercial centers.

No stranger to the eccentricities Berlin had to offer, she had only second-hand knowledge of their salacious diversity. The city's red light districts were rumored to be decadent corrupters of boys and girls alike. On the outskirts of such "pockets of sin," dance clubs and cabarets satisfied the most extreme tastes. Newsstands displayed lurid rags promoting every sexual variation and perversion, and, once darkness fell, the pitchmen descended into the streets hawking raunchy booklets, while street girls and rent boys displayed their most personal wares to both goal-oriented and naive tourist alike.

Nevertheless, Doro was ill-prepared as she trailed Isabel up the staircase to the second landing in a narrow apartment block off Nollendorfplatz in Berlin West. Isabel had remained tight-lipped about her "plan," offered only a frustrating "wait and see." Now, with lunch behind them, she rapped lightly at a door and awaited a response. Then tried again.

Toni opened at last. Smiling sleepily, she had clearly dragged herself from bed in response to their arrival. The slim-hipped young woman towered over Doro. Barely hidden beneath a carmine day robe, her well-muscled arms and legs suggested an athlete, and the weary eyes implied a schedule that kept her up until the earliest morning hours. Her oiled black hair was cut short and she wore no makeup. A cigarette holder pinched between thumb and forefinger jutted upward, the mannerism of a young aristocrat awakening from a bender. Only the surge of nipples beneath the thin wrap betrayed her biological gender.

Isabel gave her a friendly peck on each cheek. "You're such a love, Toni. Especially on such short notice."

"Always glad to see you, Izz." Toni's smile revealed perfect, even teeth.

Isabel put an arm around her friend's waist and squeezed. "It really couldn't wait, you see." She introduced Doro and the two shook hands.

"I'll put the kettle on," Toni said, setting aside her cigarette and running fingers through her slick hair to restore its masculine styling.

The two guests took seats at the only table. Their hostess produced three delicate teacups from the cupboard above the sink. She wiped the dishware with a towel and checked the spoons for spots before setting one beside each saucer. A canister of sugar and a beige ceramic teapot completed the setting. "I'm afraid these don't get much use," Toni said "My schedule doesn't allow for much entertaining or housekeeping." She pried the lid from a tin of Darjeeling. "A gift from an English admirer," she said, filling a tea ball.

The flat was tastefully decorated with a velour sofa in rich purple flanked by mahogany side tables, a brass standing lamp, and a leather fauteuil. A credenza below one window held a porcelain vase of dried flowers. A bathroom and a clothes closet flanked either side of the short hallway leading to the sole bedroom. Isabel already knew that any feminine apparel took second station to the varied menswear in the closet. A well-cut black tuxedo hung at the bedroom door and a top hat rested haphazardly on the back of the couch.

Doro's curiosity got the best of her. "Isabel says you're an entertainer?"

"I'm not sure how entertaining—" she flashed Doro a smile as she placed the kettle on the gas ring and lit a match, "but it's what I do." She joined them at the table, reversing her chair to straddle it, her arms resting on the back.

Doro was intrigued by this first personal encounter with a world she only knew from rumor and innuendo. "Is your work nearby?"

"Not far. The Toppkeller," she made a vague gesture to the north, "in the Schwerinstrasse. You've heard of it?"

"No, not really." Doro noted a studied gruffness to the woman's voice, something compellingly masculine. For a woman, she made a most attractive man, though clearly not the Jürgen type. For the moment Doro was simply mystified. "Sounds like fun. A nightclub?"

"Of sorts…a gathering place for the like-minded." She smiled sweetly. "I emcee most evenings."

"Sounds charming," Doro knew nothing more to add.

Isabel interrupted, eyes sparkling in anticipation. "So, is everything ready?"

"As requested, Izzy." Toni rose to fetch an armload of clothing from the alcove shelf. "Two common laborers, a bit down on their luck, right. Though I thought you told me it would be you and some man."

"He couldn't make it," Isabel said, sounding a bit peeved, "but happily Doro here came to my rescue."

Doro turned to Isabel with raised brows. "Come on—no more delays, Izzy, out with it now—just what's in store for us?"

"You and I are about to become men!" Isabel ignored Doro's look of astonishment as she pushed aside the tea service and sorted the used men's clothing into two piles. "How'd you get these, Toni? Not quite up to your professional standard, I must say."

"My uncle owns a used-clothing business, and items do occasionally go missing, you know," Toni shrugged in feigned concern, "at least temporarily. We can alter as needed. I have pins and such. Just return it all tomorrow and we're fine." She disappeared into the bedroom.

Isabel had already abandoned her shoes. Now she checked out the brown trousers. They would be baggy but work with suspenders. "Come on, Doro. Off with the old, on with the new."

"I'm not so sure about this, Izzy." She hesitated. "The two of us as men?"

"It's our only ticket in, my friend. No women at these meetings. But when my story appears, the world will know that women were up to the task."

Toni returned with a lacquered tray of grooming implements. "First things first, 'gentlemen.'" She studied Doro's stylishly short haircut with an approving nod. "All you'll need, my dear, is a good slick of pomade and a tight body wrap and you'll be convincing enough, though you are a bit on the small side. But as for you, Izz, that fabulous hair of yours must go."

Isabel shook loose her shoulder-length tresses. "It's all yours, darling—no sacrifice too great for a story." She took to the chair and Toni draped a bedsheet around her shoulders. Scissors made quick work of the longer locks before Toni reached for hand clippers and styled a bob cut. Warming the hair grease between her hands, she sculpted the hair back from Isabel's forehead and admired her handiwork. "As for the makeup and mascara—for your purposes away it goes." She unscrewed a jar of cold cream.

Doro stared in amazement at the gradual transformation. In the dim light of the apartment her friend could now pass for a young, somewhat effeminate male. With luck, tonight's meeting would be poorly lit. She found herself excited by the masquerade despite her understandable fears. That close call of the previous week had nearly killed Jürgen, but she had to admit that she and Isabel were looking totally different than their appearance at the brawl.

Twenty-five minutes later the job was complete. "All right, the two of you, take a look at what we've got." Toni handed them a mirror, her grin contagious.

"Good Lord!" Isabel turned her face from side to side, admiring her reflection. "You've outdone yourself!"

"All in a day's work, but don't forget your voices. Izz, yours is naturally husky—"

"It's all those cigarettes." Doro gave her friend a scolding look.

"Well, whatever you're doing, it's working, so keep it up. You'd make a fortune at Toppkeller. As for you, Doro, you are a bit high-pitched. So listen—here's what all my girls do: first off, hum deeply to yourself. Just part your lips slightly and lower your chin to your chest. Add a bit of the nasal, and keep it low in the throat." Both women practiced the humming. "Excellent, now breathe deeply." They inhaled. "No, no—" she placed a hand on Isabel's lower ribcage, "from the diaphragm, not so high in the chest. Just keep that deep hum in your voice while speaking." They made several attempts until Toni pronounced herself satisfied. "Don't worry—cinching in your tits helps force the air lower. And for God's sake, relax those throats."

Doro gave it several more tries. Her voice came out a bit scratchy. "I'm not sure I can do this." She turned to Isabel. "Maybe Toni should go instead?"

Toni jumped in: "Thanks but no thanks, my friends. I've enough problems with those goons without sticking my neck out." She reached for her lighter. "I never look for trouble." A curtain of smoke enveloped her. "Trouble looks for me." She inhaled again, deeply. "You'll both be fine. Worst case, claim a sore throat. Everybody's sick right now anyway, what with the miserable weather."

Toni had them strip down to panties, and Doro was glad to have worn her only really nice pair. "What lovely titties all around," Toni observed, "really a shame to hide them away!" She shook out the old bedsheet, then used her foot to gather the hair clippings on the linoleum and scoot them under the table. "I'll get around to that later." She tore long strips from the cloth and bound their breasts, securing the wraps with safety pins. Finally they donned the rest of the costumes, ultimately exchanging waistcoats for a better fit. Doro's trousers were far too long, requiring needle and thread to hastily baste the cuffs.

Toni brought out several pairs of scuffed men's shoes. She lined them up on the floor beside the table. "For comedy skits at the club. The fit usually stinks, but their worn condition is *de rigueur* for what you're pretending to be." A bit of trial and error and they arrived at a decision.

"Okay, you two, now show me what you've got." Arms linked, Doro and Isabel strolled toward the bedroom and then back to the table, all the while doubling over with laughter. Toni gave them a critical eye and finally nodded her approval. "Do keep in mind how men walk—very full of themselves. Otherwise, they'll take you for *Bubis*. Our butch sisters aren't the usual Brownshirt cup of tea," she took another drag on her cigarette, "though a few of Hitler's boys do fall for them from time to time." Toni suggested the gray fedora for Isabel. Doro preferred a worker's billed cap, a tighter fit.

"So what's next?" Doro looked at Isabel imploringly, hoping this would all turn out to be another of her jokes. She took the last sip of her tea.

"We take in a picture show in these duds, then grab a meal in public before the big event. Our dress rehearsal, so to speak."

"My knees are already shaking. I'm not sure I can pull this off!"

"Relax, darling. You're a natural. Just follow my lead and we'll both be fine, and I'll owe you a big one."

While not fully convinced, Doro had to admit the get-up was passable. Toni gave her professional seal of approval as she saw them to the door. "I'll put in a good word with my manager." She stifled her laughter. "She's always got an eye out for new talent. Now get the devil out of here, and remember—walk like men!" They hugged all around. "And get those duds back to me by tomorrow afternoon so I can return them to my uncle's shop."

Gasthaus Schmidt evoked the Bavarian origins of the National Socialist Party. Isabel knew the choice of locale was intentional. Every weathered tabletop spoke of spilled beer and greasy food. Massive posts supported oaken beams traversing the hall, and the wood-paneled walls bore faux medieval shields. Years of smoke masked their originally bold colors. In stark contrast, a swastika flag hung from the speaker's dais in black and white on crimson. Horst Wessel, the newly-minted martyr to the Nazi cause, stared into the distance from a large framed photograph flanking the speaker's rostrum. Isabel and Doro sat against the rear wall of the basement meeting hall. Two Brownshirts boxed them in.

The local cell leader welcomed the gathering, drawing the audience's attention to propaganda pamphlets and books for sale at a side table. Each attendee had already coughed up a full mark just to gain entrance. Normally a fifty *Pfennig* contribution to Party operations would have sufficed, so this was certain to be a noteworthy occasion. While awaiting the arrival of his guest speaker, the master of ceremonies encouraged a rousing chorus of *Die Fahne hoch* in honor of Wessel, the song's creator and fallen hero. Some twenty local Nazi leaders had already gathered up front, with lesser minions packing the remaining tables.

Isabel sat in the rear but didn't feel like singing. She worked against the shoelaces binding her hands at her back. The attempt only further abraded her wrists. Doro slumped forwards in surrender, making no attempt to weaken her ties as she scanned the crowded hall and threw Isabel terrified glances. Who could blame her? They were in deep trouble, and Isabel fiercely cursed herself for putting them at such risk.

They should have turned tail while they still had the chance, having first held back to observe the goings-on from across the street. The tavern had appeared benign from the exterior, its signage limited to a carved wooden plaque above a stone arch. A solitary lantern over the entry illuminated the sidewalk. Isabel had anticipated finding a couple of Brownshirts guarding the entrance. Stormtroopers went everywhere in pairs, as if fearful of being out alone. But for this gathering, six men hovered outside with wooden staves at the ready.

A few guests pulled up in automobiles. The guards stood at attention as their leader waved the important men inside. The drivers left the curb in a hurry, clearing the impostors' view of the proceedings. The SA gatekeepers referred to a list as they screened newcomers. Most arrivals produced some sort of identity card, likely Party ID's. Others, clearly recognized by their comrades, exchanged a few words at the door before bounding up the steps. Many came in crisp brown uniforms with leather belting, others in business suits. Very few wore workers' garb, and none wore clothing as grubby as the women's disguises. Something special was certainly about to happen here, given the security precautions and dress.

"We'll go for it anyway," Isabel had insisted to Doro's dismay, "we'll bluff ourselves in." The name of one local Nazi bigwig was fresh in her mind. She intended to use the knowledge to their advantage. Before Doro could protest, Isabel strode out into the street and Doro hurried to catch up. They approached the entrance as boldly as they could muster, remembering Toni's advice and mimicking the confident gait of the two Nazis they saw approaching to their right. Isabel softly reminded Doro to deepen her voice.

The first guard gave them a quick once-over and sneered: "So what do you *gents* want?" Taking a closer look in the light from the doorway, he raised an eyebrow in mock surprise. "Did our little boys lose their way home?"

Isabel held her voice firm and husky: "Herr Hallinger invited us." In her head she heard only the voice of a pre-pubescent boy trying to emulate a man.

The guard appeared unimpressed. "Herr Hallinger, eh? You *boys* got your Party cards?"

"The Führer is Germany's future, and we're here to enroll tonight." Perhaps they wouldn't catch the growing edge of fear in her voice. Doro's jaw remained tight, an uncertain smile on her lips. Isabel sensed she was tempted to cut and run. The gatekeeper continued to scrutinize them with a patronizing grin.

"Any problem with our joining up?" Isabel tried to break his silence. "Somebody has to put the damn Yids and Bolshies in their place, right?"

The man eyed the brown-shirted comrades now gathering directly behind the impostors and gave them a wink. Their laughter burned. *In for a penny, in for a pound,* so Isabel added emphasis to their commitment to the cause: "Give us a chance to bust heads for Germany—we'll give those mongrels what they deserve!"

"Well then, head on in, *Jungs.*" He grinned as he stepped aside. "I'm sure Herr Hallinger will be delighted to have you at his table." He made a broad gesture of welcome and his Stormtrooper pals closed ranks behind them, pressing up against the women and forcing them up the steps.

"Oh my God!" Doro whispered, making no attempt to deepen her voice.

In the shadows of the foyer lurked a heavy-set man in a broad-brimmed fedora and dark overcoat. He crushed a smoldering butt beneath his heel and stepped forward to face them. Beneath the wide hat brim glared a boxer's mug and Isabel stopped short, grabbing Doro by the elbow. It was a brute she and Ryan had seen on the street on their way to the bloody brawl. Less than an hour later his brass-knuckles had pounded Ryan mercilessly until a club-wielding Reichsbanner trooper dropped this thug to his knees.

Now that battered tough towered over them, his bad teeth showing in a supercilious smile. He addressed Isabel in gutter slang, his voice ripe with sarcasm. "What a pleasure to see you again, *Liebling*. Two quick questions for you: where's your pretty boy tonight? We've unfinished business, me and him. And second," his eyes raked first her body and then Doro's, "I see you've traded cock for cunt?"

Doro was visibly shaken. Isabel remained silent. The man motioned to the nearby Brownshirts. "You two, wrap them up good and tight and stick them in back for now!"

The taller of the men remained motionless. "We've nothing to tie them with, Herr Storm Leader."

"Use your belts if you have to! Now get the fuck in there and on the double! I've plans for these two. They owe me from last time and tonight I collect what's due." The guards reacted to the raw power of the man and followed orders. They led the women into the dim-ly-lit back row of the hall and forced them to remove their shoelaces. "Nice and tight at those delicate wrists," the tough said, examining the bonds. "We can't have these *boys* leaving before they share their beauty secrets, right?" He ran a finger down Isabel's cheekbone, "Ah, smooth as silk," then abruptly grabbed her by the crotch and squeezed hard. Isabel winced but bit her tongue. "Why, just imagine, comrades—this one's so scared his cock's gone missing!"

The troopers laughed a bit too enthusiastically. The older guard, broad-headed and of smaller stature, shared the thuggish appearance of the Storm Leader. The second was a decent-looking type in his early twenties, handsome if not for the ridiculous SA cap with narrow chin strap giving him the look of a bellhop or elevator operator. Perhaps she could win him over once the bastard-in-charge moved on. Then she remembered her masculine look with bound breasts and dropped that idea. She missed her curves, the long hair and red lipstick, feminine tools to turn any man's head.

The brute gave Doro's jaw a light slap. "One word from either of you—" he pulled brass knuckles from his pocket, "and your lips are sealed with this, *verstanden?*" He held his armored fist beneath her nose. "Don't worry—you can open your mouths for me later," he jerked a thumb toward the well-dressed Nazis gathered before the rostrum, "but the fun must wait till our guests have left. So sit down and enjoy the evening.

You might learn something useful, but don't count on any good coming from it."

He headed toward the rostrum to whisper something in the ear of a VIP at the front table. That well-dressed man turned, smiled directly at them, and said something in reply. The brute grinned broadly and nodded in agreement. Rising from the table, the man came to the back of the room accompanied by the big thug.

"I am Johann Hallinger," he said, bowing slightly. "Word is we are already acquainted."

Isabel's voice quivered despite efforts to keep it calm. "There must be some mistake."

He turned to the brute. "Can that possibly be, Sturmführer Veidtner? Do we ever make mistakes?"

"Never, sir." A malicious grin emphasized his battered teeth.

Hallinger's civilized demeanor suddenly hardened, his smile gone as quickly as it had come. "On your feet when you address me!" Isabel and Doro stood. "Now show us your asses." They turned to face the wall and he lifted the flap on Isabel's jacket. "Comrades, I believe we do make an occasional mistake after all. These are certainly neither men nor boys. I do believe these are misguided women badly in need of a good fucking."

"My thoughts exactly," Veidtner said.

"So here's what you do, Storm Leader, and with my blessing: once tonight's gathering comes to a close, take these 'ladies' out to the shed for a little rest and relaxation. Get them out of those ridiculous clothes, ride them till they scream for a break, then ride them some more." Doro lost control, sobbing as Hallinger continued. "Were I not having a nightcap this evening with our guest speaker, I'd gladly join you immediately to assure their pleasure goes on and on."

"Don't worry, sir. I know plenty of tricks they'll never forget."

"I bet you do, Veidtner. Just make sure this is the last gathering they ever attend. Can't have party-crashers spoiling our fun, can we?" He gave Isabel a mirthless smile as he and the brute strode away, rejoining their compatriots up front.

Isabel heard the younger guard release his breath. She and Doro collapsed on the chairs. The two Brown-shirts took seats to either side, bookending the bound women. Isabel missed the slender switchblade she normally carried in her garter when she thought she might encounter a personal threat. She'd shown it twice in tight situations, and each time the would-be assailant had backed off. In the dim lighting of the basement hall she might have reached the knife had she worn skirt and stockings, but she'd left the blade at Toni's when she'd donned male clothing. Another stupid mistake.

The younger guard watched the staircase, awaiting the appearance of the guest speaker. From time to time he cast a sidelong glance at her. Bending forward, she caught his eye. "These laces are cutting into my wrists," she whispered. The guard looked to the front. The brute who had ordered their silence was bent over the front table, speaking again with Hallinger. She gave the guard an imploring smile. "Any chance of loosening them? If only a fraction?" He turned slowly, a first hint of weakness. *Perhaps something to work with after all?*

He motioned for her to twist to the side and he freed her hands. She rubbed her wrists and found friction burns but no broken skin. The man retied the laces, leaving a bit more play. Her fingers brushed gently over his as he tested the first knot, and she caught a flicker of a smile before he returned his attention to the rostrum. Neither Doro nor the thuggish guard on her far side appeared to have noticed the help.

Loud cheers and riotous applause rose in the hall. Through the dense smoke Isabel spotted the guest speaker descending the stairs. She recognized him immediately: Dr. Joseph Goebbels, Hitler's propagandist. He stepped to the rostrum. She mentally kicked herself, for here was a Nazi meeting certain to demand full security if ever there was one, and she had been ill-prepared. It might as well have been their Führer himself. What a great story here should they get out alive! And if she ever saw that Inspector Brandt again, what an earful he would get for passing along this particular lead!

Goebbels' sharp features and obvious limp belied a brilliant and manipulative mind. She'd heard rumors he was a ladies man, though she found nothing about him attractive. His weasel-like face displayed an obvious cunning. The room quickly quieted for him to speak. She had already witnessed his public act with Ryan. At the big nighttime rallies the torchlight played off his bold gestures as he ranted and wheedled, gesticulating with a finger held high to wield a threat against the Party's enemies or throwing back his shoulders, arms at his sides, to emphasize through stance the power of his words. The theatrics also helped overcome his diminutive physical stature. Here tonight his words might foretell some important revelation only for the ears of the Party's most committed followers in Berlin.

Isabel could foresee their fate. She knew that unwanted guests usually landed in the gutter after a thorough pasting, often with a broken bone or two. But any spy or known enemy was rumored to end up as one more unidentified body in the city morgue. So were she and Doro still there simply on a whim of the Storm Leader Ryan had pissed off the other night? Or did Hallinger himself intend to interrogate them more thoroughly once they'd been sexually violated by his brutal henchman?

Surviving this night would be a miracle.

The black Ford raced through the streets, the women rocking from side to side in the rear seat and unable to steady themselves with their hands bound. Their blind-folds were filthy rags taken from the trunk, the sharp odor nauseating Isabel. Her swollen wrists ached from the tension of the ties, and she knew her skin was chaf-ing raw. Doro was also clearly suffering, but the orders were to keep their mouths shut and they were obeying. They were headed for "the shed," and Veidtner had promised to come along later for a "personal interroga-tion."

A siren warbled in the distance, growing steadily louder. Had someone discovered their plight? *No chance.* They were in it up to their necks. Isabel wished their headlong rush through the city might lead to a col-lision, anything to draw the attention of the authorities. But the emergency vehicle passed them by. Moments later they sped beneath tolling bells; anyone's guess which church with so many in the city. Completely disoriented, she knew things had taken a likely fatal turn and had no idea what to do about it.

Goebbels' speech had been incendiary enough, his audience enraptured by every word. The establishment of a National Socialist dictatorship and brutal suppres-sion of dissent across Germany was to be but the first step in an aggressive political and economic conquest of all Europe. The ultimate goal was control of natural resources and transportation hubs necessary to make Germany the most powerful nation on earth. The Nazi leadership was not yet ready to threaten the Versailles powers by revealing Hitler's grand aspiration, but for that select group of Party devotees the speech was designed to inspire even greater commitment to the first stages of demolishing the Weimar Republic.

But there was no great scoop there. She'd heard it all before. A wasted evening likely to be the end of her. Of Doro.

"The shed" was a looming, disused factory somewhere on the outskirts, likely one of the many commercial and industrial enterprises doomed by the worldwide economic collapse of the previous year. *Grossmanufaktur Eisenstein GmbH* stood in faded lettering above the entrance, but any remaining signage was either missing or lost to the car headlamps. To the left of the structure lurked the remains of a long-abandoned outbuilding, its roof canted away from the warehouse, its surviving walls now nothing but ragged piles of brick rubble barely a meter high. No lights burned anywhere. A glow on the horizon suggested a commercial district not far beyond a pine woods.

The younger guard removed their blindfolds while the other approached a side entrance to the main structure. "What about our hands?" Isabel asked quietly, hoping to take advantage of the amenable one. "Mine hurt like hell and I've lost all feeling."

She looked expectantly at Doro, who nodded agreement. Her friend's voice came as a whisper: "I can't feel my fingers anymore."

The guard shrugged, almost embarrassed. "Sorry, orders are you stay like that until the Storm Leader gets here."

Isabel gave her most winning smile. "Look, what can we possibly do with free hands? Attack two big men? Don't be silly. And we sure can't run in shoes with no laces." She lifted her foot to emphasize the disability. "Plus, we've no idea where we are, much less how to get back into the city, and, in case you haven't noticed, it's cold as the devil out here. I for one want to get inside now."

The younger man looked over at his frustrated companion. The oafish one was working a stubborn lock in the glare of the headlamps. His shadow played above the doorway like some monstrous marionette. The guard, surrendering to Isabel's persistent pleas, used a pocketknife to slit the laces. She smiled in thanks and gently rubbed her wrists as he turned to release Doro's hands.

In that second of inattention Isabel abandoned her flopping shoes and ran into the darkness toward the collapsed outbuilding. The frozen ground stabbed at her feet, her woolen socks providing scant protection. One false step could break an ankle, one broken bottle tear open a foot and bring a quick end to her escape. Nothing mattered but reaching the ruins and the blackness beyond. The startled guard shouted as he saw her bolt: "Hey, you! Get the hell back here!" His companion forgot the lock as he realized what had happened.

Reaching for his flashlight, he cursed the younger man: "You asshole, what've you done now? We'll be in for a shitload!"

The young man, ignoring the insult, grabbed a flashlight from the car and headed out after Isabel. He shouted over his shoulder to the brutish colleague: "Watch the other! The runner's mine!"

Isabel glanced back long enough to see his light piercing the darkness. She barreled past rotting crates and disappeared amongst them, but quickly enough her pursuer spotted her again. Now the beam held her fast, its light spreading beyond her shadow and helpfully illuminating the pitfalls ahead. Close to the threshold of the ruined building she dodged a pile of bricks and fell headlong into the debris. "My ankle, I think I broke it!" Her voice shaky, edged with pain.

She moaned as the young man approached her. "A fool's errand, *Fräulein*. Let me see that foot." He squatted beside her. "You never should have run—" His rebuke stopped short. Isabel had bolted to her feet, her right arm cutting a wide arc and gathering momentum backed by all the strength she could muster. The heavy brick did its work, smashing into the side of his head and sending his cap flying. The flashlight hit the ground as his hands shot to his head. She heard his grunt before he collapsed at her feet.

Surprised at her own success, Isabel felt a surge of triumph. She reached for the light and knelt beside the fallen man. His left ear was a shiny mess, blood matting the closely-cropped hair above. Fierce-looking abrasions marred his jaw. She waited a long moment before placing a hand on his unmoving chest. She shone the light on his nostrils and mouth and made certain no breath shimmered in the chill air. Satisfied, she cautiously made her way back to the doorway.

Her abandoned shoes lay scattered beside the Ford, gathering a dusting of snow. They remained unwieldy, but felt good on her cold and bruised feet. The laces had been cut to strands by the trooper when he had freed her hands. With a silent curse she chided herself for forgetting to take his small knife. Now there was no time to return to the corpse. Who knew what Doro was facing? Tension gripped her every fiber. She inhaled deeply and released a billowing cloud of vapor, steeling herself to take on the remaining guard.

The side door was ajar. She eased it open onto a vast industrial space. Row upon row of huge lathes stretched into the darkness, colossal soldiers at parade rest. The frigid air smelled of metal and oil. She stopped to listen but picked up only silence. They were in there somewhere. She allowed the beam to scan the immediate area at ground level. Wooden racks along the wall held steel panels in tight rows and varying lengths of iron rod. She quietly pulled out one the length of her arm and tested its heft. It would do. She abandoned the cumbersome shoes, feeling again the deep chill as her stockinged feet met the concrete. She would have to walk the long aisles in sequence until she stumbled on her prey and his captive. The search would require stealth.

The first aisle yielded nothing. She took a chance and swept the space ahead with the flashlight as she took the turn. Nothing appeared out of place, just more rows of bins and machinery. Then a glint caught her eye. In a distant corner of the vast space she saw the outline of a man-sized door, a sliver of light escaping the frame. *Got you, you bastard!* Approaching the target, her light picked out a small sign: *Achtung! Eintritt ohne Zulassung Strengstens Verboten.* No entry without permission—*like hell,* she thought. Large metal barrels lined the exterior wall of the storeroom, the twisted tabs on the lids suggesting they now sat empty. Skull-and-crossbones and names of industrial acids showed their former purpose. The door, scuffed by years of mistreatment, bore faded record sheets beneath a block-lettered sign reading *Aufsicht,* supervisor.

With an ear to the door she heard only muffled sounds, but her nose picked up a disturbing stench. Her editor father had sometimes sent her on off-putting assignments, perhaps hoping she would abandon real journalism. A story on new efficiencies at a Chicago slaughterhouse forced her to witness workers stunning cattle with blows to the beasts' foreheads. Many still twitched and bellowed as the men winched up the carcasses and opened their neck arteries with curved knives. She now recognized that salty mix of blood and sweat. The stench confirmed that these violent assholes were capable of any mayhem.

She held her breath as she peered through the keyhole, allowing her eye to adjust to the interior glare. A lighting fixture hung from the ceiling of a large room, illuminating only the center of the space and leaving the remainder in deep shadow. At first she saw no movement. Then an image at the edge of the circle caught her eye and her guts began to churn. She knew she deserved every bit of damnation for what was happening there. The brutish guard had Doro on her knees, her face pressed to the concrete. He'd wrapped her head in the jacket, all other clothing piled to the side. Her butt was fully exposed under the glaring light. The assailant's dun-colored trousers pooled at his ankles, his stubby cock stood erect. "Spread 'em wider, bitch!" he snarled. "Gotta loosen you up for the Storm Leader."

All hesitation forgotten, Isabel shoved the door wide open and reached the attacker in seconds. "You fucking bastard!" Her shout echoed in the closeness of the room. The iron rod split the man's upturned face, his nose a spray of tissue and blood, but Isabel could not let up. As he keeled over, she beat him repeatedly over the head before ramming the bar into the softness of his exposed belly. He twitched several times before his chest collapsed and he lay still.

Isabel finally exhaled. She felt lightheaded, almost faint. She had never killed before that evening. Now she had, and twice.

She helped Doro to her feet. Together they removed the jacket encasing her head. "Come on, love, it's over now. Get yourself dressed as best you're able. We have to get the hell out of here!"

Doro was trembling, her head shaking from side to side in denial. With Isabel's help she pulled on the soiled clothing and shoes and blew her nose on her sleeve. Isabel searched the impaled attacker for keys to the Ford and retrieved her shoes as they neared the exit. She guided Doro by the arm out to the car. Doro finally found her voice, a hoarse whisper as they climbed in: "Please tell me you can you drive a car."

Despite all the horror, Isabel couldn't help thinking her friend had finally mastered the throaty, masculine voice, the errant thought helping relieve the pent-up tension of the last few minutes. "You bet I can." They clambered into the Ford. The engine caught on the first try and Isabel eased the car into gear. It lurched forward, stuttered, and the engine fell silent. "A little rusty at this," the excuse more for herself than for Doro. She tried again, and the car lunged once more before dying. In the pale glow of the dashboard she saw Doro still trembled. She forced herself to be calm. Having once learned to drive years before on her grandfather's farm, she had never needed the ability either in Chicago or Germany. She quickly rehearsed the release of the clutch and balanced pressure on the gas pedal, then gave it another try.

This time the car inched forward and she allowed the engine to rev higher, hesitant to up-shift for fear of killing it again. They covered less than a hundred meters on the pitted road when lights pierced the darkness in the distance. Another vehicle was heading toward the metal gate now in the reach of their high beams. She went for broke, slamming into second and accelerating, knowing that if the car bringing that bastard Storm Leader reached the entry first, they'd be at the devil's mercy. They gained on the exit but the other car was closer still, its driver obviously more skilled. They would miss escape by a few meters, and once blocked, their fates would be sealed. Isabel brought the Ford to a halt, its brakes squealing as it slid on the loose gravel.

She handed Doro the flashlight and yelled: "Get the hell out of here and don't look back!"

"But—"

"No buts, love—get going!" She pointed to the woods on the horizon. "Hide in those trees, then find your way back to Toni's. She'll look after you!"

Doro abandoned the car, stumbling in her untied shoes before disappearing into the dark. Isabel jammed back into gear and accelerated, intending to barrel headlong into the other vehicle. With any luck they'd all be killed and she'd be spared a far more painful death. But then, shifting up again, she killed the engine and this time it refused to turn over as she rolled to a stop. The other car had now passed through the open gate, its headlamps blinding her as she repeatedly turned the key in the ignition and cursed a blue streak.

A man leapt from the other vehicle while still in motion. She recognized the cruel-faced Veidtner. He took off running, his flashlight seeking out Doro. Isabel screamed "No!" at the top of her lungs, but the windows were up and she heard only the futile echoes of her own impotence in the face of this disaster. She sprang from the Ford as the other car came to a stop a half-meter from her vehicle's grill. The driver was already out with a revolver in hand. Isabel stopped short, her eyes now pinned on the black field off to her right. A flash of light pierced the darkness, the crack of a pistol shot close on its heels, and then another. Isabel heard a scream, and she knew Doro was finished. A moment later a third shot rang out. The flashlight beam wavered in the gloom before pivoting back to head her way.

Tears of fury, frustration and bitterness flowed down her cheeks and she began to sob. She had only herself to blame for this fiasco. She offered no resistance as the Brownshirt slammed her against the hood of the Ford and twisted her around, kicking her legs out to the sides. "Stay where you are, Jew-cunt, until we say otherwise. You'll soon wish you were dead." He hissed into her ear: "And once we're through with you, you'll thank us for ending it all, understood?"

She nodded. She did.

❖

Berlin, Germany
December 1941

"My God, Ryan—Do you see what I did? Doro died because of me! I pulled that trigger as surely as I killed the bastard who was raping her!"

Ryan slid over on the sofa and drew her close. All thoughts of keeping his distance had dissolved in the horrors of her tale. He would have offered his handkerchief but knew she was beyond caring about tear-smeared make-up. "Go ahead now, let it out. You've held it in too long."

"That's just it, darling, there's no letting it go, the guilt never leaves. Every single day it gnaws at me, begging for release. I often awaken with my pillow drenched and can't fall sleep again for the shame of it." She squeezed his hand. "You're the first in years I feel safe telling this to, so please know how grateful I am to have you back in my life. It's as devastating as the night it happened and won't stay buried!"

Ryan nodded. "You'd be surprised by what I do now, by what I've become. I have blood on my hands, too. I wish I could tell how to move beyond it, but I'm still seeking answers. You simply have to look beyond the guilt and find ways to help right a world gone terribly wrong."

"Believe me, I've tried, but this is so personal, so damning of me and who I was. I tell you, Doro never wanted to go to that cursed meeting. I manipulated her; I appealed to her convictions." She wiped the tears with her hand. "For me, it was one more lark—always the new challenge, always the new adventure. I was so damned determined to prove myself anyone's equal—man or woman—I ran roughshod over my best friend and she suffered a horrifying death for it." She pulled away long enough to look into his eyes. "I know it must have been difficult for you, as well...my silence."

Her sobs were easing at last. It felt so natural to hold her in his arms, to feel her familiar body against his. He nestled her closer, and silently cursed himself for feeling aroused in the depth of her misery. What a story she told, but many things left unexplained. How much of it to believe? Isabel had always had a calculating streak and a flair for the dramatic. She rested her head on his chest as if no time had passed in the decade since he'd last held her. He gently kissed her forehead but found no further words of consolation over such agonizing loss.

"Why do they do it, Ryan?" Her voice was softer, the crisis passed for now. "I thought only of myself and caused Doro's death, but these people live for such behavior. They crush anyone they think weaker and never give it a second thought. How can anyone be so cruel?"

The same question plagued him endlessly. "There's no explaining this shit away. It's just there!

For them the world's a test of strength where they must constantly prove themselves the victors. Only winners and losers, and no place for compassion. It must come from feeling inferior, from coming together so late as a nation. All those little German principalities and king-doms had warred against each other forever, each de-manding to be seen as something special. Well, now this Reich is something special all right: their might makes right, and the bullies can do as they wish to any-one they choose."

She stared vacantly across the room. He knew she saw only her horrid memories. "It's just not fair."

"You know as well as I that fairness is the greatest of lies." He gave voice to his bitterness. "An innocent child slips and drowns in a river. Who or what justifies that? Century after century some live in luxury while others slave in poverty. The poor watch their children die from hunger, from lack of proper medical care. Is any of that fair?" He shook his head in disgust. "And now Europe is under fascist control and the bastards slaughter innocents right and left! No, I've given up on 'fairness' in life. Twice I've tried to make a difference, and each time I've failed." He paused, recalling efforts thwarted by powers beyond his control. "I no longer look at things the same way. I just do my best for a cause I still believe humane and right."

Ryan wanted to express the depth of his hurt back in '31, to reveal how responsible he'd felt for sending her into that fateful night alone. He'd carried her presumed death as his personal sorrow. As much as she condemned the ruthlessness of the Nazis, this beautiful woman had also behaved callously, and yet he wanted desperately to forgive her. The sharp edge of her self-blame scored him deeply, and he wouldn't add to her burden.

How had she survived, and why had she never reached out to him? She could easily have sought him out in Marburg before he left for the States. If not that, surely the university would have shared his forwarding address. She was a reporter, after all, and knew his origins in Lawrence. Just what had she done with that entire decade? And most troubling of all, why was she now working with those SS bastards at a concentration camp? Too much yet to learn. He fought against surrendering to her despair, against letting go of memories of the emotional pain he'd suffered at her hands. He still had a story to hear. And to find credible.

"This guilt and sorrow are difficult to leave behind, Isabel, but the world is now so different from back then. The Nazis were just one of many parties, dangerous players but seemingly no threat to the world. Now times have changed, and clearly you have, too. But I'm also a different man, no longer that greenhorn who abandoned himself to whims at the drop of a hat." He gave her arm a squeeze. "I've become harder in the face of my own challenges."

A bit of the old Isabel surfaced: "You were always hard enough for me." A wry smile brightened her face at last as she reached for his handkerchief and blew her nose. "I think I'm ready to tell the rest, but promise me one thing—you'll still think fondly of me when you learn the whole truth." He offered only the hint of a smile in return, unwilling to commit himself fully.

And she continued the tale.

CHAPTER TEN

Berlin Outskirts
February 1931

Isabel knew what was sure to come. Rumors of Nazi torture and brutal murder were widely shared among foreign correspondents. Her mind raced. No time to mourn Doro for she herself would soon be dead. Or worse still, they make her suffer horribly for hours or days before tiring of it. She remembered Hallinger's chilling order to make it the last meeting they'd ever attend.

Leaning over the hood of the car, she trembled, tasting bile, her guts churning. How long before her knees buckled? *I'm the worst kind of fool*, she thought, *so self-centered I've sacrificed Doro and myself, and all for nothing.* Should she reveal her identity as a journalist? Could she bribe this Veidtner who had just murdered Doro? *My God, I've just killed two of their men!* There's nothing left to trade.

The brute emerged from the darkness, still gripping his pistol as he gave an order to the SA man: "Go bring back what's left of the little bitch." The Brownshirt moved off in a hurry, his flashlight retracing the route of the Storm Leader. Veidtner caustically called out after him: "Careful of all the blood!" He turned to Isabel. "Now, what the hell have you done with my men?"

She desperately hoped to buy time, but why even bother? He'd soon find his henchmen's bodies. She went for broke anyway, weaving a seemingly plausible story: "The older guy wanted to rape us before you got here, but the other said to obey your orders and wait, so he called the young guy an *Arschloch* and much worse. They threw punches and when the younger one stormed out, the other followed and came back alone." Isabel couldn't see Veidtner's eyes beneath the hat brim, couldn't tell if he was buying the story, so she plunged on: "The older guy must have killed him—he came back splattered with blood." The lies came more easily now. "Then he said 'why should Veidtner be first with the fun?' and he stripped my friend naked. I managed to break loose while he was raping her, and when he turned on me I hit him with a metal rod. It was self-defense—you must believe me!"

"So both are dead?"

"As far as I know."

"And this because one of them tried to make a fool of me?"

She saw a glimmer of hope. "Yes, it's true!"

He slipped the pistol into his pocket and grabbed her by the base of the neck. "Then let's have a look." His grip felt like a pincers. "Get moving!" She nearly lost the loose shoes as he shoved her into the sedan. The engine caught and they backed up, then swerved past the Ford and covered the distance quickly. "*Raus!*" he commanded. She got out, shuffling alongside him as they headed toward the glow of the office.

The scene inside the torture room almost paralyzed her. *God, what a horror!* When she'd come to Doro's defense she'd paid no attention to the surroundings, but now they hit her like a brutal blow to the gut. A tall wooden rack resembling a cross hovered over the circle of light. Hand restraints hung on either end of the arm, just beyond the reach of any captive. A repurposed billiard-cue stand held bludgeons and whips. Worse still, a metal table was outfitted with hand and foot cuffs at either end, and a nearby table displayed glistening bladed tools, an automobile battery with jumper cables, and bottles labeled for various toxic and caustic substances.

The second man she'd killed lay face up, his features barely recognizable. The metal rod extended from the man's belly. Veidtner forced her to sit on the cold concrete so close to the body she could smell the blood that had pooled around it. He removed his hat as he squatted to examine the corpse. A thick scar gave one eye a downward tug, and a recent welt shone red behind his left ear. When he looked up she knew he wasn't buying her story. "You think you're so clever, don't you?" He smiled and his raspy voice assumed a falsetto sing-song: "Time to pay the piper, *Fräulein*." He stood up and tossed his hat aside. "Now lose the clothes or I'll do it for you!" He snapped open a switchblade. "I get clumsy with sharp objects, so might just cut you a bit in the process."

Her whole body trembling, she slipped off the shoes and began to disrobe. "You can't do this to me— I'm an American citizen and a reporter. You must set me free, and now!"

He grabbed her by the throat and squeezed hard. "I don't give a rat's ass if you're Hoover himself! Now show me all you've got." He slit the suspenders and yanked down her trousers. She shuddered as a low whistle escaped his lips. His knife made short work of her panties and he forced his free hand between her thighs. "You'd better wet up soon or I'll hump you dry, and that won't be fun for either of us." He reeked of beer and cigarettes. "Ah, but of course, we do keep something for that around here." He pulled his hand free and reached for a jar on the cluttered tabletop. "This isn't the first time I've serviced a bitch here."

In that moment of distraction she tried to back away but the trousers at her ankles slowed her. He viciously grabbed her crotch again and jerked her to him, causing her to cry out in pain. She fought the tremor in her voice. "I'm just a journalist trying to share your Nazi story with the world!"

"You think we don't know what crap you write about us?" He leaned in closer, whispering in her ear. "Your big mistake was siding with the Bolshies last week, missy. I was all set to put down that pretty boy of yours when some asshole planted one on me." The welt behind his ear shone livid. "As Dr. Goebbels said tonight, we will exterminate all you vermin and remake Europe in our image." He bit into her earlobe, then spat out the blood. She flinched at the pain. "What would your readers think of us if you printed such a thing?"

"If that's what you want written, I'll do it—I'll write anything you say!"

"No, *Liebchen*, no more pretty words. The only thing coming out of you will be blood and whatever else I stick in there. And you'll beg for it all to end and happily join your sister in the Spree."

She gritted her teeth in silence, trying to remain on her feet as her knees threatened to buckle.

"And don't think I won't make mincemeat of that boyfriend of yours either, because you weaklings always underestimate us. I promise your pretty boy won't get off as easy as that slut out there in the field." He glanced toward the door and laughed again. "You'll hardly recognize what's left of that pretty face when my guy gets back. Your little bitch was totally expendable—not enough meat on the bone to make me hard—but as for you, I like your looks." He squeezed until she cried out, then pulled his hand away and licked his fingers. "Now, off with it all! Every stitch!"

Isabel inhaled deeply. She had nothing more to say, no new plea to make. She shrugged the coat to the floor. "Now we're getting somewhere, so lose the fucking vest and shirt!" He laughed at the sight of cloth binding her chest. "Get moving—I'm beginning to really feel it." When she fumbled with the pin, he ran the blade between her breasts and jerked upward. The cloth fell away, leaving an angry cut. "Prize winners," he said.

She would soon join the nameless bodies in a Berlin morgue. Veidtner tossed aside the knife and grabbed her ass, hefting her onto the cold metal of the table. "Now open 'em wide. First comes my fun, then your pain." He unbuttoned his fly and smeared his erection with petroleum jelly. She stared over his shoulder, her mind seeking escape. *Poor Ryan. He wouldn't know they were coming till too late.* Veidtner's man appeared in the shadows of the threshold, the burden in his arms so tiny in death. Isabel was grateful for the darkness as he lowered Doro's limp body to the concrete.

Despite herself, she glanced down. His cock was fully engorged as he spread her thighs. She pinched her eyes shut, tears streaming, and held her breath.

Abruptly, Veidtner jerked back, releasing her legs. His muffled gasp forced her eyes to open and see him slumping before her. A man clenched a choking hand at her attacker's throat while bearing the man's weight against his own body. A switchblade was buried in the brute's ribcage and the stranger now worked it upward, twisting the knife with a vengeance. Dark blood flowed from the wound. She recognized the young man she believed she'd killed with the brick. His ear was massively swollen, his scalp caked with blood, but he still managed a smile. And his eyes were remarkably kind as he released Veidtner's convulsing body to the floor.

He saw she was trembling and reached for the fallen jacket, draping it over her shoulders. "Get dressed—time's wasting." He gathered up her other clothing and handed it to her. "We have to run, and now!

Stunned and hurting, she dressed quickly with no concern for modesty. "I've no shoes for running."

"Take his." He pointed to the feet of the fallen Storm Leader. "He won't need them."

She couldn't look at Doro as they passed her body at the threshold.

The Ford again refused to start. Instead, her unexpected savior guided Veidtner's black Mercedes through the gate and onto the road toward the city. They sat in silence for what seemed ages. Light snow whipped at the windshield as they crept along, the rhythmic snick-snick of the wipers doing nothing to distract from the turmoil in her mind. She tried to grasp all that had happened, stunned to the core by Doro's brutal death and her own ability to kill, reliving every moment of the past hours. So senseless, and for nothing, yet her first step off that curb had set it all in motion, committing

186 | PATRICK W. O'BRYON

them to that cursed meeting and all the horrors it had brought.

Could she have handled it differently and somehow saved Doro? What if the damned Ford hadn't failed her? Or should she really be cursing her own incompetence with the clutch? She tried to concentrate on what would come next, anything to avoid confronting the brutality she had found within: bashing her savior in the head and thinking him dead, then thrashing and stabbing the trooper in a white rage. She surrounded herself in a self-induced fog, turning her back on the grisly and painful details. *Yes, better to focus now on what was yet to come.*

"And just who the devil are you?" Her question no more than a whisper.

"You don't need to know."

"But you were dead. I killed you!"

He chuckled softly. "Obviously not. But I will say this—you gave it a solid try and have my thanks for backing off when you did."

His glibness was infuriating, but the man had just saved her from Veidtner's rape and torture, so she tempered her response. Somewhat. "Damn you, Mr. You-Don't-Need-To-Know, you weren't breathing! I checked!"

"I couldn't let you hit me again, so I held my breath to avoid your *coup de grace*. Rule number one—if you fall in battle, play dead." He downshifted into a turn and she thought of her failure with the clutch. They were now approaching the center of the city. Her mind drifted back to that horrid moment of lifting that brick, that first realization of her desire to kill. She was grateful when he picked up the thread: "I thought you'd never leave. And next time, check for a pulse. Far more conclusive." He slowly worked his jaw and flinched. "Damn but that hurts! His light-heartedness was ill-suited to the moment and disconcerting.

"They'll know you helped me escape, so what's in it for you?"

His hint of a smile turned to a frown and she heard the bitterness of past experience in his words: "Torture is despicable, and no one deserves what these assholes dish out!" He stared ahead for long moments, his thoughts clearly elsewhere. *How much had this man witnessed before in that chamber of horror? Had he participated in such grievous crimes?* She watched him in the dim light of the dashboard, trying to grasp the incongruity of his coming to her aid. "I'll be leaving the city first thing," he said at last. "My Nazi comrades don't take kindly to betrayal."

"Then why'd you do it?"

"Seems you'd run out of ways to save yourself, though you did give us—give them—quite a run for the money." He accelerated past a car stuck in the slush, wheels spinning.

"Where's the one Veidtner sent for Doro's body?"

He peered beyond the scrape of the wipers. "In hell, I hope, swapping stories with Veidtner."

Tears coursed down her cheeks. When she spoke, her trembling voice was almost lost to the rumble of the engine. "Why couldn't we have saved her?"

"That's on both of us—I was still groggy and carried only a penknife to go up against Veidtner's pistol, and you might've handled the clutch better and beaten them to the gate."

That hit home, and his casual attitude to the horrors of the night stretched her to the breaking point. "God, how I hate you! So flippant and unfeeling when Doro's dead!"

He nodded, accepting her anger. "We'll all die, but for a better cause than theirs, let's hope."

She swallowed her anger, still wary despite what he'd done for her. He might just as quickly revert to Nazi ways. Finally she begrudgingly gave credit where due: "But you did save my life, so I owe you a debt I can't repay."

"Doesn't matter." His eyes still on the slick road ahead, he reached over and gently touched her forearm. "I was going to stop them before they harmed the two of you anyway, but you messed with my plan. Taking risks comes with the job."

"My words of a few hours ago, but now…I really don't know. What the hell is your job, other than saving my skin?"

"From what I've seen—and felt—" he gingerly touched his swollen ear before returning his hand to the wheel, "you were doing a decent job of saving yourself." They came to a stop, the traffic light glowing pink under falling snow. "You were simply outnumbered, and I was there to help...no thanks to you and that brick!" He looked increasingly trustworthy despite the bloodied SA uniform, but he still hadn't answered her question. Instead he posed one of his own: "So where can I drop you?"

Suddenly, she didn't want to be alone. She couldn't go back to her place—they would be watching it by morning—and the last thing she needed was to lead them to Ryan, so his place was also off limits. "Where will *you* go?"

"Far from Berlin, that's for certain—they'll be on my tail the minute they find us and this car missing. I'll lay low till morning, then contact a friend and plan an exit."

"Do you have a hide-out?"

"Only someplace temporary, like a hotel somewhere while I arrange new papers. What about you? You've been marked."

She thought a moment before giving in. If this man had risked all to save her, she would have to put her trust in him. She would rely on her gut: "I know where we both can hide, at least till tomorrow."

"And that is...?" He pulled to the curb, awaiting instructions.

"Can you get us to Nollendorfstrasse? I know the way from there."

They crept along in silence, her head filled with questions and self-blame as they searched for familiar landmarks. She needed rest and her tongue felt thick, her mouth dry. The snowfall had eased for the moment but the roads remained treacherous. Hoarfrost made reading the signs difficult. Here and there streetwalkers sheltering in doorways defied the weather. One hooker saw them slow for a turn and blew a kiss through the flurries. They eased to the curb and Isabel cranked down her window. The woman tottered over on high heels, likely hoping for a quick transaction in a heated sedan. Her face fell when she learned they sought directions to Greifingerstrasse, but she accepted his fifty-Pfennig coin and described the route before teetering back toward her shelter.

Toni wouldn't be home for many hours, but a key to the flat lay hidden near the top of the stairs. Gaining entry to the apartment house shouldn't be a problem either, since the front lock hadn't worked in years. Worst case, she would wake the concierge, an old acquaintance. They circled round and parked in an alleyway outside a low-end hotel several blocks away. A police patrol would surely chance upon the car by morning and trace it back to the Party.

He grabbed a flashlight from the glove box. They set off on foot, staying close to buildings and watching for ice on the sidewalks. The snow was picking up again, swiftly obscuring their tracks. Neither had outerwear and their clothing was splattered with dried blood. She shuffled along in Veidtner's vastly oversized shoes, laced to the limit. One nightclub was still in full swing, bouncer at the door, music and laughter spilling out into the dark night. They hurried past to reach the entrance to the apartment house.

Luck was with them. The street door opened without a problem and they climbed to Toni's third-floor flat. The radiator felt barely warm to the touch, the basement boiler long damped down for the night. The apartment was chilly, but nothing compared to the brutal cold of the abandoned factory. They were just happy to be out of the weather. "Let's ditch these filthy clothes," Isabel suggested as she headed to Toni's closet. She emerged with an armload of men's clothing. "Bound to be something here that fits."

He started to pick through the pile. "What about you?"

"My things are over here." She gathered her sweater, skirt and bra. Doro's abandoned clothing caused an ache in her heart, but she shoved the thought aside. Time enough later to face all that.

He was already changing trousers and shirt without a glance in her direction. He pulled on a knit sweater, carefully avoiding contact with his swollen ear. Adjusting the collar, he pointed to the telephone on the credenza. "Any problem ringing up a friend?"

"Help yourself."

"Time to get things rolling."

She found panties in Toni's dresser and retreated to the lavatory to wash and change, automatically closing the door behind her. *How absurd,* she thought, *the man's seen me naked.* She examined her torn earlobe in the mirror and tentatively touched the cut between her breasts, painful but crusting over. Once tepid water filled the basin she scrubbed the blood and filth from her face and washed between her legs to rid herself of the disgusting assault. Shampoo removed most of the hair oil and she made a turban of a thin towel before dressing. After checking herself in the mirror, she emerged shivering but energized. Her overcoat made her feel warmer and stronger already.

The refrigerator held beer and little else. Something with a kick would be more welcome on this shittiest of nights. She opened a bottle and filled two glasses, then remembered a flask of brandy Toni kept bedside and grabbed that, as well. Almost as an afterthought, she fired up the gas ring and put on the tea kettle. Unscrewing the cap, she took a swig of brandy and enjoyed its heat going down.

He was still standing beside the telephone, pensive, the receiver back in its cradle. She handed him a glass of beer and the uncapped brandy. "What does your guy say?" He took a swallow of the cognac, then downed half the beer. "He'll get back to me. I gave the number on the dial. I hope your friend won't mind, but I need to act fast with my cover blown. Once Hallinger finds the bodies he'll turn the city upside-down, and he has friends with the police who'll make the job easier." He lit a cigarette from the lacquered box on the side table and offered her one. "How safe is this place?"

"Safe enough for now. Toni won't be home till around three or so." She inhaled deeply, grateful for the warmth in her lungs. He returned the flask and she took another nip as they sat down side-by-side on the sofa.

"And this Tony...is he trustworthy? I mean really trustworthy? Our lives depend on it."

Isabel smiled. "Toni's a girl. Antoinette. We're close." The memories were nice: the briefest of flings, a few weeks, and afterwards just good friends. What pleasure to bed someone who knew a woman's body as well as her own. Their affair had been short but very entertaining, and Toni had understood when Isabel decided to move on. No regrets. Toni also liked men. Isabel recalled her sweetness just hours earlier, encouraging Doro to go along with that asinine plan. "I'd trust her with my life."

"We're about to do just that." He stubbed out the half-smoked cigarette. "I'm told there's a man called Lemmon, another American?"

Suddenly she was again on edge. "How do you know about him?"

"Veidtner. He told us he didn't get a fair shake at the brawl, thanks to the two of you, so he had you in his sights. Then word came your friend is also a foreign correspondent." He gave her a quick glance. "So this Lemmon fellow is your current guy?"

"He's the one." She pictured Ryan, better off now for his lack of courage. Or rather—as she had to concede—for reasonable caution.

"Why not hide out at his place? Might be safer to lay low with another foreigner." His fingers drummed a beat on the sofa arm, marking his rapid thoughts.

"Not sure he'd be up for it, plus he rooms with a wealthy family out in Grunewald when in Berlin. It would draw too much attention...and besides, he took quite a beating and still isn't on top of his game. We need someone fearless, someone like Toni." Suddenly she bolted upright. "Oh my God, I do have to let Ryan know—the bastards were already on to us!"

"No, not yet—not a word! Stay out of contact for twenty-four hours. At least till I'm long gone, then you're on your own."

She let it ride for the moment, still trying to figure out this man and too exhausted to think clearly.

They finished a second beer and drained the brandy before she finally spoke. "Let me take a look at that ear." He tilted his head under the floor lamp to display the damage. "My God! What a horrible mess I made of you!" She warmed a washcloth with water from the kettle and returned to dab at the wound. He endured the ministrations silently, flinching only occasionally. Having rinsed out the cloth, she returned from the sink for a second go. Finally she saturated the cloth with cold tap water, wrung it out and folded it neatly. "Hold this to your ear. It'll help reduce the swelling. Had I known...well, you know...I'm really very sorry for all this."

He shrugged his shoulders. "You and me both."

The kettle began to whistle. She filled the tea pot in the kitchen as he picked up the thread of their earlier conversation: "Look, with regard to notifying your boyfriend, that torture factory out there is only known to Hallinger and a few of his close buddies. They won't miss Veidtner and the others for at least a day or two. But if your friend Lemmon raises a stink about what happened to you, word will spread and we're all done for, him included." He accepted a cup of tea. "Berlin is finished for you anyway, so consider a move to Dresden or Vienna. Big cities, easy to lose yourself in the crowds. You'll both be safer there. But meanwhile, give me a day to get out of town before telling your reporter friend what's happened."

She began to relax, the horrid memories becoming muddled. Likely the alcohol at work. Returning to the sofa she tucked in her legs. "I suppose a day or two can't hurt." A concession, and was that a fleeting smile? She wasn't certain. "You never answered my question. Why *did* you save me? And who are you *really*?"

"Long story."

"I have time...thanks to you." She needed the truth. Could he be using her to identify her other friends? But then why kill his comrades, and can one ever trust someone who betrays his buddies? Too many questions. She started with the easy ones: "So why this conversion from Nazi to savior of tortured women? You like girls dressed as boys?"

He hesitated, clearly wondering how much to divulge. This time she was certain of that grin. Gentle. Open, not cynical. "I've been undercover for almost a year. A few of us operate within the local Nazi cells."

"Bolsheviks or Socialists?"

"A little of both, perhaps. It makes no difference— we despise all that Hitler stands for."

She focused on his eyes, watching for clues. "So you're spies."

"Germany needs them more than ever if it's to survive." His demeanor changed again, worry creasing his brow. He looked vulnerable with that washcloth plastered to his brutalized ear.

"You've seen me naked," she reined in an urge to smile at the surprise on his face and then confessed, "and I watched you change out of that horrid uniform. I believe we've shared enough for me to know your name?"

"We won't be together that long." He glanced toward the telephone, thoughtful, finally yielding. "But Karl will do."

There was something attractive there, very masculine, and not simply because he'd come to her rescue. She sensed kindness as with Ryan, but a strength and courage she'd seldom encountered in Europe, much less back home. She fetched the teapot and set it on the table beside the cups from earlier. "Okay then, Karl it is. I'm Isabel, but you probably know that already, since you know about Ryan. So, what comes next, Karl?"

"Get to safety somewhere, as I said. Berlin has nothing more for either of us. They know your name and where you work, and will eventually track down your remaining Commie friends if they don't do the smart thing and go to ground." She sensed he'd learned something from his call but was hesitant to share the information. She waited for him to continue. "It may be too late for the tall one with the beard, the one who took a blade to the throat at the warehouse melee. The bastards went after him this afternoon but I couldn't break free to warn my people. Had to leave a message."

"Doro's Jürgen? Dead?"

"Likely. My friends will have intervened if it wasn't already too late, but don't count on anything."

She felt another bolt of sadness. Grieving for her losses would have to come later. For now she carried the suffocating weight deep in her throat.

Her pain seemed to touch him: "Sorry, but it must be said: I know for a fact that even with Veidtner dead the search for you won't end. That goon was just an enforcer, a sadistic thug, and I'll admit it felt good to gut the bastard, but Johann Hallinger's our real danger from here on out. He's a more 'civilized' Nazi—if such a thing exists—educated, but as ruthless as they come. He issued the orders to wipe out your entire group. He knows how you bested his men the other night; you made them look foolish. He's smart, vicious and rising fast in the Party. Your people stained his reputation and he's out for blood."

Isabel knew all this would never have happened had that cop not encouraged her to attend the meeting. Her cheeks began to burn. "So that damned detective Brandt who sent me knew I was walking into danger! That Kripo sonofabitch set me up."

"Well…not exactly." He placed the bloodied washcloth on the coffee table, then thought better of it and took it to the kitchen. He returned to join her on the couch. "Your 'damned' Inspector Brandt is actually one of ours." He hesitated as this news sank in. "Hate to admit it, but he's the one I just reached by phone, and he concedes this wasn't his brightest idea. He's damning himself already, but only after he cursed me for waking him at such an ungodly hour. The man's horrified at all that's happened but had no idea Goebbels would show up and security be so tight. Our good inspector does mean well and he has connections we can use. He'll set you up in another city and do whatever he can."

She clenched her fists, fighting an urge to lash out at someone, anyone. "He can't bring Doro back...or Jürgen."

"Brandt is convinced the world must learn the threat these Nazis pose. And I agree. I know first-hand. They'll do anything and everything to get control of the country: sabotage, assassination, blackmail, extortion. Tonight you saw what some of them are capable of. Fear and unrest wins votes, and they're already getting delegates to the Reichstag. The other parties are divided, but these Nazis have one purpose. If Hitler makes good on his dream, all hope for Germany goes out the window."

"So your Brandt thought I'd slip right in, find an angle for a great story, and then come out again in one piece to publish it?"

"He put me there to keep an eye on you, but things got out of hand the moment you showed up with another woman. And, my God, dressed as *Garçonnes*? I guess we should have known you'd try something crazy, given that hooker get-up you wore last week when all hell broke loose in Wedding! Now *that* outfit sure drew everyone's attention!"

She shrugged. "I thought I was dressing appropriate for such a shady neighborhood." She eyed him intently. "So you were there in Wedding. Saw it all."

He appeared uncomfortable as he took a sip of tea. "I was there. Had to be. But I held back in the fight as much as I could." He set down his cup. "Veidtner wasn't even supposed to be there tonight—he was off to Hamburg to settle some matter. But the fact is he already had a personal grudge against you for that drubbing at the warehouse. He'd spotted you and Lemmon on the street, and once the fight broke out he was set to take out your friend when someone bashed him over the head. He said you watched it all and laughed at him as he went down."

"Very likely. It happened so fast I couldn't really say."

"One thing's for certain—the man hated lack of respect or ridicule. He demanded deference. So when his boys found where you work, he came back early. I learned too late that he'd returned to the city so couldn't update Brandt. They were going to snatch you off the street tomorrow anyway and hold you prisoner until he could teach you a lesson. So when you showed at the tavern tonight in that ridiculous disguise, your game was over."

She sniffed back tears as the vivid memories resurfaced. "Yes, he promised us he'd go for Ryan once done with me."

"I'd told him I wanted to screen for uninvited guests so was able to step in as one of your guards." He hesitated, gathering his thoughts. "But there's something more you should know. What was happening in that cursed 'shed,' that was the first time I'd been there. I never believed the rumors but now I know those cretins deserve what they dish out and more!" He had taken her hand as he spoke, but now seemed embarrassed and released it again. He leaned his head back on the couch. "My mind was made up to kill the bastards the moment I saw how they treated you."

She felt a sudden urge to comfort him but remained silent, unnerved by his anger, suppressing her own, feeling obliged to explain her own brutality. She had destroyed a man's face with an iron rod and impaled him in unquenchable rage. When she finally spoke, tears remained but her voice was calm and accepting: "That *Arschloch* was raping her, you know…my friend Doro. I couldn't spare her that before the end."

He again picked up her hand. "Far worse for her had you not taken him down. They were on her trail no matter what you did tonight. I can't say whether I could have gotten you both out—that was my plan, and my duty—but at least you're here now and safe for the moment."

She pulled her hand free to hug herself, eyes shut to block out the memory. "They're ruthless criminals, each and every one of them, if you ask me. And the Veidtner types are beyond insane, taking such pleasure in others' pain."

"Hallinger's just as evil, so don't underestimate him. Perhaps even worse, since word is he mastermind's the torture and abuse. The 'shed' was all his creation." She began to rock back and forth and he tried to divert her thoughts. "Well, in any case, they're far more dangerous than your Chicago gangsters, at least from what I read in the magazines. At least your bad guys don't have a political agenda." He struck a match and let it burn out, watching the curl of smoke ascend. "Brandt tells me you're from Chicago?"

"What else does he know about me?"

"He's a detective, after all, and determined to prevent another mess like that warehouse fiasco and fire, so he does his homework." Karl tossed the burnt matchstick and ignited another, watching it burn for a moment before lighting a cigarette. "And what we do know about these Nazi bastards—what I've witnessed personally for months—is that they'll use any means to get their way, to manipulate others, to gain leverage." He released a stream of smoke. "Often as not they succeed."

"They got nothing of value from Doro and me tonight. All that horror gained them nothing."

"That's why we have to get moving. And soon. When word does get out, Hallinger must explain to his big boss Himmler how this happened, and he'll need to cover his tracks. As Goebbels said, Hitler wants Germans to view them as the savior party to be trusted, the only one who can put this country back on the map and destroy the Versailles oppressors. What you witnessed tonight as a reporter makes you especially dangerous to them. You've experienced firsthand their brutality, their lack of self-control. The everyday German can't be allowed to see this side of the Party, and they want the outside world to view them as respectable leaders. So you must disappear, as was supposed to happen this evening. It's the way their organization works."

Isabel was exhausted, drained mentally as well as physically. "But I'm not personally involved, not really taking political sides. I'm just doing my job as a correspondent, trying to report on all the warring factions in this godforsaken republic of yours!"

"Judging by what you've already seen and done, I'd say you've now definitely chosen a side." He gingerly tested the damage to his ear and jaw. "And we can agree on one thing: Hitler can't be allowed that first step. Should he seize control, all Europe could be next, and the whole world will have hell to pay. You had a bitter taste of that tonight." His voice was leaden, all banter forgotten. "Once you and I leave the city, Brandt can direct his efforts to putting the brakes on Hallinger's search. He's good at his job."

"Not very good tonight."

Karl checked his watch. It was approaching two in the morning.

Mid-afternoon, Toni discovered visitors asleep on her couch. Isabel's head slumped against the shoulder of a young man, good-looking were it not for horrible swelling of one ear and red scrapes down his jaw. At the foot of the sofa lay a pile of badly bloodied clothing she recognized as an SA uniform.

Toni gently nudged her friend awake and Isabel made groggy introductions. She explained that poor Doro had died in Nazi hands and this man Karl had saved her life, and now the filthy bastards would be out to get them both. Barely controlling her tears as it was, she spared Toni the gruesome details.

"Izzy darling, come with me." Toni took Isabel by the hand. "We need to do something with that wild hair of yours." In the bathroom she did her best to style Isabel's chopped locks into a feminine bob. Pomade made her hair look halfway passable in the mirror. Isabel tried to tell more of their story but her friend shushed her. "Later. For now, let's make you human again." A little rouge on the cheeks and a touch of lipstick and Isabel almost appeared herself.

She gave Toni a hug. "Thank you, love. Is it okay if we stay here a little while?"

"Nothing to thank, Izz. You've clearly had a hell of a night. Staying here won't be a problem. Now a bite to eat for the three of us and I hit the sack. I'm bushed." After changing into a day robe and making a thorough search of her cupboard, Toni rounded up a makeshift lunch for her guests. "You know I sleep most days till eight-thirty or so, then back to the club." She set out half a loaf of bread, a chunk of hard cheese, a length of salami and two bottles of beer. "Sorry, slim pickings. I don't eat here much." She laughed as she cleared away their empties from the night before. "I'd swear I had more beer in there."

They came back out to the living room to find Karl with his hand resting on the telephone receiver. He appeared pensive. "I left a message for my friend. I hope I'm not taking advantage using your phone without asking."

"Everything here is at your disposal, Karl. I so appreciate you rescuing Izzy from herself. She usually gets out of trouble on her own, despite the odds." She wrapped her arm around Isabel's shoulders. "Glad you were there to help, though judging from that ear, you may have preferred being elsewhere." She stuck a cigarette in the long holder and lit up. "You're both welcome to stay as long as you wish. After I grab a few hours' shuteye I'll go out and get us some groceries."

"A gracious offer, but I'll be gone by evening. No need to overstay my welcome."

Toni was insistent: "Seriously, this place sits empty most of the day and you'll need time to make plans. Don't rush it." She sat in the chair and crossed her legs, revealing a bit of thigh. Isabel noticed her friend assuming a more feminine pose. "Plenty of room for you on the sofa, Karl. Isabel and I can share the bed." Toni smiled slyly, assessing him with her eyes, giving Isabel a knowing look. "Or if the couch is uncomfortable, the bed for the three of us, perhaps?"

206 | PATRICK W. O'BRYON

Karl looked away. A blush was a rare trait among the men Isabel knew. "Thank you, darling," she said, flashing her friend an innocent smile, "but time is pressing. We're waiting for Karl's friend to get us out of town till things cool down."

Karl's embarrassment faded to a dark frown. "I don't think you understand the gravity of our situation, Isabel—things aren't about to cool down. They're going to heat up. The danger won't go away, so don't think you can lay low for a few days and return to work in this city. It's simply not going to happen."

"I know, but—"

All three turned as the phone rang. Toni stubbed out her smoke as she put the receiver to her ear. She turned toward Karl and nodded as she listened to the caller. "Yes, he's here," she said at last. Covering the mouthpiece with her palm, she smiled. "You seem to be the only 'pleasant-looking man with a cleft chin,' so I believe this call's for you."

He was already reaching for the receiver. "Yes, yes," he repeated several times, his brow furrowed, adding "that makes sense" and finishing at last with "understood." He hung up and turned to Isabel. "We didn't get the break I expected. Hallinger's already on to us and raising hell. He's calling in every marker and he's got no shortage—powerful men in both the municipal and criminal police. They have my photo from my SA card and an artist's sketch of you as both hooker and male imposter." He creased his brow, obviously worried. "Stormtroopers are posting to all train stations, S-Bahn lines, bus terminals, even Tempelhof. Your office is under surveillance, and your apartment address known to the police so you can't return there."

"My God!" Isabel already had the phone in her hand. "I can't wait any longer—I have to call Ryan!" Karl depressed the cradle and cut the connection. "No, wait!"

"We can't afford to wait!" She pushed Karl aside in near panic. "Ryan has to know they're after him!"

"That's just it—Brandt says Lemmon isn't even in their sights! He's not a target!"

"How's that possible? Veidtner told me specifically Ryan would be next."

"Hallinger must have arrived at that cursed place right after we left last night, likely hoping to still enjoy the horror show. Instead, he found Veidtner and the others dead and us gone with the car. Now he has no choice but to rub us out quickly to protect his tarnished reputation. I must die for betraying the Party and for helping you escape. To maintain his own standing, he'll have to show Himmler he's covered his tracks and shown what happens to traitors."

Isabel surrendered the phone as she followed the rest of his reasoning. "Go on."

"Let's face it—I've set a very bad example for the Party faithful. But we know that bastard Veidtner wanted to deal with you personally, to make you pay in blood and suffering for his humiliation. He told you as much, so would have kept your role in the warehouse brawl hidden to deal with you in his own way on his own terms."

"So he never even mentioned Ryan to Hallinger?"

"That would explain why no one's out looking for Lemmon. It makes good sense. But all that changes if your contact him. If there's the slightest hint your boyfriend knows what happened out there, he also becomes a target to be dealt with. He's a reporter, after all, and the Nazis sure as hell don't want this kind of publicity as they consolidate their strength with more moderate types."

"So you and Brandt are saying I just disappear without telling Ryan where I've gone?"

"Far better for him if he knows nothing."

She looked down at her clenched hands. "That so cruel, leaving him totally in the dark." She shook her head in disbelief.

"Not as cruel as signing his death warrant. Hallinger wants us rubbed out and now before you can tell anyone what you know. He won't rest till he puts us both in the ground." Karl glanced around. "May I?" He gestured to the cigarette box and matches.

"Be my guest." Toni offered her gilded lighter, clearly unconcerned that the ashtray overflowed with evidence of those consumed in the preceding night.

He blew a stream of smoke and turned to Isabel. "Brandt suggests hiding out for a few days to buy him time to come up with a sure escape route."

Toni gave Isabel's shoulder a reassuring squeeze. "Remember, you're both welcome here."

"Most grateful," he said, "but we'd be trapped should they get on to us. I checked out your fire escape. The courtyard down below appears to have only one exit, so it's too big a gamble. And I won't put you at risk, either."

"Then I know the perfect place." Toni gave a bright smile. "The Toppkeller has upper rooms for private tête-à-têtes. The cops never bother us there thanks to 'contributions' to their widows and orphans fund, and some of the girls share special favors with the bulls, too. You'll be safe from prying eyes, and a phone closet in the hall will keep you in touch. I'll get you the number and a key. What do you think?"

Isabel had visited the club numerous times, although never the rooms designed for private assignations. The specialty clientele at Toppkeller was mostly attractive *Garçonnes*, young types like Toni who wore French male fashions. She did her best to live up to their motto, "For Friendship, Love and Sexual Enlightenment," as Isabel could personally attest. After further discussion, they accepted the offer. It seemed unlikely Hallinger's goons and corrupt cops would search for the fugitives in such a notorious cabaret.

Karl phoned Brandt with their decision, then volunteered to slip out to the nearest shops for food and drink. Toni insisted on his wearing a fake mustache from her stage kit and a suitable fedora and overcoat. They waited out the remainder of the day at the flat with Toni napping for a few hours. She was excited and concerned, but anxious to help any way she could. Once dusk faded to black they made their way on foot to Toppkeller.

CHAPTER ELEVEN

Berlin, Germany

December 1941

"So I was meant to spot you on the Alex and track you here?"

"It took a couple of tries, darling, until it dawned on me that the red hat and scarf might catch your eye."

"Well, it certainly worked. I'm here and listening, but sure as hell don't understand why. The minute you mentioned Brandt I knew you'd taken me for a ride. So what's the name of the game and how do I fit in? Why not approach me directly?"

"Brandt recognized you from that Gestapo flyer but had no idea if you were still around. He thought you'd have made yourself scarce after that bank thing. Then one of his snitches, a forger, brought in your photo and new identity for his weekly update, and Brandt took things from there."

"So why's Brandt so interested in the two of us?"

"He was the one who brought me back to Germany six months ago and got me the job at Sachsenhausen. For years he's carried the guilt for all I've been through, so he's determined to set things right. And now we're under pressure to move forward with something important, but first he wants to see if you're up for it, have the skills required, and can be trusted with the secret."

Curiosity gripped him. "So what's your report so far?"

"Well, you obviously know your covert tracking. I never spotted you once, but his guy was waiting for you to make it to Oranienburg."

Ryan thought for a moment. "The station cop with the toothache?"

"You got it."

"He appeared too lax for a real control."

"And the fact you're sitting here tonight shows you know your stuff. Brandt thinks you're a spy." She looked into his eyes. "Is he right?"

Ryan ignored the question. "So what other skills must I display to meet his standards?"

"Impersonating a German, but I can attest to your acting skills from the old days so no worries there."

"And who am I to be?"

She shook her head. "Only Brandt can give the go-ahead. It's his show, and there's too much at stake."

"For whom?"

"For me." She quickly glanced away. "And others, as well."

"Well if I'm to be involved, the least you can do is tell me everything that happened back then."

"Well, now you know about Karl."

"You fell for him, didn't you?"

She appeared relieved he'd caught on. "You must understand how much that night changed me. You and I had a good thing, Ryan, always fun and exciting." She touched his cheek. "And you were wonderful in bed, of course, but we never found that spark. Neither of us was ready for that." She spoke more quickly now, anxious to get it all out. "Karl was different. Though I saw his concern in that cursed beerhall, when push came to shove I still hit him with that brick. I wanted him dead. The other guy, too. But the more time we spent together later, the more I knew it felt right, and not just something physical. More than that, much more. And not simply because he saved my life, either. We just belonged together from the start."

"Couldn't you have left a message with the von Haldheims when you disappeared without a trace? Brandt led me to believe you were dead, your body left to rot in the river?"

"It wasn't just Brandt. I was in on that, too. I wanted so much to tell you. It hurt so much keeping silent, because I had real feelings for you. Real friendship." She squeezed his hand. "I still do, and that's what makes this all so painful. In those first days you turned the city upside-down, knocking at every door to find me. For me we'd been a fling, but then I saw how devoted you were." She wouldn't look at him. "Brandt's men quickly spotted the Nazi on your tail once you showed up at my landlady's. Every step you took, one of those bastards was right there behind you, and one of Brandt's men was one step back. When you searched for Doro and Jürgen in Wedding, their comrades knew better than to say anything, even had they known where we were hiding, and both my friends were already dead anyway, don't you see?"

"The Nazis wanted me to lead them to you, so you had the inspector throw me off the trail with that newspaper clipping." He hesitated, his suspicions clicking into place. "The woman in the river—that was Doro?"

She nodded, biting her lower lip at the memory, then finally spoke: "We knew you couldn't find me, but had to put an end to your search before they added you to their kill list. You were still out there raising questions and we wanted Hallinger to move on."

"And the Daily News? Were they in on your deception?"

"As much in the dark as you. I couldn't even let my father in Chicago know." She looked up at him. "No, that's not exactly true. I could have sent him a cable or even called. But you know what? I didn't want him gloating over my failure. He would never have let up with the ridicule for botching the assignment I'd set for myself."

"Does he now know?"

"He does...he did." Her eyes dropped to her lap and her voice thickened. "He's gone now, but I was home for a number of years by then and he learned what I'd been through. In the end I think he realized just how strong he'd made me." She wiped her eyes with her fingertips. "But he never really admitted it, even so. He was a hard-hitting man. That same toughness and lack of understanding drove my mother to an early grave, and it hardened me, too, and not necessarily in a good way. But he deserved the truth rather than thinking what you believed—that I was dead." Her eyes glistened and she accepted his handkerchief. "One more haunting regret, along with Doro's death, thanks to me."

"Didn't I deserve that same truth? Why not let me know you were alive once the pressure was off?"

"Brandt tracked down your address in Marburg and I wrote to the history department, but it came back with a handwritten note that you'd completed your doctorate and returned to the States, and I decided to let that sleeping dog lie."

"Well, this hound is now wide awake and demands to know more."

"I see you haven't really changed." She patted the top of his head before heading off to the kitchen for a bottle and two small glasses. He accepted the Cointreau. With France under the Nazi thumb, French luxury brands were available to anyone with enough money or a connection.

Ryan took a sip, welcoming the warmth of the liqueur. "So what made this Karl so special?"

"Thrown together in that sordid room above the club we shared everything: meals and stories and personal histories. I soon realized I'd found the man I hadn't known I was looking for—committed to some valiant cause, accepting of me as a fully capable person as well as a woman, a man willing to sacrifice everything for me, even kill for me."

"Ten years ago I didn't know I had that in me. Now I do. Time and events change a person."

"Confronting danger really wasn't your strength back then, was it? Your heart was open and sweet and you had a naïve sense of adventure. We were children playing at a game. In reality, we played with a fire that almost destroyed us."

"Then why single me out that night we met? I was just one more American guy, not your usual conquest, shall we say…not that I've ever regretted that you did."

"I never told you?" She hesitated. "No, of course not. I kept such things to myself. Well, it's time you knew—I was sleeping with a professor at the time, but when I saw you in all your bored, charming handsomeness at that university function, I knew I had to have you instead. It's just the way I was then—taking charge, using all the wiles and wits at my disposal, proving to myself I was as daring as any man at finding new lovers."

Taken aback by her candor, Ryan suddenly felt close to her again. "I am sorry I didn't show more courage, wasn't there when you needed me."

"Don't feel bad—I was just as naïve, perhaps more so, since I ignored the dangers. Only in true commitment to a cause did I find a place to achieve something real, and in the process I learned to love."

"Your Karl."

She nodded. "Karl Wittenberg. Originally Weissberg. His father was a Jew."

He sat back, considering the implications, the risks involved. *A Jew undercover in a Nazi cell? What chutzpah! The man was fearless!* He had spotted the wedding band on her left hand. "So what's with 'I. Friedrich,' the name downstairs on the bell?"

"Ah, yes," she said, rising from the couch. "There's more to this story, of course. Can you hear the rest now? It's getting late and curfew is coming."

"Screw the curfew. Just try to kick me out now."

"Then first some cheese and crackers to go with the Cointreau—and you'd better prepare yourself for another hour. The story gets stranger." She was already at the door to the kitchen when she added: "And far sadder."

She returned to kiss him on the forehead and then returned to the kitchen. Ryan remained on the couch, absorbing all he'd just heard, searching in vain for holes in her story, gaps in the narrative. He thought of her smiling at the SS officers earlier that day, her flirtatious banter while boarding the bus for Sachsenhausen. She was right about how young and immature he'd been back in '31. It did not seem the affront he might first have imagined, learning she had abandoned him for a man better suited to her mental and emotional needs. At the time he was in no position to make any commitment, even had he wanted to.

She returned with a tray of cheese and crackers and picked up the tale.

Berlin, Germany
February - March 1931

A well-known lesbian spot in Berlin West, Toppkeller was unimpressive—even seedy—by daylight. From scuffed parquet flooring to dark wainscoting to petite tables decked with white linen and delicate flower vases, the look was faded and passé. Garlands of paper herons swooped down from the beamed ceiling and odd wall murals—strange erotic nature scenes fronted by cutouts of familiar entertainers—added a whimsical

if kitschy touch to the establishment. But come evening, the place began to hop and continued swinging
through the night hours, drawing everyone from lesbian
cross-dressers to professional working girls of any per-
suasion. Straight men could find everything from conventional encounters to bondage under the whips of a
Domina. The stage hosted a four-piece brass band, live-
ly cabaret shows thick with innuendo, and boisterous
contests for the prettiest calves or breasts. At midnight
a tongue-in-cheek Black Mass was celebrated. Whatever one's pleasure, Toppkeller delivered, drawing famous stage and screen artists, singers and dancers, and
the whole panoply of sex workers to satisfy local and
tourist alike.

Weeks passed in the close quarters above the club.
Brandt reported that Hallinger was still offering sizable
bribes for any word on the fugitives' whereabouts.
From ticket sellers at transportation centers to police
controls, many were on the lookout for the couple
sought for the brutal murder of "innocent SA men."
Any premature attempt to leave the city would be extremely risky. Brandt said a powerful friend could get
them out by private vehicle, but he was in southern
Spain to escape the winter cold and wouldn't return
until the following month. Equally troubling, Brandt
knew Ryan was still rattling cages as he tried to find
out what had become of her, so finally—and at Isabel's
insistence—Brandt paid him a visit to discourage any
further inquiries. Afterwards Brandt reported things
had gone well.

Meanwhile, their days were filled with tedious waiting. Toni brought additional clothing, a radio and the latest magazines, and became the nightly courier for food and necessities. Each slipped out after dark, alone and in disguise, for exercise and a break from the boredom, but they kept such excursions short. Their nights were filled with the sounds of boisterous partying in the lounge below and rutting in the adjoining rooms. Nothing helped to muffle the cacophony of giggles and grunts, moans and cries, thumps on the walls and low laughter.

They shared details of their past lives and future dreams and discovered a remarkable connection. She told of her early years under the thumb of a harsh and demanding father, of her college studies and journalistic endeavors as she made a name for herself. He spoke of the early death of his parents and of growing up in the home of his uncle. He described his childhood on the streets of the city, his apprenticeship and journeyman experience learning the trade of a printer, and his discovery of democratic ideas and ideals. A minor run-in with the law—he didn't go into detail—brought him into Brandt's office and the opportunity to volunteer for an undercover role within the Nazi cell. Despite the occasional moments of friction—expected when sharing such close quarters—they shared much in common and grew closer by the day.

At last she'd thrown caution to the wind and invited him to join her beneath the comforter. She sensed their weeks together without physical contact had been hard on him, as well. "You're sure about this?" he asked. She drew him to her with a kiss leaving no reason to doubt the sincerity of her offer. It had felt right—his arms around her, his tongue a quick learner once she'd shown him the ropes, a hungry if inexperienced bedmate. In that sleazy setting there was nowhere she would rather be. And afterwards, lying in the crook of his arm, her fingers toying with the dark hair of his chest, she already wanted more of this man. Together they would take on the world, and as equals.

Very early one morning Isabel heard the incessant ring of the hall phone and answered the detective's call. A female floater had been sighted in the Spree, long in the water and decomposing badly. Brandt had put out word on behalf of Isabel to be informed should this occur. A Water Police patrol boat was already dispatched to bring it in. "Probably what we've been expecting," he reported.

"I want to be there." Isabel knew she owed Doro that much. Her friend had suffered miserably and died because of her. The least she could do was witness the recovery, to be present for her, to confess in spirit her guilt and sorrow so as to never again take a friend's safety lightly. Never again betray someone who placed trust in her.

Brandt conceded but remained dubious, as he explained over the phone: "Some boys spotted the body on their way to school. The water officers will bring the remains to shore, but we take things from there. Cover yourself well and be downstairs in ten minutes. I'll make a call and slow things down till we get there. You can certainly watch from a distance but you may regret this later. It's never a pretty sight." She had. It left her hollow, the ache of guilt and loss so painful she thought she would burst.

With each additional day in hiding, concerns grew that someone might give them up. Service personnel talked, and there was no telling when word might reach some Nazi or reactionary cop out to earn points with the likes of Hallinger. It might be the man who delivered the booze each morning and haul away the empties, coming up to gather 'dead soldiers' from the landing. Any residual liquor was conserved for his personal consumption. A few mornings before he had surprised her on the way to the hall bathroom and she hadn't liked his staring look, so she was on her guard. Also suspect were the two women who tidied up the club each afternoon, including the upstairs rooms. When hearing any daytime activity out on the landing, Karl crouched on the fire escape and watched for a surprise entry by their enemies. He longed for a pistol but would use his knife if push came to shove.

Their one-way ticket out entered the club a few days later. Shortly before noon the place was finally empty. Early evening would bring the first guests looking for a good time, but afternoons were usually quiet. Only the stale odors of dirty ashtrays and spilled booze lingered downstairs, permeating table linens and draperies. Occasionally a customer might descend nursing a hangover after a night spent upstairs and would leave in a hurry, but there was little else to disturb the lethargy of the joint.

On Brandt's request, Isabel had left the front door unlocked and waited in the main lounge, nervously smoking, still upset over what she had witnessed at the river. He was finally bringing the friend who could get them safely out of the city by private car. Brandt suggested she meet him and their savior alone and wearing her most attractive dress. Toni had come through again, this time with a short-skirted number that showcased Isabel's legs. Saying good-bye to such a trustworthy friend had been difficult, but Toni handled it in her usual casual manner. "Come back to see me when we're free of the Nazi bastards, okay?"

Now Isabel chain-smoked in anticipation of meeting Brandt's mystery guest. Karl concealed himself behind a wooden stage curtain. He would observe through holes used to display breasts or other appendages of beauty contestants while hiding faces to avoid undue influence on the cabaret audience. Although they trusted Brandt, their growing uncertainty demanded a back-up plan in every case. Karl knelt on the boards of the stage, his blade ready.

The detective strolled in with a nattily-dressed gent in chalk-striped suit and high-winged collar. The dandy set his walking stick and bowler atop one of the tables and made himself at home. Isabel stubbed out her smoke and came forward. Brandt introduced her to Anton Kessler, and Isabel recognized a regular she'd occasionally seen in the old days at the club when she and Toni had been an item. Kessler was reputed to run shady enterprises in the underworld of Berlin West, so Isabel was surprised to find the notorious gangster and man-about-town completely at ease around a top cop. She had heard from Toni that this swell was particularly popular for his free-spending ways and his affinity for *Gougnettes*, expensive call girls who indulged either sex.

Brandt immediately explained the odd partnership: "Herr Kessler and I go way back—a few scrapes in our youth made us comrades, and we fought our way out of mutual trouble often enough. Anton took a somewhat different route to his dubious success, but his heart's good and his word's his bond." He lit up a cigar and chuckled. "Besides, I have enough on this criminal bastard to take advantage of his friendship from time to time." Kessler, unfazed by either the joke or the insulting moniker, grinned at Isabel. He took in her face and legs in obvious appreciation. Toni's dress worked its magic and the boyish haircut accented her high cheekbones. He shook her hand.

"A pleasure to make your acquaintance, Herr Kessler?" She glanced toward Brandt for reassurance.

"Well, my dear, the pleasure's all mine. Our beloved inspector here says you wish to leave our fair city in a rather secretive manner. If there's one thing I know well, it's how to by-pass more conventional exits and means of transport." He turned his grin on Brandt. "My detective friend knows nothing about any of this, of course."

Brandt blew cigar smoke high over his shoulder and feigned distraction, muttering: "About what?"

Isabel wondered if she should bring Karl out from hiding. "We would be most appreciative of your help, Herr Kessler."

Kessler appeared surprised and pivoted to Brandt. "We? I only recall hearing of this lovely lady's need for a ride, my friend, and since she's all I imagined and more, I thought perhaps to accompany her myself."

Brandt laughed through another cloud of smoke. "Do you really think my trust extends to allowing a woman of such class to fall into your clutches? The lady has a traveling companion, a young colleague of mine, by the way, and most capable of protecting her honor." He tapped off the ash. "Just in case you get any ideas, he must be around here somewhere." Brandt made a show of glancing around the empty lounge.

"Then it's my loss, Gregor." He grinned again at Isabel. "Can you leave this evening, miss?"

"The sooner the better."

"Excellent. Consider it done. Meet my driver in the first alleyway a block to the north as you leave the club. Eight p.m. exactly. A dark blue sedan will take you as far as Magdeburg. From there you're on your own."

"My sincere gratitude, Herr Kessler." She shook his hand again. "You're a life-saver."

He hesitated releasing her hand. Bending closer, he whispered: "And should you ever return to the city unaccompanied, feel free to get in touch." He handed her a business card. "I believe you and I might have much to enjoy in common." He winked with obvious intent. "Now, if you will excuse me, the inspector and I have a luncheon engagement." He reached for his bowler and cane.

She walked them to the door. "And thank you so much, Detective Brandt, for everything you've done for us."

"A pleasure, Fräulein. May you and Karl find happiness wherever you two end up." He took a thick envelope from his breast pocket and put it in her hand. "You'll find these useful, I expect, and I'll be sending your friend Lemmon a clipping on the recovery of your friend's remains. Let's hope it closes that door permanently."

"I'm most grateful."

He gave her a peck on the cheek. "Now travel safely."

The men stepped out under the overcast sky. Brandt turned and whispered to Isabel: "You should probably release our friend from behind that screen."

With a chuckle he rejoined Kessler as a dark sedan pulled to the curb. Sliding into the rear seat, he called out to her one last time: "And tell him I'll miss his fine work. I wish we had more of his kind."

Isabel remained beneath the portico until the car disappeared at the corner. Karl already waited in the lounge. She opened the envelope and extracted two slim document bundles. His newly-forged identity card listed him as a journeyman printer. The photo did him justice, showing off the strong cleft in his chin and the deep-set eyes. She couldn't help stealing a sideways glance at his right ear, still damaged from her brick attack. Would it never heal? No matter. He was still a handsome man. A letter from the printers' local put him on assignment to an affiliated union in Munich.

Her gray booklet identified her as Isabel Friedrich, a secretary and native to Dresden. She recognized the stapled photo as one taken for the municipal police file when she had registered as a foreign correspondent in Berlin a few years prior. It was clearly time to let her hair grow out again to match the picture. As she handed Karl his papers, a handwritten note fluttered to the ground. It listed several names and contact numbers in other cities, along with the notation that Brandt had alerted each to a possible future contact from trustworthy parties.

Karl scrutinized his packet beneath the pink shade of the table lamp. He ran his finger carefully over each page, holding the paper over the bulb while looking for watermarks, following the contours of an official-looking stamp covering a third of his photo. "Young Becker's work and adequate," he judged at last, reaching for Isabel's papers to give them the same treatment. "But not even close to my own." He smiled at her, his grin infectious. "I pride myself on *expert* forgery and counterfeiting."

CHAPTER TWELVE

Berlin, Germany
December 1941

The well-worn clothing did suggest a recent financial challenge, though surely it was a ruse. Maturity suited him. The wrinkles at his eyes were deeper, but he'd always been a smiler and the ruggedness only added to his looks. Those remarkable blue eyes recalled better times and could still draw her in if she gave them half a chance. One aspect of his face did show a marked alteration: the once patrician nose was off-kilter from some cruel blow.

Beyond those physical changes, she sensed an unexpected toughness and new confidence. The naïve Ryan she'd seduced was nowhere to be seen. Sitting beside her was a man with a potentially dangerous edge, honed on cruelties such as she herself had experienced. This new Ryan Lemmon would be good for what she had in mind. What Brandt had in mind. But would he be open to what would be demanded of him? Sharing her story had been the first step. He had taken it well so far. She valued the compassion shown, the

230 | PATRICK W. O'BRYON

understanding for what she had done to him and to others. To Doro.

His reappearance had certainly come as a blow. Brandt had known enough to deliver the news in person. She had laughed to hear Ryan was likely an American spy, but her laughter had rung hollow. Inwardly, she was still guilt-ridden by what she'd put him through and sensed in herself an unexpected longing for their lost times. Brandt told of Ryan's inscrutable robbery of the Reichsbank. He had taken something of such value that it threatened the self-satisfied lives of the Nazi bigwigs, and his face now graced the "most wanted" list of the Gestapo. The flyer showed a decent likeness, and she was pleased her old flame hadn't lost his sense of adventure. Perhaps she had contributed in some small way to his bold transformation.

And now, for whatever reason, Ryan was living near the Alex, passing himself off as a reporter for an American magazine, or—were one to believe his forged papers—a German engineer with the Todt Organization helping Hitler create a new Berlin. Either way, Brandt had him over a barrel. Ryan might participate willingly by appealing to his country's best interests, or through his sense of what was right. But first she had to confess everything she had experienced before she could win him over to their cause. Her disappearance had hurt him badly, more than she had expected, but he seemed to be handling the revelations well. She trusted that his suspicions or revulsion would melt away when confronted by all the horrors she had endured. In the end, she hoped to win forgiveness rather than recrimination.

Munich, Germany

1931 – 1933

Escaping Hallinger's reach had been fraught with tension, yet oddly uneventful. Anton Kessler's driver was a slender young man with an acne problem. Isabel's flirtations convinced him to forgo Magdeburg in favor of the far longer haul into the heart of Bavaria. In Munich they contacted the local printers union and were well received, thanks to Brandt's introduction, and within weeks had joined a socialist cell. Applying his impressive knowledge of printing, Karl soon found a journeyman position in a small print shop off Ulmerstrasse. Working after hours, he forged new identities and they dutifully registered with the authorities as a respectable married couple. A legal marriage would wait until the Nazis were thwarted.

Hugo Haussmann, the owner of the shop, was nearing retirement. He had fought honorably in the Great War and paid for his courage with lungs scarred by mustard gas and a weak left arm. A bullet had rendered his elbow a liability. He rarely appeared at the business, preferring to spend his days at a tavern closer to both home and ailing wife. Hugo recognized Karl's skills, shared his leftist political leanings, and gladly surrendered day-to-day operations to the young man who produced beautiful customized stationery, handbills, and advertising posters. By day. At night Karl secretly printed anti-Nazi pamphlets. For his legitimate labors he pocketed a decent 50 marks a week, allowing him to maintain a new household with Isabel while still working to undermine the National Socialists.

Leisure time didn't sit well with Isabel. Having always thrived on new challenges and expressing her own voice, she missed the action and resolved to maintain some semblance of her former life. Soon she was penning searing anonymous attacks on the Nazis and helping covertly distribute the political tracts rolling off Karl's nocturnal press. In sharp contrast to such bold activity, women in Munich who held no secretarial position or had no shop to tend were expected to focus on running their households and raising their children. Thus it was a great surprise when a maternal sensibility began to grow in Isabel alongside an unplanned child. The parents-to-be were delighted.

March of 1933 ended with hints of a warm spring to come, but the couple's mood was chilled by unmistakable and immediate threats to the Weimar Republic. Hitler had gained control of the Reichstag and much of Bavaria appeared to ignore the looming tyranny. On the last day of the month Isabel set out to cross the city on trams and buses. At each transfer she left behind political tracts for others to find. Karl would work till evening fulfilling commercial orders, then remain at the shop late into the night. A major print job was on rush to benefit their cause. She would drop by after hours with sandwiches and beer.

The socialists were taking to the streets that night to plaster the central city with posters decrying the growing menace. It was a bold and dangerous maneuver with pro-Nazi propaganda and support ramping up, but without full commitment there would be no stopping the fascist tide. They would have their hands full wrapping up the protest under cover of darkness and they knew the risks. Rumor had it a man in the Schwabing cell had already died after a brutal beating, and ever fewer dissidents were stepping forward to risk all for human dignity and self-government.

It was a hard-pressed and somewhat taciturn Karl who raised the metal shutter for Isabel around seven that evening. The soles of her feet ached from blanketing the town with pamphlets and the metallic smell of ink and oiled machinery left her queasy, recalling her bouts with morning sickness. But the concern on Karl's face seemed unrelated to her obvious exhaustion. She took a rag and brusquely wiped sweat-smeared ink from his chin. "Why so glum, darling? We'll finish in time, right?" She set down the paper bag holding his dinner.

"Yes, of course, love. But it'll be a rush, as usual." He paused to allow the apprentice to peel the damp poster off the press and lay it on the rack to dry. "You may have to feed me while we work." He reached for a cloth and wiped the platen.

"No problem, and I won't let Ludi starve either." She emptied the contents of her sack on the table alongside a growing stack of finished posters. Karl's teenaged trainee smiled in gratitude. They took several quick bites of liver sausage on rye and set the rest aside for later. Ludi, applying fresh ink to the platen, also appeared down and distracted. She opened two bottles of beer and set them near the clattering machine, and both took greedy swigs before returning to the heaving press.

Isabel climbed onto a stool to watch them work. Karl was clearly hiding something worrisome. After several anxious minutes she broached the subject: "All right, out with it, *Liebling*. What's eating you?"

His attempt at a grin failed. "You read me like a book, Izz."

"An easy read, my love." She hoped her smile would ease his concerns. "What's going on?"

He stilled the press. "We're down three tonight. Some SA assholes mouthed off at a beerhall this afternoon and went after a Jew out front, and a couple of our guys stepped in."

Her smile disappeared. "Which of ours?" Isabel knew each cell member well, knew their wives and husbands, partners and families. "Are they all right?"

Karl gave the names with respect bordering on reverence: "Hans-Gustav, Georg and Little Max." His fists were clenched. "Hans-Gustav and Georg should be okay—a broken arm, bad bruises. Georg may have busted ribs. It'll all take time."

She feared what was coming next. "And Little Max?" A skinny boy, he was barely sixteen and under-sized for his age, shallow-chested but as bold and committed as the older ones.

His eyes cut to Ludi, a close friend of young Max. "Still unconscious is all we know for sure. His mother's with him at the hospital now. They thrashed him pretty good and he'll lose an eye—one sonofabitch took a blade to his face..." He choked up. "But that's not the worst of it. They aren't sure he'll pull through."

"Oh my God!" She nearly stumbled as she came off the stool raging. "But he's only a boy!" Her jaw trembled. "Those cretins have no decency, no shame." She wiped tears with the same rag she'd used on her husband's chin.

Karl put his arm around her shoulders. "You're not going to like what comes next, darling." He hesitated. "Ludi and I are stepping in for them tonight." He hushed her instant protest with a finger to her lips. "We've no choice: the posters go up no matter what."

She wrenched herself loose from his arm and her voice rose: "Bad enough you spend every minute of every day in here." The reproaches multiplied: "Forget me, forget my needs! What the devil will it mean for our baby if you end up crippled, or worse? Some of those bastards carry pistols, you know. Must our child grow up fatherless?" Isabel crossed her arms in defiance. "If you're going I go with you, and there's nothing you can say or do to stop me!"

He tried again to offer comfort but she pulled away in protest and turned her back to him. "Come on, Isabel. The risk's too great for you and our baby. If nothing else, think of our child!"

"You've just made my point, Karl. It's too great for all three of us! If Germany falls to these brutes none of us is safe, not even this baby." Her hands cradled the bulge of her belly. "If you're going to put yourself on the line, then so will I. This child will learn exactly what his parents are made of."

Ludi had retreated behind the press, wiping his hands with a rag while awaiting resolution of the standoff. Karl leaned against the table and bowed his head as she quietly fumed. Finally, he turned back to her. "You're right, love. I can't expect less of you than I do of myself. We're in this together, come what may. Our lives are worthless anyway if we lose this thing." He took her in his arms. "What kind of world will be left to our baby if we let the bastards have their way?"

He called over to the waiting Ludi: "It's decided then. We all go out together. We win together."

By eleven their comrades began to arrive in small groups. The rear door to the alley was unlocked for the new arrivals. Lookouts stood watch at each end of the street in case word had slipped in idle conversation or someone had snitched. The chatter was halfhearted. By now all had heard about the losses. Minutes before midnight the last of the posters came off the press, and everyone helped roll up the broad sheets, fill glue pots, and assemble the long-handled brushes. Just past twelve their cell leader, Matthias, distributed hand-sketched maps and assigned key locations in the target-ed streets. There was little discussion. Each activist knew the gravity of the coming deed.

The comrades left team-by-team, quietly echoing their new slogan on the way out: *"Für Kleinen Max!"* One member of each team carried the rolls, the other a glue pot and long brush. One would slop adhesive on the surface of a wall or advertising pillar, the other slap up the poster and smooth out the wrinkles. Two spe-cialized teams were charged with handcarts carrying additional supplies. They would lie low at pre-determined locations, allowing their comrades to re-stock without returning to the shop.

Isabel, Karl and Ludi locked up front and rear on their way out. The bells of the Frauenkirche struck one as they neared the Marienplatz. The heart of the old city appeared quiet, but a patrol could suddenly appear from any of numerous side streets. Brownshirts often left the beerhalls soused and itching for trouble. Their arrival was usually preceded by boisterous laughter or song, so the drunker the goons, the greater the chance of early warning and avoiding conflict. Police patrols were more treacherous, the cops moving stealthily in teams of two. The comrades knew to keep necessary conversation to a whisper.

Ludi stood lookout. A two-fingered whistle would signal "drop everything and run." Isabel and Karl stepped back to admire their first completed job, a row of bold posters now running the length of a towering wall just north of the gothic city hall. That same stretch had been papered by the Nazi Party earlier in the week to promote the All-Fools-Day boycott of Jewish businesses set to begin at daybreak. Hitler had taken the chancellorship during the first month of the year and by February a suspicious fire had destroyed the Reichstag building in Berlin, giving the new chancellor "justification" for a widespread crackdown on Socialists, Communists and Jews. Some suspected the Nazis had committed arson to accomplish their political goals, and now, in the early hours of April, the government-sanctioned persecution of the German Jews would commence.

While her husband was the true artist, Isabel herself came up with the image for the biting posters now concealing the government-sanctioned placards. Like those postings, her version also displayed a prominent

swastika, but from its center glared Hitler's face twisted into a hateful grimace. Four bent appendages wearing Nazi armbands extended to form the hooks of the
crooked cross, in each fist a threatening weapon: pistol,
knife, fuse-lit bomb or poison bottle. In script below
the striking image was the bold warning: "For now, the
Jews. Are you next?" At first glance one might think
Hitlerites themselves had crafted the image, but a closer look would reveal the imminent threat to German
civility and humanity.

They moved on toward their next assigned target.
As they passed the iron-gated entrance to the city hall,
Ludi suddenly shouted: "Run! Run!" His cries rang out
high-pitched and terrified as he ran full tilt across the
square. There'd been no time to whistle a warning.
Karl, glue brush still in hand, grabbed Isabel's arm as
she dropped the posters and they followed on his heels.
A backward glance revealed Brownshirts raising the
alarm, stumbling in their drunkenness but already
catching up. The cobblestones made running difficult
and her legs, exhausted from the long day on the trams,
barely supported her. She managed to keep pace with
Karl despite stabbing pains in her calves and feet.

Ludi had disappeared up a side alley. Hoping to
divide the pursuers, the couple dodged to the right and
passed several dark storefronts to enter the next open
street. Isabel bent over, hands on her knees as she tried
to catch her breath. Karl positioned himself at the
mouth of the street to reconnoiter, twisting the handle

free of the brush head to wield it like a club on the first pursuer to round the corner, but the thugs had chosen the easiest target, the kid. They heard muffled shouts in the distance.

Her voice was shaky, her breathing still labored. "What'll we do? They'll kill Ludi!"

"Let's go!" He grabbed her arm. In the feeble light she saw the set of his jaw and knew they were heading for serious trouble but she pushed all fear aside.

They moved cautiously in case of a guard but the mouth of the alley was unattended. The thugs had cornered Ludi twenty meters down the passageway. He crouched in a doorway alcove, arms shielding his head, his cries muffled and pleading. The louts took turns pelting him with cobbles kicked loose from the neglected pavement. Mocking his suffering, the leader taunted with obscene promises of what lay ahead as their victim's cries grew weaker with every projectile hitting home. Only drunkenness caused some to tumble uselessly to the ground or land with limited force.

"Wait here!" Karl abandoned caution and raced into the fray, the end of the broomstick clutched in his hands.

"No way in hell!" She picked up a stone at her feet and ran toward the assailants.

So involved in tormenting the youth, the Brownshirts ignored the assault from their rear until it was too late. Karl splintered his stick over the head of the first man, sending him to the ground with hands to his face and a ragged cry of pain. Isabel slammed her stone into the face of an inebriated thug distracted by his fallen colleague, but the element of surprise was lost and the other two turned the tables. The pack leader, a huge brute, was already atop Karl, pummeling with both fists. Karl tried to defend himself but the stump of the handle got him nowhere. Fists rained down relentlessly despite the attacker's drunkenness.

Isabel, infuriated by the assault on her husband, hurled her stone at the man's head but failed to protect herself from the remaining goon. He snagged her by the arm as she ran past and threw her into the brick wall. As she staggered back dazed, he buried a fist in her belly. She doubled over and dropped to the ground. The Nazi kicked her over and over with his heavy boot until she lay still, then joined his colleague to finish up with Karl.

She awoke on her back, shivering violently. A slash of gray announced the coming dawn. The alley remained dark. Intense cold permeated her body but she welcomed the growing numbness in her heart. Tears streamed down her cheeks but she made no effort to stop them, afraid to move in the knowledge that, with the first shift of her legs, with the first timid exploration of her hand, she would find what she feared most. With difficulty, she turned her head to the side and stared into the blackness. She was alone.

❖

Berlin, Germany
December 1941

"Horrifying. Absolutely horrifying." Ryan shook his head, filled with compassion and mind-numbing disgust. "I'm so sorry for your loss, Isabel."

Subdued by the memories, she finished the tale. "Our cell leader Mathias and some comrades went out searching before dawn after we failed to return. Mathias knew our route and targets, of course. They eventually found Ludi, who had managed to drag himself out to the square. Though barely coherent, he directed them to me, and they brought the two of us to a sympathetic doctor. He had us admitted to a hospital as victims of an agricultural accident."

"What had become of Karl?"

"The bastards must have dragged him off after the fight. We'd injured two of them, so I suppose they weren't able to handle more than Karl. Perhaps they planned to return for the two of us, but who really knows? I was battered and incoherent. I lost track of him for almost a week. They said I'd never have another child. Mathias visited my ward and showed me a photo from the paper showing a filthy man with a sign at his neck reading 'traitor,' and the Brownshirts had him seated backwards on an ox." She shut her eyes.

"They paraded him around town that way. It was obvious he'd been badly beaten, but the cauliflower ear told me immediately he was my Karl."

Ryan couldn't find words to encompass such cruelty and hate. He forced himself to sound calm. "And what happened next?"

"Hauled into court and sentenced to three years in prison for defacing public property and fomenting rebellion. As for Ludi, he was released from the hospital and disappeared after that. Our printer Hugo tried to track him down but Ludi's family played dumb. Likely sent him off to relatives in the country." She dried her eyes. "I wrote Karl for the first year and received only two short notes back. They were mostly blacked out by the censors, but he did acknowledge the loss of our baby." She blew her nose. "If only I could have been with him to share our loss, our grief."

Ryan realized his fingernails were buried in his palms and forced his hands to relax. "Despicable, heartbreaking."

She turned to face him on the sofa and composed herself. "And then he disappeared. No further word. I contacted Brandt, who inquired within the prison system. Karl was supposed get out at the end of his sentence but instead they kept him in 'protective custody' in a concentration camp and he's still a political prisoner of the Reich. The inspector was able to track Karl's transfers from one camp to another, but had no direct knowledge of him or his condition until six months ago when they moved him to Sachsenhausen."

"So why on earth are you working out there, and for SS bastards yet? Especially after all you've suffered at their hands, that baffles the hell out of me."

"No wonder. I'm baffled by it all, as well. When I lost track of my husband—for that's what he was despite no license or ceremony—I was at wit's end. I had the little bit my dad was willing to send and no way to make a living in Munich, so at Brandt's suggestion I returned to Chicago. He promised to keep track of Karl and let me know when he was freed. So I returned home on my old passport and began working again at the News. If you'd known I was still alive and had been in the States you might have spotted a few by-lines, mostly society pieces, of course. My dad still didn't buy into a woman's covering actual news, despite all I'd accomplished in Berlin. That is, accomplished before everything went to hell. In any case, I struggled along for years knowing that I'd completely fouled up my life and lost everyone I'd ever really cared about."

"So how'd you get back here?" He sensed her mood lighten as she moved beyond the Munich disaster.

"Last spring a letter reached me from Brandt. He gave a phone number and said he had important information. I rang him up, and he asked me to call back in an hour on a different line. That's when I learned what was happening here. A secret SS operation needed expert forgers and had sent word to Kripo headquarters. Brandt had suggested they run down Karl in their camp system and transfer him to Sachsenhausen. Once the move was |made, our friend the inspector encouraged me to return to Berlin. I still had my old 'Isabel Friedrich' papers, and using those he set me up in the camp admin office, typing and scheduling and that sort of thing. It's been challenging living under fake cover for months, but it has allowed me to keep tabs on Karl, at least on paper. I'm never allowed into the prison compound itself, so haven't even caught a glimpse of him. Frustrating as hell, having him so close yet untouchable."

"And you wanted me to see your being buddy-buddy with those SS officers at the camp bus, right? You wanted me to question your motives."

"Had you turned tail and run, I would have understood and, quite frankly, admired your good sense despite my disappointment. Instead you're sitting here now, and that's what we hoped for. You showed guts, curiosity and compassion, and Brandt assures me you were quick on your feet in response to his 'arrest and interrogation' test. He wanted to see for himself just how well you masquerade under tense conditions." She smiled a little at last. "So that's all I can tell you till we sit down with him."

"That means I passed the tests?"

"With flying colors, but once you hear the rest you still may run for the hills. God knows, I wouldn't blame you one bit, given the way I treated you."

"What you put me through is nothing compared to the cards life's dealt you, Izz. If there's a way I can get back at that filth for what you and have Karl suffered, well, that fits right in with my personal goal. So let's get this thing underway. When do I see my old buddy Brandt?"

"First things first, Ryan." She glanced up at the wall clock. "It's well past curfew, and you can't spend the night without alerting either the concierge or my neighbors. So empty your glass, grab your coat and hat, and give me a hug for old time's sake. Then get the hell out of here as quietly as you came. Brandt will be in touch tomorrow, okay?"

He did. Tomorrow would surely be an interesting day.

CHAPTER THIRTEEN

Berlin, Germany
December 1941

They met the next evening at Isabel's flat. One of
Kessler's men had dropped by the apartment
house earlier that afternoon for a word with the concierge. Reichmarks changed hands and a bit of persua-
sion assured that any gathering upstairs would remain a
secret. Ryan arrived at a quarter to eight. Isabel buzzed
him up and offered a hug and Cointreau. He accepted
the embrace but declined the drink. He wanted his wits
about him. Isabel appeared nervous and declined any
further discussion until the group had gathered.

At five to eight a sedan pulled to the curb and dis-
charged two men in heavy overcoats and fedoras. Ryan
watched through a gap in the blackout drapes as they
made their way up the stoop. Isabel pressed the button
to unlock the front door and moments later welcomed
the new arrivals to her living room. She took coats and
hats and suggested they make themselves at home.

Brandt greeted Ryan like a long-time acquaintance.
Barely a week had passed since the interrogation in the

detective's office where the reception had been far less convivial. Ryan wasn't sure how he felt about the natti-ly-dressed gangster credited with Isabel's escape years before. Anton Kessler was clearly to play some key role in the project up for Ryan's consideration, yet the man seemed aloof, as if the meeting were taking place under his patronage but with no need for his personal input. Brandt asked permission to smoke his pipe and Isabel encouraged Ryan to follow suit. Kessler snipped the tip from a massive cigar and set it aflame. She brought out glasses of amber liqueur and the two new-comers accepted gracefully. Ryan once again declined.

Kessler immediately claimed the larger armchair while Brandt took a seat on the sofa across from Ryan. Isabel chose to remain standing behind the couch at Brandt's back. The inspector wasted no time getting down to business: "Frau Friedrich tells me you now appreciate all she has endured over the past decade. It falls to me to present a plan to help make her whole again while simultaneously doing something valuable to others. While I'm sure you're most curious by now, what we discuss tonight never leaves this room. Agreed?"

"Agreed. And I am, as you say, most curious."

"Let me confirm up front that you show a natural talent for passing yourself off as German. Your accent is flawless and you've mastered our demeanor. And Frau Friedrich tells me you proved your worth in that regard back in your days together."

"So that's why I'm here?"

"You appear an ideal candidate," Brandt pulled from his coat pocket the Gestapo sketch, "if this flyer speaks the truth." Boldfaced print above his image read *Sought under Suspicion of Bank Robbery*. "A decent-enough likeness. I recognized you the moment it hit my desk."

Ryan glanced up at Isabel and smiled, hoping to draw her out of her mood. "Do you think it truly captures my nose?" She offered a fleeting grin and Brandt chuckled. The attempt at humor got no reaction from stoic Kessler so Ryan moved on. "Let's get down to brass tacks—what exactly are you asking of me?"

Brandt caught Kessler's eye. "Very well, it's all quite simple, really. We want you to pinch millions of pounds sterling."

Ryan shook his head in disbelief. "Surely you can't mean robbing the Bank of England?"

"Well, technically, Reichsführer-SS Himmler is already masterminding the robbery, and right here in a nice neighborhood of Berlin. We've simply come up with a better use for the loot."

Ryan looked to Isabel. "What should I make of this nonsense?"

She gave him an encouraging smile. "You'll understand soon enough. Just hear him out."

Brandt smoothed his mustache with two fingers and began: "Himmler has a major counterfeiting operation underway. He intends to blanket the world with fake British notes—a grandiose plan to weaken our enemy." The inspector leaned back, puffing to keep his pipe alight as he spoke. "After all, if word gets out the pound sterling can't be trusted, who will subsidize the Allied war effort? Even you Americans will think twice before chipping in, I believe." He cleared his throat. "So we suggest you help us close down this operation."

"Why me? And why would you of all people want to help England?"

"On that first count, you come along at a fortunate moment and with valuable attributes. As we discussed, you're clearly excellent at impersonating a German, a role central to our plan. Rumor has it you were in and out of the Reichsbank without anyone's being the wiser. And secondly—even more helpful—you're already a criminal suspect in the breach of a major Reich depository. If our plan were to go sideways, you—or more precisely your persona—would be the primary target of the secret police. That takes the heat off the rest of us, right?" He couldn't restrain a broad smile. "Finally, I might add that your obvious connections with, shall we say, operations outside the Reich put you in an excellent place to get away with the caper."

Ryan still couldn't believe what he was hearing and offered a wry smile. "I thank you for this great honor."

Brandt gave his pipe a sour look and scraped the plug of unburnt tobacco into the ashtray. He worked a pipe cleaner through the stem as he spoke. "As for our providing aid and succor to an enemy of the Reich, I might instead make the case that we are protecting our great country *and* our beloved Führer." His sarcasm was obvious. "Should fake banknotes threaten the British economy on any massive scale, you can bet the Allied bombers will paper our skies with equally fake Reichsmarks. Our citizens will put such unexpected bounty to good use and no one comes out a winner. Throwing a large monkey wrench into the world economy is a serious risk to all the powers that be. The world has already lived through one massive inflationary economy, and no one wants another, you'll surely understand."

Ryan understood. But he wouldn't reveal his espionage role no matter how obviously Brandt was on to him. In truth, his lines of communication with both Ellington and Canaris appeared severed so he'd get no outside help should he sign up for this scheme. "Just how do you intend to get proof of this devious enterprise out of the country? Aren't border controls extremely tight?" He thought of his experience at Weil am Rhein.

Anton Kessler finally spoke up: "I don't know to what extent my friend Gregor has told you of my enterprises, so allow me to clarify. I specialize in the movement of goods and people into and out of the Reich. My network of routes and pliable border agents makes for a very lucrative trade." He tapped the ash from his cigar. "Two of my best people are waiting down in the car as we speak, ready to work with you on this. They handle difficulties in an efficient manner, so you needn't give a thought to international borders."

Ryan accepted this information with a nod and turned back to Brandt. "Such an operation requires careful planning and is extremely high-risk. How soon do you need an answer?"

Brandt had refilled his pipe and was tamping down the tobacco. "You are here right now, so that shows a willingness to work on behalf of Frau Friedrich. And your current legal situation remains precarious, given you're an active target of a Gestapo manhunt and your cover story is at best tenuous." He grinned. "So I believe we already have your answer. The rest is mere logistics. But it is imperative you know that time is of the essence. We've only two days to make a go of this."

"Two days? But that's impossible!" Ryan impatiently ran his fingers through his hair. "Okay, fine. So tell me exactly how this theft helps Isabel?"

She came around the sofa and put a hand on his shoulder. "Just hear him out, Ryan."

"Let me explain the rush," Brandt continued. "We have an engraver working inside the print shop, a trustworthy man, and we also have a deliveryman who serves as our eyes and ears. After hours he drinks with two of the guards, so we know pretty well what's going on from their standpoint." The inspector glanced up and Isabel's nod encouraged him to continue. "So here's the story: this SS operation of Himmler's has been a fiasco from day one. Every petty faction within his Berlin security apparatus wants control so they can take credit should it succeed. And it's literally a money-mill, so they're certainly siphoning off fake currency along the way." He set the pipe aside without lighting it. "They started with civilian printers under SS oversight and the product proved shit. Next they brought in a guy they call 'the professor,' a mathematician and physicist considered an expert in serial numbers and the like. He authenticates the finished product but understands little of the creative process itself. It seems counterfeiting is a fine art. Anyway, Himmler is fed up with delays and turnover. He's fuming and his lackeys are under extreme pressure to produce the goods."

Ryan considered for a moment. He had practical concerns. "Surely the place is well guarded. How do you make this happen without bloodshed?"

Brandt exchanged another glance with Kessler. "I'll get to that in a moment, but first you need to understand what we're dealing with. After a number of failures someone finally suggested scouring the prisons for professional counterfeiters, a captive work force whose continued existence will depend on producing a satisfactory product. Naturally, the word went out to the Criminal Police detailing the type of inmate being sought, and I knew a particularly fine candidate. I arranged his transfer to Sachsenhausen and he now lives at the shop around the clock."

"Your engraver."

"As you've surely guessed," Isabel took a seat on the arm of Ryan's chair, "it's Karl."

Ryan gave her an understanding smile. "I suspected at the word 'counterfeiter.'" So isn't it time you told me why you still work at that horrible camp now that Karl's somewhere here in Berlin?"

"First hear the inspector out, then you'll understand."

Ryan looked to Brandt. "So, if I've got this straight, Herr Kessler's men and I waltz into an SS print shop under German guise, have Isabel's husband slip me a printing plate or fake banknote or whatever, and then I stroll over the border with proof of Himmler's scheme?"

Brandt, his pipe finally lit, shook out the match. "More or less. It does get a bit more complicated, since Karl must get out with you."

"The devil you say! It goes from grand theft to aiding and abetting a prison escape?"

"Listen, Herr Lemmon. I am personally responsible for getting Karl into this mess. Over a decade back I arrested him for small-scale counterfeiting and forgery. During interrogation I discovered a kindred political spirit and a fine young man, so instead of putting him behind bars for years, I put him undercover. I needed someone to keep an eye on Nazi thugs. But that decision put me on the hook for everything he and Isabel subsequently suffered. I am cleaning up the mess if it's the last thing I do, and should our plan fail, it may well be."

"And Isabel goes with us?"

She spoke up: "Though I work here as 'Isabel Friedrich,' I still have my American passport squirreled away. The inspector had a forger update my journalism credentials, so I can leave anytime."

Ryan turned to Brandt. "Our mutual friend Becker, I presume?"

"As you know, he does make a convincing document."

"So if you couldn't get Karl released from prison through your own channels, how were you planning to get him out of the counterfeiting shop before I entered the picture?

Isabel's eyes filled with hope as she explained. "We hadn't arrived at a definitive plan when you showed up and the solution became clear. "You, Ryan, are our godsend. Once we know Karl's free, I leave Berlin and he joins me in Zürich."

Ryan was convinced. Helping Isabel reunite with her husband was reason enough. Getting Ellington and the COI solid proof of this counterfeiting operation would be icing on the cake. "Listen, inspector, I'm willing to move forward, but I'll need twenty-four hours to think this through and strategize with Herr Kessler's men. This will have to run like clockwork if we're to pull it off."

"Understood," Brandt said. "But just to clarify— we'll need your thoughts and proposals by morning."

Fed up with surprises, Ryan wanted the whole picture. "Why in God's name's this infernal rush?"

"An untimely change of command. Isabel learned of it at Sachsenhausen just a few days back, and the clock is ticking. Himmler wants harsher oversight for this 'Operation Andreas,' especially as they bring in convicts as the primary workforce. He's chosen a man known for working inmates to death by the hundreds if not thousands and enforcing discipline with torture."

Isabel's voice turned brittle as she interrupted the inspector. "It can't get worse than this, Ryan—it's Johann Hallinger, the same man who destroyed our lives!" Her fists were clenched, her jaw trembling. "That son-of-a-bitch is now a lieutenant colonel in the SS, and he'll recognize Karl the minute he steps into that shop. We're talking the devil incarnate!"

With the memory of Gestapo torture seared in his own flesh, Ryan understood her fury and her fears. "And he takes over in two days?"

Brandt fished eyeglasses from his vest pocket and cleaned the lenses with a handkerchief. "Hallinger's been in charge of one of the concentration camps of a growing complex in the Ostmark called Mauthausen-

Gusen. Apparently he anticipated a promotion to full command of the whole operation as a reward for his innovation and performance, so this Operation Andreas assignment appears to him a major career setback." He removed a small photograph from his wallet. "His plane arrives tomorrow evening at Tempelhof, and we don't expect him to arrive happy." Brandt put on the glasses and glanced at the photo before handing it over to Ryan. "Decent likeness, I'm sure, though a few years old, taken covertly when he was a rising Nazi thug on my personal watch list. He's close to your size and build."

Ryan noted closely-cropped dark hair, an arrogant twist to the mouth, and soulless eyes. He returned the picture. "So why the charade? Why not pull a nighttime smash and grab before Hallinger shows his face?"

"There are night guards, of course, and the Gestapo would be on your tail with a Reich-wide alert within hours. This needs to happen quickly and quietly, and with no alarms until you've made a clean get-away."

"Does Karl know he's about to be freed?"

"Not yet. But now with you on board, we'll let him know something's in the works." He put the photo back in his wallet. "We thought we had more time."

"What's the layout?"

"Our delivery guy says twelve or so working a twelve-hour dayshift in the main rooms. He's made us a sketch. At least four SS guards on duty at all times;

one at the front gate, another at the building entrance or the rear gate when a delivery comes, two always inside. Plus there's the shop foreman Ehrlich, an obnoxious type, we hear. Langer, the math 'professor,' stops by most days to keep tabs on the finished product, but always on his own schedule and never mornings. A late sleeper."

"And when does Hallinger actually inspect his new command?"

"Day after tomorrow at nine a.m. Thanks to Frau Friedrich's access at the camp, we know his schedule from the time of his flight to where he'll stay upon arrival. That's why she still heads out there daily—to make sure there aren't any changes to foul us up."

"So you delay him long enough for me to assume his role, then Herr Kessler's men and I spirit away Karl and proof of the counterfeiting."

"Frau Friedrich said you were a smart one." Brandt broad smile revealed tobacco-stained teeth. "Yes, Herr Lemmon, you are to become a brutal Obersturmbannführer." Brandt promised to go over everything when they next met. "Finally, Herr Lemmon, I took the liberty of having our forger Becker create identity papers mimicking Hallinger's. Our mutual friend happened upon a photograph of you and I must say the work is excellent, as always."

Kessler wrapped up the meeting with few words for Ryan: "My men will follow your lead, and personal risk and violent response aren't a problem. It's what they do, and they're well compensated for it. But the success of the actual enterprise rests on your shoulders, so I suggest you be at your best." He rose from the chair. "We meet tomorrow morning at ten. Gregor will get you the address of my townhome."

"I'll have to call in sick again for the morning," Isabel clarified, "but I must be at the camp by afternoon to confirm Hallinger's schedule."

Brandt put away his eyeglasses and smoothed the wrinkles from his waistcoat. He rose cautiously, holding on to the arm of the chair. Ryan suspected arthritic knees. "Let me know what else you'll need and I'll get it for you." The inspector gave the smiling Isabel a fatherly hug. "I've waited years to make this right for you, dear lady." He requested his coat and hat.

Kessler snuffed out his cigar and stood ramrod straight as he awaited his own outerwear. "Welcome aboard," he said to Ryan as they shook hands all around.

After observing the sedan pull out from the curb, Ryan closed the narrow gap in the blackout drapes and broke the silence. "If you don't mind, Izzy, I believe I could use that Cointreau now."

CHAPTER FOURTEEN

Berlin, Germany
Delbrückstrasse 6a
December 1941

Karl leaned away from the magnifying glass and flexed his back muscles, helping to relieve the pain between his shoulder blades. Nearly a decade of incarceration and foul treatment had taken a toll on his body. He removed the wire-rimmed glasses and gently rubbed his eyes. His forging of the fifty-pound bank-note was approaching perfection, but he fully expected his shop mates to botch things on the production end. Many notes would be ill-cut and unable to fool the most myopic bank teller. On others, the loose fibers in the rag-based paper would reveal something amiss, even if one overlooked the odd texture of the paper it-self. One press run might place the watermark too high with respect to the seated figure of Brittania in the up-per left corner, then the next might show a faded black tint obvious to any practiced eye. The fault wouldn't lie with his expression of the soul of the note in the plate before him. This ill-trained team simply lacked the mo-tivation to perfect their counterfeiting skills, and the procurers of supplies had yet to duplicate the precise nature of the British product.

He observed the others toiling in the shop. The men's brows were constantly furrowed in concentration, their ears long immune to the mechanical clank and clunk of the nearby presses. Some hunched over tables, tearing the rag paper to mimic the edges of genuine banknotes. Others mistreated the pristine banknotes to give them a patina of rough usage, then pricked the currency to mimic the banking practices of the British, who favored pins over rubber bands. Still others bundled approved product for storage in the room known as their "Bank of England."

He sighted the length of the shop and spotted the blond and balding foreman. A true devotee of his Führer Adolph Hitler, Ehrlich bossed with a discipline as rigid as his posture and his lips pursed as tight as his sphincter. His ultimate task was evaluating the finished bills as they arrived at the bundling station. True to form, very few made it past his approval stage.

Weber, Henning and the others manned the presses and followed the routine procedures, inspecting their personal stage of production with only a casual eye. Luther, the only other engraver, tried his best but lacked the gift and hand that made Karl's plates shine. Everyone knew that, in the final approval stage, Ehrlich would leave no doubt how incompetent he found his underlings. Sadly, the man lacked the skills to show a better way.

Some workers wore uniforms beneath their smocks, others neat civilian garb with white collars and dark neckties. Karl's required dress was different. He alone wore the blue-and-gray stripes of a camp prisoner. His tunic bore a five-digit prison number on the chest, the cloth badge a red triangle identifying him as a political prisoner and an overlapping triangle in yellow for his Jewish heritage. Together they formed a Star of David.

At day's end the others left for home but Karl remained behind, confined to a closet beneath the stairs with a cot and no window. Two guards stood watch for the night. For Karl it was a paradise of privacy after years of communal suffering, and the available food seemed decadent, almost sinful, after the starvation rations of the camps. A solitary cupboard held his personal possessions: a few smokes, a safety razor, a bar of shaving soap.

Tucked in a seam of the cot's iron frame was a tiny photo sent by Isabel during his first year of incarceration. Suspecting it might be tossed by the censors, she had cleverly secreted it behind a false backing within the envelope. With bent edges and an image now faded by time and wear, the 35mm contact print showed a woman against the imposing backdrop of a cathedral. But that woman, her features unrecognizable, was the love of his life. Their baby had not survived, but had she lived beyond that last letter? Before sleep each night he dwelt on the image, recalling her features and crafting stories of her current whereabouts. Had she married another? Was she now a mother of beautiful children and living again in Chicago?

The disparaging attitude of his colleagues paled in comparison to the harsh physical treatment he'd experienced at the hands of camp guards, yet it remained a constant aggravation. The printers made no effort to hide their disgust with taking direction from a *Mischling*, a half-Jew in prison pajamas. This attitude was aggravated by Karl's disapproval of their printing efforts. Ehrlich berated that same apathetic production of his colleagues, but saved his special physical punishments for Karl's slightest infraction: failing to rise quickly when addressed by an SS officer, daring to light up without permission, or nodding off after the long, tedious hours. Any error in demeanor and he would forego all meals for a day, sit cross-legged for an entire 12-hour shift, or squat on his heels until his legs buckled. "Strength through obedience," Ehrlich barked.

At times Karl had considered adding the tiniest of errors to each of his engraving blocks, perhaps a subtle alteration of one of many markers the British already hid to call attention to forgeries. But, despite the conviction he would never go free and thus had little to lose if discovered, he couldn't bring himself to spoil his own creations. His engravings remained perfect.

A decade had passed since he'd committed his life to fighting fascism. Those years had not been easy. Already bruised and hurting from the fight that robbed

264 | PATRICK W. O'BRYON

him of wife and unborn child, he was dragged to a cel-
lar somewhere in the city and forced to down liters of
castor oil. They repeatedly beat him across his bloated
belly until he soiled himself, adding one more level of
humiliation. Then the heroes of the new Germany led
him through the streets seated backwards on an ox, a
sign at his neck branding him "Jewish traitor to the Fatherland." Following this public degradation, they beat
him senseless and delivered him to a cell. He recovered
only because other political prisoners nursed him back
to a semblance of health. The court trial that followed
was a mockery of justice, the prosecutor and his ap-
pointed defender both making the same case for his
condemnation and incarceration.

That first year in prison was the hardest, for he still
hoped to reunite one day with his beautiful Isabel. Soon
her letters stopped and he received no further word.
After serving out his sentence, the guards thrashed him
again for good measure before transport first to the Esterwegen camp for political dissidents, then later to the
Dachau concentration camp. He was deemed an unde-
sirable, socially unfit to live and work among solid citizens of the Third Reich. At Esterwegen the SS had not
yet assumed full security duties and a few SA guards
involved in his initial arrest and mistreatment singled
him out for ongoing abuse. His survival relied on the
selfless acts of other political inmates.

For years he endured cruelty, inhumane living
conditions and starvation rations. While witnessing the

heinous and often fatal treatment of his fellow prisoners, he fared marginally better due to his organizational
talents. The concentration camps were profit centers for
the SS overlords, providing slave labor to local industries in return for financial compensation. The SS had
initially put the career criminals in charge of barracks
operations, but they proved so inept and corrupt it im-
pacted those profits. The wardens ultimately singled
out competent political prisoners to handle that task.
Karl was one of the lucky few. In this role he was able
to identify political convicts and place them in less
dangerous work details and barracks where the resist-
ing dissidents held greater sway. Dangerous felons who
had previously collaborated in the mistreatment of inmates received the most abhorrent of work assignments, and some perished at the hands of the men they
had earlier mistreated. Slowly but surely, he'd helped
foster a subtle but effective resistance movement, aiding the survival of some and encouraging sabotage and
disruption in the factories and quarries where the prisoners were forced to toil and die.

For no discernable reason, he was then abruptly
transferred to the Sachsenhausen camp northeast of
Berlin. He returned to cruel work details and brutal roll
calls favoring group punishment for individual infrac-
tions, but overall he was harassed less frequently. This
change left him baffled. Was some guardian angel suddenly handing down orders from above? And one day
seemingly no different from all the rest, the guards had
come for him. Laying on shackles, they yanked a cloth

bag over his head and cinched it at the throat. He was certain that tight cord signaled a noose in his future. They hustled him into a waiting prison van where the guard answered his muffled questions with a sharp *"Maul halten!"* and a rap on the shins. He shut up. For nearly an hour they lumbered down uneven roads and onto smooth urban streets, and he felt death drawing nearer with every kilometer. But much to his amazement, no scaffolding or guillotine awaited him. Instead he'd been released into this print shop and a new routine, the familiar odors of ink and solvent and press machinery so welcome after a long separation.

The others were free to venture out into the city to join family or friends, but Karl hadn't seen direct sunlight in many months. He did eventually learn the location of the facility. A deliveryman called Heini had left an address label on a packing crate: Delbrückstrasse 6a. Karl recognized the name of a pleasant residential street in the upscale Charlottenburg district. He could picture the neighborhood grid, though the knowledge did him no good. Nevertheless, it was nice to know precisely where he was, to know he was now imprisoned closer to his Berlin home.

And then this morning his life of terror and tedium took a sudden and heartening turn. The same delivery man who had revealed the shop's address handed him paper samples along with two whispered words: "Be patient." Midway through the stack he found a duplicate of his most treasured possession, that snapshot of

Isabel, only now in a print large enough to reveal detail under his magnification lens. Karl slid the find into the pocket of his smock and waited out the day in heady anticipation. Once Ehrlich had put away the engravings for safe-keeping and the guards locked up for the night, he dared examine his gift in detail. Tears came as he made out the blurred features of his beloved wife. Overcome with emotion, he barely slept, fearing the foreman might discover his secret.

Isabel lived, and somehow she had tracked him down! If she could deliver a treasure like this into his hands, more good news was sure to follow. He would be patient. After all, what choice did he have?

Gusen Concentration Camp

Mauthausen Complex

Ostmark, Greater Germany

December 1941

Johann Hallinger tapped his foot incessantly, anxious to move things along. His flight out of Linz couldn't come soon enough, though first he had to officially welcome Lieutenant Colonel Wilhelm Dettmüller, an old SS colleague replacing him as commandant at Gusen. It was Hallinger's duty to make Dettmüller comfortable in his new domain, but the outgoing deputy commander was quietly fuming over his transfer back to Berlin. Hallinger had created the most efficient concentration camp in the SS system, yet Reichsführer-SS Himmler was pulling him out to oversee some misbegotten counterfeiting scheme. Hallinger's decade-long upward path to success in the Party now appeared to be heading on a downward trajectory.

During tomorrow's formal change-of-command ceremony the entire prison population would gather on the *Appellplatz* to witness his humiliating departure. This morning however had been all business, introducing Dettmüller to the facilities and quarries. And now, as the group of gray-uniformed officers approached, Hallinger prepared to play the convivial party host. The officers already held flutes of fine French champagne. The demonstration about to commence, offered as pure entertainment, called for appropriate refreshment.

Hallinger muttered under his breath to his adjutant, Reinhold Steuer: "Let's make this damned thing happen."

"At your orders, Herr Obersturmbannführer." The exiting commandant's foul mood was not lost on his aide, who regretted having openly expressed his personal delight at returning to the heart of the Reich. Steuer left the stand to pass along instructions to the chief SS guard as Hallinger turned to greet his colleagues.

Gusen—the camp, not the lovely nearby town—prided itself on deriving maximum productivity from the adjoining granite quarries. The facility was subordinate to the main complex centered on a hilltop in nearby Mauthausen. Both occupied the lush green countryside of what had been called Upper Austria prior to the 1938 *Anschluss*. Hitler had then declared the region of his birthplace the "Upper Danube," and the former imperial power Austria was subsumed within the Greater German Reich and designated the Ostmark.

Before Gusen's recent construction the prisoner workforce had come over from the main camp to work the demanding stone pits in thirteen-hour shifts. Now those slaves who remained standing by the end of each grueling day marched to and from their barracks on foot. Both the main complex and Gusen sub-camp were Grade III facilities designed to handle the "incorrigible" enemies of the Reich. They specialized in the subjugation and extermination of more educated prisoners, the social elite gathered from the farthest reaches of the empire.

Thanks to Hallinger's brilliance, the year-old compound at Gusen already outshone Mauthausen proper in both mortality rate—equated with deriving maximum value from every expendable worker—and in resulting financial gains for the SS. With such proven successes to his credit, Hallinger had been floored to learn that he was not to assume full control of the Mauthausen camp network. Colonel Franz Ziereis appeared to be firmly ensconced as commandant of the entire complex and was going nowhere. Hallinger guessed the reason why. Ziereis must have been tipped off to his personal ambitions by someone in Berlin—likely Heydrich himself—and arranged to rid himself of his strongest competitor.

So now Hallinger would return home to manage a failing counterfeiting operation which had proved frustrating for the Reichsführer-SS. He had already created a magnificent and successful money mill in Gusen. Physically fit workers were brought to their knees in the granite quarries until every last breath had been worked or beaten out of them, generating enormous profits for the SS. Other capable workers could be farmed out to local industrial concerns like nearby munitions plants to further fill the Schutzstaffel's coffers. What enjoyment could he possibly find harassing a dozen criminal forgers into greater productivity after exploiting an unlimited workforce that lived and died at his whim?

Even more impressive, those physically or mentally unsuited to the rigors of the stone works or other enterprises were a burden on society and of no economic value to the Reich, and Hallinger had won praise for inventing innovative methods for their quick extermination. By mid-summer an *Erholungslager* was up and running in nearby Hartheim Castle. This officially-designated "convalescent camp" accepted only those selected by the main camp's medical commission for "mercy killing." Code-named *Aktion 14f13*, the Zyklon-B gas process had proved a grand success, sure to be duplicated elsewhere and adding another feather to Hallinger's cap. For that action alone he deserved the top leadership position at Mauthausen, and everyone knew it as well. Including Franz Ziereis. Hallinger's "promotion" back to Berlin was clear retribution for aiming too high too fast.

His second bold idea had won praise not only for its expediency but also for its entertainment value. Resident SS officers and non-coms, prison functionaries, and visiting guests from Berlin all found it a splendid diversion. For this reason, and despite his bitterness at the transfer, Hallinger had chosen to make his newest brainchild the highlight of the afternoon. But now, with mere hours to go before he surrendered his leadership and all hope of a further ascent in the SS camp system, he was having difficulty stifling his anger at Ziereis, Heydrich and Himmler. He wanted the whole charade over with, and quickly.

Dettmüller and the staff officers had gathered around him on a platform overlooking the broad concrete basin. Steuer handed his boss a champagne glass. Guards and functionaries holding bludgeons and whips took up positions encircling the basin. Hallinger lifted his glass with a toast to his friend: "To your success!" They touched flutes and he crushed his spent cigarette beneath his boot. "I'm most confident you will enjoy the spectacle, Willy. We've had it up and running for a couple of months and it's already proving its worth."

Dettmüller sipped from his glass and looked toward the doors where the condemned would soon appear. "How many are processed at a go?"

"Tops out at three hundred." Hallinger glanced at his watch. "But I would recommend somewhat fewer at a time to make house-cleaning afterwards easier." Hallinger caught his aide's eye and nodded. Raising a Hitler salute, Steuer dropped his right arm abruptly, miming the descent of a guillotine blade. "And we're off and running, gentlemen," Hallinger declared.

The doors swung open and a parade of naked men filed in. The ailing prisoners came slowly at first, then faster and stumbling as they balked at the sight before them. The guards herded the captives forward with shouts and curses until two hundred malnourished and trembling men crowded beneath multiple ranks of overhead plumbing. A few shouted out in protest in some Slavic language. The majority suffered silently, all hope and energies exhausted by rigors already endured. Those who had fallen to their knees in the surge were helped to their feet by compatriots to escape the thrashing whips of the guards. Once the basin was full, Hallinger's aide turned back to his commander to await the next order.

"What sort do you have for us today?" Dettmüller squinted, trying to discern the racial makeup of the crowd but falling short. Disease, infirmity and mistreatment had rendered all but a few haggard specimens indistinguishable in the huddled mass. "All Jews?"

"Mostly Soviet POWs. A few Poles and Republican Spaniards for good measure. The first transports from the south of France are just now arriving, so you'll see plenty of French Jews soon enough."

"Excellent." Dettmüller arched his brows. "But am I missing something? I see no women!" He looked to his officers for confirmation. "That sight might enliven the proceedings a bit, right?" The underlings laughed and nodded in agreement.

"My apologies, Willy. Time was short or I would have trucked some younger ones down from Ravensbrück. I was intending to set up an incentive brothel here, anyway. Nonetheless, I think you'll enjoy the spectacle, so let's get things rolling." Hallinger nodded to Steuer and the aide relayed the order. Four SS men at gate valves spun the large iron wheels in unison and an infernal hissing rattled the maze of plumbing. Air gave way to the rush of ice-cold water and across the basin high-powered jets blasted the naked men amid a howl of pain and protest. Brutal cold rained down from the overhead shower heads, forcing the weakest to their knees under the relentless drenching. The strongest struggled to escape the downpour but were beaten back by the guards. Truncheons and whips tore into flesh and stained the water gathering in the basin. The backs of those directly beneath the powerful blasts ran red under the piercing onslaught while many of the weaker men were trampled underfoot. If they tried to rise above the water's surface laughing guards trod on their necks until their struggles ceased.

Dettmüller took another sip of champagne. "Most entertaining, indeed—you've choreographed a true 'Dance of the Dead,' Johann." And how long does the show last?"

"At most thirty minutes. The majority suffer circulatory collapse well before then." He pointed to the center of the group as ever more fell to the floor, their bodies covering those already drowned. "Look over there—it's working like a charm!" Despite his foul mood, the sight couldn't help but lift his spirits a bit. Hallinger offered Dettmüller one of his cigarettes. "Extremely efficient, and cleanup so much easier than with pesticide gas."

Dettmüller accepted a light off Hallinger's match. "Have you named this innovation of yours?"

"Indeed I have." The cries had given way to a communal moan. Sunken ribcages shook violently and stick-like limbs quivered as on one great dying beast. Hallinger smiled at his own cleverness. "I call it 'The Death Bath Protocol.'"

Dettmüller smiled. "Splendid. Perhaps we'll soon be offering such baths throughout the camp system."

"My friend, I regret I shall miss out on your first trial with females." Hallinger emptied his glass. "Always more satisfying to watch women bathe, *nicht wahr*?"

CHAPTER FIFTEEN

Berlin, Germany
December 1941

"What's up with Herbert tonight?" The SS driver clearly knew his regular guards on the Sachsenhausen-Tempelhof route. He seemed surprised to encounter an unknown face at the airport field entrance. The blue-on-black Mercedes 260D idled at the gate, exhaust trembling in the frigid air.

"Word is he's down with the flu." The substitute sentry grinned as he switched on his flashlight. "Likely taking the cure with a brandy bottle, if you ask me." After giving the sedan a quick once-over he examined the sergeant's identity card and noted the arrival on a register. "Name's Heinz. I normally work over on the freight side." He secured his pencil on the clipboard. "Who you here for?"

The driver eyed the gloom beyond the reach of his shielded headlamps. "Some lieutenant colonel in from Vienna." His fingers drummed the steering wheel. "Say, can we hurry this along? My guy's landing any minute, and I'm supposed to be out there saluting his majesty."

The sentry glanced skyward. The airplane had yet to appear, but the rumble of heavy engines above the clouds announced an imminent landing. Ground lights blinked on abruptly to reveal the runway. "Paperwork looks good," the guard returned the driver's documents and stepped away from the window, "but I'd check out that right front if I were you. You've a gash on the sidewall and it's sitting pretty low. Wouldn't want to keep your special guest waiting while you change out a tire."

The man slammed a palm against the wheel. "*Scheisse!* Who needs this crap?" He left the car idling and came around to squat beside the wheel in question. A quick look found nothing. "So where the hell's the damage?" He looked up just as the guard's flashlight descended his way.

"On your head, comrade." The driver lay sprawled at the feet of Kessler's man Heinz. Ryan appeared from beyond the gate to help drag the stunned chauffeur into the hut. Kessler's other minion Gerhardt side-stepped them on his way out. Already dressed as an SS sergeant, he guided the Mercedes out to welcome Obersturmbannführer-SS Hallinger to Berlin Tempelhof.

The plane dropped below the cloud cover and touched down, wing lights bouncing as its wheels met the frozen ground. The Junkers-52 cut a wide turn across the field and rolled up alongside the waiting sedan. Two men appeared in the doorway and hurried down the steps, hats gripped tightly against the wash of the propellers. Gerhardt saluted smartly and opened doors for the colonel and his adjutant. A crew member helped stow their valises in the trunk. Gerhardt had barely turned the sedan when the plane rumbled off toward a distant hangar.

Heinz stood before the airfield gate, his left hand holding the flashlight at his side, his right held high to signal a halt. Ryan remained out of sight behind the guard shack. He released the safety on his pistol even though they expected no difficulties. Gerhardt came to a stop beneath the dull glow of the lamp post.

Hallinger aimed his frustration at the driver. "Whose asinine idea is this? Doesn't that fool know who I am?"

"No worries, Herr Obersturmbannführer, it's only a formality." Gerhardt's eyes met Hallinger's in the rearview mirror. "Rumors of airport saboteurs, so everyone's on high alert."

Heinz rapped his flashlight on Hallinger's window glass and demanded *"Papiere, bitte."* The SS officer lowered the pane with his left while reaching for his papers, ready to tear into the guard once he proved his rank and authority. Frigid air rushed in followed by the muzzle of an automatic pistol, and the colonel lurched back in disbelief. The adjutant's hand barely reached the flap of his holster before Heinz's Walther spit twice, splattering gore on the far window. The aide pitched forward, his peaked cap falling to the floor as blood seeped from his temple. Gerhardt had already swiveled to train a second weapon on the colonel. Eyes uncomprehending and ears ringing, Hallinger slowly raised his hands.

Ryan rounded the sedan with a shout: "Inside, and quickly!" Kessler's men confiscated Hallinger's sidearm and hustled him into the hut. Ryan righted the fallen aide's body. The head wound said it all. Wiping his bloodied hands on the dead man's trousers, he was less than pleased to have a corpse to deal with.

He entered the shack. Against the wall lay the unconscious SS driver, hands and feet bound with thin cord. The "ailing" airport guard—the one called Herbert—lay tied and gagged beside him. Heinz had heavily doped both with a sedative. All of this was per plan, but not the gruesome mess in the sedan. "We'd agreed there'd be no bloodshed."

"The guy ignored your memo—" Heinz grinned at his cleverness, "he went for his rod."

"So now we have a problem."

"Best laid plans, right?"

"When does the swing shift come to relieve poor Herbert?"

"I asked before I wished him 'nighty-night.' The new guy comes at two."

"Herbert knows only that some stranger roughed him up and left him drugged. The airport police will assume a saboteur and search the airfield and buildings, including the passenger terminal. The missing sedan and driver shouldn't draw attention till word comes from Sachsenhausen, and even then it'll take hours to locate the flight crew and find out their man actually arrived tonight."

Hallinger finally found his voice and growled out a protest. "Do you bucket-headed idiots have any idea whom you're dealing with here? I'll have your heads on a platter!"

Heinz's pistol abruptly swept across his jaw. The colonel staggered back, bleeding from the corner of his mouth as his tongue probed for damage to his teeth.

"So any ideas on disposing of that body? We sure as hell can't leave it here."

They'd been dropped off an hour earlier by another of Kessler's men and approached the gate on foot. The intent was to leave with the colonel and trussed driver in the trunk of the Mercedes and Ryan in the back seat. No one anticipated Hallinger's bringing along an aide.

"I saw concrete pipe out beyond the fence when we snuck in," Gerhardt said. "Looks like they just put in a culvert or something. I'll find room for the stiff." He was already out the door.

Ryan ordered Hallinger to undress and tossed him a pile of civilian clothes. Hatred shown in his eyes, but he did as told. While Heinz watched over their captive with drawn pistol, Ryan tried on the colonel's gray trousers, loose in the waist, the inseam almost perfect. The glowering colonel, his damaged jaw already swelling, shivered as he made do with the replacement wear. Ryan donned the SS tunic, which fit adequately. The high- peaked hat with death-head emblem sat too high on his head, so he slit the inner band with his knife to give it more play, then sat on the stool to pull on the tall black boots. Heinz handed him the colonel's commandeered holster and belt. "It's show time," Ryan said, strapping on the weapon and taking to his feet in the confident posture of the Reich's paramilitary elite.

Ryan scanned the register on the guard's clipboard. He noted no further arrivals or departures scheduled for that evening. He pocketed the sheet and rehung the clipboard beside the door.

Gerhardt entered, fresh from entombing the dead aide. "How'd it go?" Ryan asked.

"Fit like a glove." A roll of gray clothing was tucked beneath his arm. "Didn't want to waste a good uniform," he explained with a smile. "The trousers were shot, but the rest might come in handy down the line."

Ryan acknowledged the logic with a nod. "So tie up our colonel here and ditch his luggage where you hid the aide. The swing shift can free our buddy Herbert when we're long gone."

"Sir, if I may—" Gerhardt stepped forward, "their baggage likely contains some valuable items. The Boss would want us to secure the contents, not chuck them. Waste not, want not, right?"

Ryan gave it a moment's thought. "Very well, the bags remain in the trunk and the driver joins them, and our lieutenant colonel rides in the rear with me. But I'll be damned if I'm going to sit back there with fresh brain tissue smeared across the window."

"At your service, sir." Heinz hefted a janitor's bucket and cleaning supplies from the corner of the shack and headed out to do some clean-up.

Ryan wondered what else could go awry in the coming hours. These days, he preferred working alone.

Both the reliability of motor vehicles and recent Wehrmacht demands for equine power in the field had shrunk Berlin's horse and mule population. Many stables in residential neighborhoods had gradually converted to other uses. Such was the case for a neglected building in the Bremergasse belonging to Kessler. From the street it appeared abandoned, but the interior told a different story. Several bays housed crated merchandise "liberated" by his criminal enterprises and awaiting resale or distribution. The blue-on-black SS diesel now occupied the center aisle. Kessler's men had parked themselves in the back seat to smoke cigarettes and enjoy the rush of methamphetamine. The popular drug Pervitin promised increased energy and enhanced stamina, so much so that the Wehrmacht was giving it to both pilots and ground troops alike. Ryan had politely declined the white pills, assuring his accomplices that his enthusiasm for the coming robbery would carry him through just fine.

The long night was finally dragging to an end. The window panes had gone opaque from years of neglect, but he could still see the black of night surrendering to pewter skies and the promise of more snow. Ryan counted the minutes as he leaned on the door frame of the former stable master's office. He knew that the sedan would soon be reported missing along with the SS driver now stretched out on the floor behind him. Heinz was as adept with hypodermic needle as with pistol, a veritable pharmacist and problem solver in one. The rusted coal stove was no match for a bitter early December cold. Ryan raised his collar and stomped his feet as he awaited Isabel's arrival. She was due any minute.

Hallinger, bound to a wooden chair at wrists and ankles, stared vacantly. His civilian garb offered little protection against the chill, and the gag over his injured mouth spared the captors further threats and rantings. Isabel had set the rules for his treatment, specifically ordering he not be seriously injured or drugged. She wanted him fully alert.

She had spent the previous afternoon out at Sachsenhausen, arranging the fiction of a day's delay in the colonel's arrival while assuring the airport pick-up stayed on schedule. Before arrival at the stables she would have arranged her hair to match the photo in the American passport and be ready to catch the next flight to Zürich after interrogating Hallinger. Once word of the print shop caper spread, suspicious Gestapo investigators might notice the sudden disappearance of "I. Friedrich," but by then she would be in Switzerland awaiting reunion with Karl.

Shortly before seven Isabel finally entered the stable. Heinz, buzzing from his latest methamphetamine hit, welcomed her as a long-lost co-conspirator despite having only met the previous morning. Gerhardt was also feeling euphoric and chattier than usual, but Isabel had no patience for small talk. She had waited far too long for this moment. "Where are you holding our bucket of filth?"

"All trussed up and awaiting your pleasure, Frau Friedrich." Heinz made an exaggerated bow as he gestured toward Ryan and the office. "Please follow me."

Ryan spotted nervousness in her eyes. He placed a hand on her shoulder as she reached the doorway: "You up for this, Izz?"

"I've waited ten years to close this book, Ryan. No one can do it for me."

"Understood." He stepped aside, revealing Hallinger dozing fitfully against his bonds.

"Get that one out of here," she commanded in a subdued voice, pointing to the sedated sergeant beneath the workbench. "Boss" Kessler had specified that her orders were to be obeyed to the letter, so his minions deposited the SS driver on a pile of moldering straw out near the sedan. They returned and faux-saluted Isabel, requesting further instructions.

"I'll take it from here," she said, her voice stronger now. She seized Hallinger by his close-cropped hair and pulled his head back. He opened his eyes, groggy and momentarily uncomprehending, and she slipped down the gag, leaving it loose around his neck.

"Who the hell are you, lady?"

"Take a closer look, *Arschloch*. You'll remember." She pushed back her hair to reveal her face in the dim light. "Think back to '31." Her smile could have etched glass. "Coming back to you yet?"

He dropped his gaze to her chest. "With tits like those, I'm about to blow my wad. Let me guess—I gave you a good fucking and you've missed me ever since?"

Ryan's fist landed hard. Hallinger bent forward, coughing, struggling for breath. "Treat the lady with respect," Ryan hissed, "or the next one guarantees you never fuck again!"

Isabel restrained Ryan's arm as he readied to make good on his promise. "I've got this, darling—alone."

Hallinger's breath came in shallow gasps. She tapped him lightly on the damaged jaw. "Now, let's get back to my question, Lieutenant Colonel. Think carefully now—it's 1931. Your Party holds a meeting in Wedding, your buddy Goebbels at the podium." She could see him dredging through memories and offered more clues: "Two uninvited guests. You had them detained, much as you are right now, all trussed up nice and tight, then came back to admire the handiwork of your ass-licker Veidtner?"

His eyes abruptly lit up. "The two dykes? That was you?" He shook his head as the revelation set in. "Of course it was. So that's what this is all about. You and your little friend fucked over two of my men. Cost me a fortune trying to track you down."

"And you—you piece of shit—you destroyed three of my friends in the process!"

"Gatecrashers can't complain if they don't enjoy the party, right?"

Ryan stepped forward, fists clenched, but she held up her hand to block him. "Well this one is lodging a complaint in person." She signaled Kessler's men. "You two, untie this bastard!"

"You're sure about that, lady?" Heinz's pupils showed black, dilated by the drug.

"Can you handle him if he tries something stupid?"

"Damn right, and with pleasure." Heinz pointed to the pistol in his belt and giggled.

"Then set him free, hands and feet, but no rough stuff without my say-so."

Heinz cut the cords while big Gerhardt stood behind the captive with an arm around his neck. The Nazi rubbed his sore wrists and gingerly felt along his bruised jaw. "You bastards broke a tooth last night."

Gerhardt released his hold. Heinz held his pistol to the back of the colonel's head. "I'll break more than that if you give me trouble."

The prisoner's sudden torrent of words betrayed his growing apprehension: "That unfortunate business with Veidtner was all his work, you know. The man was a crude sort—an animal, really. Brutality his stock in trade, no finesse. Surely a lady wouldn't resort to his tactics." He stumbled on through her silence, desperation finally surfacing. "We've outgrown all that as a nation, that rough stuff. Necessary back then, you know, to win over the country. We're a new Germany now. Unified. Civilized. No longer need unsophisticated measures, right?" She stared until he felt forced to speak again. "So how do I make it all up to you?"

Isabel gave a bitter laugh. "Make it all up to me? You'll learn soon enough." She approached the workbench, taking stock of old bridles, bits, and wagon traces. She manipulated heavy, long-handled pincers, then rummaged through a wooden box of curry combs, nail pullers and hoof scrapers. She appeared deep in thought, allowing his anxiety to grow. Abruptly, she turned to Ryan: "Perhaps you should leave for this next part, darling. You say you've done rough stuff before, but you needn't be part of what comes next."

"No way."

"Then step back. Wouldn't want to spoil that nice getup of yours." He'd momentarily forgotten the SS uniform. She took a coil of rope off the wall and brought it to Gerhardt. "Can you fashion a noose for me?"

"Consider it done."

"As for you, Obersturmbannführer, you will now strip naked."

Hallinger looked around for support and found none. "It's so damn cold in here!"

"Every stitch, unless you want my men to do it for you." Her smile was brittle. "Don't worry about privates, colonel. "Your man Veidtner didn't hesitate to expose mine on your orders." With trembling hands he did as instructed. "Shoes and socks, too." His body shook in the drafty room; his hands shielded his groin. Isabel gave Gerhardt's rope skills a nod of approval. "Throw it over that beam up there." On the third attempt it cleared the rafter.

Heinz's pistol had never left the captive. "Should we string him up?"

"Yes."

"Please, no!" Hallinger raised his hands in submission, his voice shaking. "I can get you whatever you want—how about money? More money than you can imagine, it's all yours! Gold, too. Diamonds, even. I have ways. And nothing happens to you and your friends. This all goes away if it ends now. Just let me out of here and all's forgotten, forgiven!"

Gerhardt started to loop the noose over the head of the cringing captive.

"No," Isabel said. "He's not getting off that easy. Around those skinny ankles, and bind the wrists again."

The Nazi trembled, but no longer from just the cold. Fear and fury had finally taken the upper hand. "You'll never get away with this, you know!" Gerhardt tightened the bonds while Heinz pressed the automatic to the base of his skull.

She turned her back on Hallinger and gave Ryan an enigmatic smile. "Take him up," she ordered over her shoulder.

Gerhardt yanked on the rope and Hallinger landed on the litter-strewn floor. He began to ascend in erratic tugs. Heinz put away his pistol and helped hoist until the head of the enraged man was at her eye level. She directed the men's attention to a run of hooks above the bench. "Now tie it off, nice and tight."

Malice distorted Hallinger's swollen face. As she stepped into range, he spat. Ryan lunged forward, fists clenched, but Isabel ordered him back. "Mine alone, remember?" She retrieved his shirt from the floor and wiped her cheek. At her direction, Heinz gagged him again. "I'd hoped to hear more talk of bribes, more protests at the unfairness of it all, but since you can't behave civilly in your new 'civilized Germany' you will suffer in silence." She took a step back, considering her words. "My friend Doro had no chance to protest the terror that took her life, and you work inmates to death at Mauthausen, delighting in new ways to prolong their suffering. So why should you fare any better? Perhaps you'll even enjoy your own suffering?"

Isabel took a baling hook from the bench. "Lower him a bit, gentlemen. I believe it's time I did something with his cock and balls." Hallinger wrenched from side to side, fighting the hold of the ropes, his face crimson from fury and gravity's pull. "He'll have no use for them where he's headed," she turned to address herself to Ryan, "and personally, I find them offensive, dangling there so weakly on such a proud officer of the Reich."

Ryan stepped closer and gently lifted her chin, encouraging her to meet his eyes. "You sure about all this, Izz? Will you be any happier looking back?"

Her jaw began to tremble and she dropped the hook to the floor. With her head pressed to his chest, she released the tears. He held her close until the weeping subsided, then she pulled back and her grief came forth in words: "These Nazi assholes are so damned rotten, stinking up the world and everything good in it! Doro had a right to happiness, to enjoy her youth and life with poor Jürgen." She pinched her eyes shut, tears flowing anew. "My unborn baby had a right to sunlight and laughter, Ryan! But these fucking bastards steal everything, ruin everything, rip families to shreds, and then they dare to claim they're a 'master race." She cleared the tears away with her hands and turned away from him. "But you're right, my dear friend. I can't see this through, not as I imagined for so long. I really never thought this time would come, and now that it's actually here, I fail myself. I don't have what it takes to be as despicable as they are, to make someone suffer so long and so horribly."

She straightened her shoulders and addressed Kessler's men: "You two may leave us now."

"You're sure, Frau Friedrich?" Heinz looked dubious, disappointed.

She nodded. "We'll be fine."

"Very well, then—as you wish." He left the office and Gerhardt followed with a last glance back.

"And now what?" Ryan said. "Shall I cut him down?"

"No." Isabel exhaled in resignation. "I'll do the cutting." She reached for the fallen hook and swung it with both hands, burying the point deep in Hallinger's neck and twisting with all her might. She released it and stepped back. Stunned by the sudden move, Ryan barely caught the hiss of her words: *"Für Doro und mein Baby!"* Retching into his gag, Hallinger jerked about, a fish on a line, blood splattering the floor below. She pivoted toward the door, ignoring the blood on her hands. Her jaw was clenched, her smile frozen.

Ryan struggled to contain his revulsion. Death for the suspended man would come soon enough and he would not help the process along. He put his arm around her shoulders to guide her from the office and closed the door behind them.

CHAPTER SIXTEEN

Berlin, Germany

December 1941

He still heard the gurgle of the man's torn throat, still smelled the iron and salt of blood and the sweat of fear. Her act had left him deeply troubled, but the bastard surely deserved his fate for all the horrors he'd called down upon her, for all the lives he'd destroyed in the camps. Ryan had clearly misunderstood her. She had questioned her ability to extend the torture but not her resolve to finish him off.

Would she ever recover her old self again, or had the Isabel of earlier days fallen victim to events in that cursed factory and Munich alley? To kill under duress or in self-defense was one thing. To kill defending liberty was another. But to take life so coldly and consciously smacked of evil, no matter how justified. Or perhaps he just kidded himself, his Presbyterian upbringing nagging at his gut. Was he simply trying to diminish his own guilt over lives he had taken?

She had not spoken as he led her to the basin to wash the blood from her hands. She'd said nothing as they walked out to the waiting Daimler, another Kess-

ler minion behind the wheel. At the idling car she finally broke her silence, stating simply: "Done is done."

"Will I see you again?"

"You thought you'd seen a ghost a few days back,"
Isabel squeezed his hand, "and you know what the
French call a ghost?"

"Un fantôme."

"I was thinking *'revenant.'* She brought his fingers
to her lips and kissed them. "The one who comes back.
Who knows with the two of us, right?" She gave a
wistful smile. "You be safe."

"I'll keep an eye out for the two of you. Go meet
Karl in Switzerland and find happiness." He opened her
door. "You both deserve it."

"Thank you for being there for me, Ryan." She got
in and rolled down the window. "One final thing, darling." She took something from her handbag. "Please
see Karl gets this so he knows how to find me." Ryan
slid the envelope into his pocket. On her signal, the
driver pulled from the curb. She turned to look back
and waved once before rolling up the window.

He had no time to consider what her future might
bring. The day ahead would be demanding. Perhaps he
should have accepted some of Heinz's Pervitin, but he
needed his wits about him. That ass Ellington would
soon see the value in personal initiative and diligence,
and COI would surely be pleased to share proof of this
forgery enterprise with the Brits.

❖

At nine sharp the Mercedes rolled to a halt at the high gate on Delbrückstrasse. Manicured gardens shielded the impressive stone mansion housing Operation Andreas. The shutters on nearby houses remained closed in this upscale neighborhood west of downtown. Neighbors would know that any operation so closely guarded by the SS was off limits to prying eyes. Rumor had it the facility had been used for some time as an SS training school and forgery operation. The guard checked papers, saluted smartly, and waved them through. Heinz pulled the Mercedes up to the portico and switched off the engine, then hurried around to hold the door for Ryan and his sham aide-de-camp Gerhardt.

Shop foreman Ehrlich, clearly anxious to make a good impression, pushed past the SS man at the door and rushed down to greet his new boss. "A hearty welcome, Lieutenant Colonel Hallinger! We are so fortunate to have your leadership here at the facility." His words couldn't come fast enough. "Allow me to introduce myself," he snapped his heels together, "Print Shop Foreman Gustav Ehrlich, at your service." He was clearly suppressing the urge to salute despite his lack of military rank.

Ryan took a moment to observe the building and gardens before acknowledging the introduction. "Show me what we've got, Ehrlich." He strode up to the entrance with Gerhardt on his right, the foreman tagging along to his left. "The Reichsführer-SS tells me previous directors have really mucked things up."

"All too true, Herr Obersturmbannführer, all too true. But you'll find I run a tight ship, given what I have to work with. Under your leadership and guidance we'll turn production around in a flash."

Ryan returned the salute from the door sentry as they entered the shop rooms. Parquet flooring and wainscoted walls betrayed the house's origins as a private residence for some wealthy family. He kept his greatcoat buttoned, his leather gloves tucked in the belt. A dozen workers stood at attention to either side of the long work tables. Ryan was surprised to see many men of an age and fitness suitable for combat duty. Surely this enterprise ranked high on Himmler's list of priorities. "Put the men back to work," Ryan ordered. "Allows me to better understand the process and why it's broken down."

"Of course, sir." Ehrlich dismissed the men back to their work stations. The sorting and cutting resumed, chemicals sloshed and water ran at the rinse basin, and presses began their steady rise and fall.

"Now take me through the procedures step by step."

Ehrlich began at a high table. Two men on stools bent over magnifying glasses as they inscribed fine lines into copper panels affixed to wooden blocks.

Ryan recognized Karl by his cauliflower ear and the blue-and-gray stripes of a prisoner's uniform showing beneath his smock. Isabel's husband was a handsome-enough fellow despite a sallow complexion from years of imprisonment and poor nourishment. He focused on the metal plate before him and avoided eye contact. Ryan gave Karl a sour look before approaching the second engraver, who moved aside quickly to give the new commandant opportunity to examine the detail of his work. "I take it this is where most errors occur, most delays in production?"

As the civilian engraver began to respond, Ehrlich interrupted: "Sometimes, sir. But we seldom have problems with the blocks themselves. Most difficulties arise in the cutting and handling of the finished notes. We've also had hitches with the quality of the rag paper and how the finished product shows under ultraviolet light."

"Who's assuring the serial numbers conform to Bank of England issues?"

"Professor Langer handles that. We've exported a few notes via diplomatic pouch and had our people pass them at unsuspecting banks. No problems arose, so we seem to be doing fine with the alphanumerics. The professor will be in around noon to introduce himself. Anxious to meet you, of course, as we all have been."

Ryan nodded, knowing full well his crew would be long gone before Langer came around. He glanced at his watch. "Let's see the rest of the operation."

"Yes, sir. Right this way, sir."

They entered an open work area with clattering presses flanked by stenciling and numbering machines. An adjacent station smelled strongly of some solvent used for cleaning the finished plates, its large washbasin flanked by a sign warning "Flammable, Smoking Forbidden!" Ehrlich explained the procedures for the sorting area where he himself cast his critical eye on the banknotes before giving final approval.

At each stop Ryan showed the appropriate interest and impatience. In the rear of the building he viewed a photographic laboratory, a washroom and a WC with several toilet stools. At the end of a hall was a tight, windowless space beneath the stairs with a cot, a tiny mirror and an open cupboard holding personal items. A single lightbulb with pull string hung from the underside of a tread. They passed a few additional closets for cleaning supplies. On a door sealed with hasp and lock someone had affixed a sign reading "Bank of England." Ryan gave the foreman a quizzical look. "For the finished product awaiting distribution," Ehrlich explained. Across the aisle was the foreman's personal office.

Ryan's expression darkened. "That'll do for now. I've the general idea. We'll address specifics later. Let's get back to the engravers, where I spotted something very troubling." Ryan led the way to the high stools at a fast clip, Ehrlich on his heels trying to catch up. He gave Karl another thorough up-and-down, then targeted the foreman with his piercing look. "This worker is clearly a felon, a traitor or a Jew—perhaps all three."

"Yes, sir." Ehrlich's jaw twitched.

Without prelude, Ryan jerked back the collar of Karl's smock to reveal the cloth badge on his prison uniform. Karl kept his eyes down. "Well, perhaps you can explain to me, Foreman Ehrlich," Ryan abruptly slammed his palm on the work table and his voice rose in anger, "why we are using such vermin if a purebred and loyal German can do this same work!" He pointed to the civilian engraver at the second station. "This fellow, for example!"

Ehrlich, perspiration on his brow, pivoted to Karl and shouted: "On your feet!" The order was so zealous that men the length of the shop looked up briefly. Karl stood to attention beside his stool. Ehrlich stumbled over his words as he cringed under Ryan's gaze: "Allow me to explain, sir..."

"No," Ryan raised his hand, "I'll hear it directly from the Jew." Ehrlich stepped back with head bowed. "So what exactly do we have here?" he demanded of the engraver. "Identify yourself, prisoner, and tell us what crimes earned you this cushy life?"

"Karl Wittenberg, sir. Prisoner 29501. Sachsenhausen."

"Well, Prisoner 29501, what the devil's wrong with that ear? Did some Aryan girl reject your filthy advances with a right hook?"

"Yes, sir, something like that."

Ryan spotted the flicker of recognition in Karl's eyes. "And your crime or crimes?"

"Running a print shop, sir. In Munich, some years back. And for being a half-Jew."

Ryan turned to Ehrlich with raised eyebrows. "Really, Ehrlich? Have we not enough forgers and counterfeiters who are neither degenerates nor half-breeds?"

"Yes, sir, you see, sir—"

"I do indeed see," he broke in, returning his attention to Karl, "and what exactly did you print that landed you in Sachsenhausen?"

Karl hesitated a split second before replying: "Only the truth, sir."

Ryan struck him across the face with his folded gloves. Pivoting to Ehrlich, he demanded: "You permit such impertinence, and from a Jew no less?"

"Never, and he pays for it on the spot!" Ehrlich motioned an SS guard forward. "The prisoner will spend the day on his haunches, understood? Beat him should he get up or fall." The nearby printers focused on their work, avoiding all eye contact.

"No!" Ryan barked. "Not good enough! I shall personally show this cockroach how we whip laborers into shape at Mauthausen, *verstanden?*"

"As ordered," Ehrlich said, nearly completing a salute before withdrawing his hand. "But may I suggest sparing his eyes and his hands, Lieutenant Colonel. For the moment we can't afford to lose his skills if we wish to keep on schedule."

Ryan addressed the guard directly: "Hold the Jew in the washroom. He's not to leave your sight but he may sit. He'll need his strength for when I personally teach him respect for his betters." The guard saluted and shoved Karl toward the rear of the shop. "Now," Ryan said, tucking his gloves back in his belt, "I believe I've seen enough to understand why this whole operation has gone to shit."

Ehrlich wiped his brow. "What do you mean, sir?"

"I mean to make major changes around here, starting with this incompetent crew you've assembled. Your operation has had abundant time to get it right yet it still fails, and Reichsführer-SS Himmler is fed up with delays." Ryan signaled Heinz and an SS guard to his side. "Clear this place out, on the double. Every last one of them."

Ehrlich saw a threat. "But sir, the others are all civilians. Wittenberg is our only Jew."

"I don't care. Who knows what other traitor undermines the mission and reveals our secrets?" He glowered at Ehrlich. "I want them all out! And now! I shall examine all personnel records and take a closer look at your failures. For the moment, we shut this circus down until I sort this all out, then I'll personally interview each and every worker and determine his fate."

"But, sir—"

"Your fate, as well, Herr Ehrlich. You have a problem with my orders?"

"Not at all, Herr Obersturmbannführer. Whatever you wish, sir." He stepped away to join the guard and Heinz as they spread the word through the shop. The presses came to a standstill. The workers dropped everything in place and headed for the door. In the antechamber the men hung up their smocks, donned overcoats and hats, and headed toward the exit. They only began to whisper amongst themselves once they reached the garden path to the gate. The shop was eerily silent after the steady beat of presses at work. Gerhardt stood by, awaiting Ryan's cue.

"Ehrlich," Ryan said, "show me the 'Bank of England.'"

"Right this way, sir." The foreman led him to the storage room and unlocked the door. Boxes rose to shoulder height. Ryan removed a lid and fingered the currency, carefully aged and worn and—to his eye— indistinguishable from the genuine article. "These are ready for distribution?"

"Pretty much the best so far. All but an expert would find them impeccable, but we store the very finest banknotes in a safe to serve as production standards."

"Quite a bounty should they fall into criminal hands. How are the plates secured when you shut down for the night?"

"This way, sir." Ehrlich unlocked the door to his office. Gerhardt tagged along. Two desks and a row of glass-fronted bookcases lined the west wall. Ryan scanned the titles, most dealing with currency and mathematics and many in English. "The books belong to Professor Langer. We share the office."

A massive safe hugged the opposite wall. "Open it up," Ryan said. Ehrlich worked the large dial, his fingers betraying his nerves, and the handle refused to budge. He cleared the tumblers and reentered the combination, this time holding his ear to the mechanism to catch the distinctive clicks. The handle surrendered with a solid thump and the door swung open to reveal bundles of banknotes bound with ribbon and a wooden box holding metal plates affixed to wooden blocks.

Ehrlich turned to gauge Ryan's reaction. The butt of Gerhardt's pistol dropped the foreman to the floorboards. "He'll be out for a while. Shall I finish him off? He's quite annoying."

"No, just stick to the plan and be sure he stays put. There's sure to be cord around here somewhere." Ryan held one of the large twenty-pound plates in his hand

and ran a finger over the fine texture of the engraving while Gerhardt stepped out into the hallway.

Heinz appeared outside the office to confer with his partner. Moments later, Gerhardt stepped back in with some cord in his hand. "Three guards out of commission, the last still watching your Jew in the washroom."

Ryan signaled Heinz to join them. "Take care of the last guard now and bring our engraver here. It's time to tell him he's free."

Heinz smiled as he downed another Pervitin. "Consider it done." With a nod to his partner, he left the office.

"We'll take a finished plate and a few of these perfect twenty-pound notes, then get the hell out of here." Ryan set the engraving block atop the safe.

"Well, not exactly." Gerhardt's voice sounded odd and Ryan turned to see what troubled him. "Orders have changed," he checked his watch, "direct from The Boss."

"What do you mean they've 'changed?'"

"Heinz just phoned in with a progress report. Herr Kessler confirmed our truck should arrive any minute now."

"Our truck?" Ryan fought to keep his temper in check. "The plan was for a car!"

"We're to clean this place out from top to bottom, including paper and ink if there's room. The Boss doesn't want to miss a bet when there's good money to be made." He laughed at his joke.

"My God, Gerhardt, this puts us all at phenomenal risk! Does Brandt know about this nonsense?"

"According to The Boss, the inspector is on board and plans to join us once we clear the city."

"Why on earth would he come with us?"

"Beats me, but you can ask in person soon enough." He compared his watch to the wall clock. "An hour or so from now if we're on schedule."

A bewildered Karl appeared in the doorway. "What's going on here? This fellow," he looked at Heinz, "says you can explain."

He held out a hand. "My name is Ryan. I'm an old acquaintance of your wife."

Amazement spread across his face. "Isabel's here? She's well?" He vigorously pumped Ryan's hand. "Can I see her?"

"In a day or two, but in Switzerland."

"You're busting me out?"

"Both you and all your expert handiwork here." He pointed to the open safe. Sheer joy spread across Karl's face and his eyes glistened. Ryan couldn't resist a smile of his own. What a revelation for a man who had spent eight years not knowing if he'd see wife or freedom again! "And while we're at it, allow me to apologize for that slap. Had to look authentic, you know?"

"Felt authentic, too." Karl brought a hand to his reddened cheek and grinned. "As soon as you mentioned my ear I knew you were the one I was 'being patient' for. Ryan Lemmon, right? Isabel once told me you weren't bold enough for all the trouble she got you into, but I think she read you wrong."

"No, she had me pegged." Brakes squealed out back and Heinz and Gerhardt hurried out. "Sorry, Karl. No time to chat. We're on the clock. The guards are down for the moment, so go swap out those pajamas for an SS uniform."

"After all such uniforms have put me through these past eight years, I may have to hold my nose, but believe me, the discomfort will be well worth it."

Kessler's men propped open a back door, bringing chill air into the rooms. An Opel Blitz with covered cargo bed waited at the loading ramp, its canvas flaps already wide open to receive the loot. A driver, Uwe by name, joined Kessler's team to bring out boxes by hand truck. In less than thirty minutes the "Bank of England" was cleared of currency and they went to work carting printing supplies. Ryan and Karl pitched in, each rolling out a final stack of cartons while Kessler's men finished packing the hold. Finally, they emptied the contents of the foreman's safe into two large canvas satchels and carried them out. Uwe wished them luck and left on foot through the garden.

Heinz would drive and Gerhardt ride upfront in the two-seater cab. Ryan and Karl made room for themselves and the satchels in the tight space remaining at the rear. As Karl rearranged a few boxes, Ryan entered the shop for one last time and returned with a couple of wool military blankets and a flashlight. While Heinz cinched down the flaps, Ryan and Karl encased themselves in scratchy wool and made backrests of the overstuffed satchels.

"Don't worry," Heinz said as he prepared to shut them in, "once Brandt joins us there'll be room to spare."

Despite the assurances, Ryan worried. The plan was already in a state of flux. Stripping the loot and plates would surely ring alarm bells all the way up to the Führer himself. And Brandt's sudden disappearance from Kripo headquarters could tie him to the enterprise, as well. What other surprises awaited them on the road to Switzerland?

CHAPTER SEVENTEEN

En Route from Berlin
December 1941

The hours passed miserably on the hard flooring of the cargo bed. Communicating with the cab was impossible, so Ryan and Karl suffered with no concept of their progress. At the first stop they sat motionless for almost an hour, not daring to lift the canvas to check on the delay. The second sounded like a service station. Shortly afterwards, the muffled voices of a police checkpoint filled them with dread as they waited to see if someone would untie the flap. Instead, muted laughter preceded a couple of thumps on the side panel and they rolled out again. Clearly Kessler's "SS men" had passed muster.

His butt began to ache and Ryan stretched as best he could. He had no idea what was taking so long to link up with Brandt. His legs threatened to cramp and he worked the muscles in the tight confines. With considerable difficulty he lifted the satchel with the banknotes over his head and settled it between his legs. The blanket now served to cushion his back against the slatted wood side of the hold. Soon Karl made the same adjustments.

Ryan had explained the original plan for the theft and his rescue, voicing suspicions that other surprises likely lay ahead and warning him to be prepared for sudden changes. He revealed that Isabel had killed Hallinger in retribution for all the pain the man had rained down on them but omitted the gory details. Karl remained silent for several minutes before expressing his satisfaction that the man was gone. He hoped his wife might find solace in her violent act, then went on to describe some of the horrors he had witnessed in the prison and camps at the hands of such men.

Karl repeatedly asked about Isabel, desperate to know about her health and where they would meet once out of the Reich's grasp. Ryan reached over her little envelope. Karl clicked on the flashlight to read her words, then sighed. It was clear the man had dreamt of such a reunion for nearly a decade. He slid the note into the breast pocket of his tunic and secured the button.

Both men settled into silence and Karl began to snore. Ryan wished for his pipe and tobacco. Having heard just a fraction of what this man had experienced, he was grateful for his own good fortune. The pervasive inhumanity of the concentration camps was worse than he could have imagined. For the moment, he only hoped that luck stayed onboard through that final checkpoint at the border.

At last the truck slowed to a stop, shifted hard and backed off the paved roadway. The dual wheels beneath them crunched on frozen ground as they came to a jolting halt. Heinz loosened the ties from the outside and lifted the canvas flap to reveal a frigid landscape. The truck stood some fifty meters into the woods on an unused access road. Their tires had imprinted their route in pristine snow. Gerhardt was already out of the cab and heading up to the main roadbed with a strip of red cloth in his hand. Ryan broke ground of his own to the nearest snow-laden tree to irrigate its trunk. Karl found his own target to relieve an overtaxed bladder. "What the devil's taking so long?" Ryan demanded, returning to the truck as he buttoned his fly.

Heinz was quick to apologize. "Brandt didn't show at the first rendezvous point. We waited an hour but couldn't let you out since we had to be on our toes. We stopped at a gas station outside Potsdam for Gerhardt to use the phone and got word that Brandt was delayed and would meet us here at the back-up spot. After tanking up, we passed through a checkpoint with no problems thanks to The Boss' generosity to the sentries."

Ryan gestured toward a dense stand of trees blanketed in white. "And where exactly is this?"

"North of Leipzig. Pretty, isn't it?"

Gerhardt came stomping back to the truck. "All these damn turnouts look alike in the snow, but Brandt has the kilometer count so shouldn't have a problem

310 | PATRICK W. O'BRYON

spotting the flag." He pulled a covered basket from behind the driver's seat. "Anyone else hungry?" He pulled out a large sausage and began to slice it on the fender of the truck while Gerhardt distributed cold beer from a tool box on the running board.

Ryan accepted a chunk of meat and a bottle. Leaning against the truck, he knew he needed to remain alert and considered asking Heinz for a couple of the white pills. Brandt's changes to the agreed plan foretold other surprises ahead. If the intent was to violently sideline him, they would likely pull something before Brandt showed up. He kept one hand resting on the holstered sidearm. Perhaps he would find sleep in the long hours ahead.

It didn't help that the landscape was mesmerizing. Wet flakes fell steadily to further burden the trees. From time to time branches dipped under the weight to release their loads and bolster the snow mounds below. It was easy to imagine wolves lurking here, ready to make quick work of any wayfarer trespassing on their domain.

Another hour passed. Each took a turn observing the main road while the others shared time in the cab with engine and heater running. As a vehicle finally slowed within sight of their marker flag, Karl trudged back to alert the group. A dark-gray Audi Cabriolet turned in and pulled nose-to-nose with the truck. *My God, a two-seater is the best they could do?* Even more surprising, Brandt was not alone. "Boss" Kessler climbed out on the far side, impeccably dressed in a heavy tweed overcoat with rubber galoshes protecting his expensive shoes.

"So what's going on?" Ryan demanded. "Why the change in plans?"

"One step at a time, Herr Lemmon." Brandt approached Karl and gave him a huge bear hug, slapping him several times on the back. "It's been so long since we last met, my friend. I'm pleased to see you here, fit and free at last!"

"Not as pleased as I am, sir."

"You look splendid, lad, especially given all you've been through. I would never forgive myself if we hadn't pulled this off, and now you're in for a nice life with that lovely wife of yours. Bravo!"

"I'm most grateful, inspector."

"First things first, it's time you met our benefactor, Anton Kessler."

The Boss came around from the car to shake hands. "Welcome aboard, Herr Wittenberg. Your reputation for printing skills precedes you."

"Most appreciative of your getting me out, sir."

"With all due respect, inspector," Ryan interrupted, "we should hit the road. At this pace we'll be lucky to reach Lustenau by midnight." He glanced again at the Cabriolet. "May I ask what brings you along on this excursion?"

"It seems my laissez-faire approach to law enforcement has finally drawn the ire of our SS overlords. My 'trusted' assistant turned out to be their snitch. I was already suspicious of his incessant inquiries, then yesterday my secretary overheard him setting the stage for my downfall." He gave a self-conscious smile. "A private interrogation revealed all, but unfortunately this discovery comes too late to prevent my imminent arrest." He clapped Karl on the shoulder. "Needless to say, at my age I wouldn't fare well in prison, so I decided to tag along."

"But why ransack the shop instead of making a more discreet exit?"

"Well, that brings us to my old friend here." He looked over to Kessler, who stood with his back to them taking in the view. "Anton will also be joining us."

Ryan watched it all click into place. "Now there's a surprise."

"Without my official protection, his head's on the block, too. Powerful people benefited from his operations and can't risk exposure. Should a trial be in the offing, he'd quickly disappear into some Gestapo basement for good. We've worked together since boyhood so I'm not about to let that happen. But with all the loot we've gathered here," he gestured toward the truck, "and with all Anton has already squirrelled away in Spain, we can run our own cash mill in a more hospitable environment, and I get to live out my days supported by the fruits of Karl's labors."

Done is done, as Isabel had said. *Had she been aware of all this?* He set that thought aside for later. "So that makes six of us," Ryan observed, trying to move things along. "Shouldn't we hit the road? Every delay raises the risk."

"I'm afraid I've bad news for you, Herr Lemmon. As impressive as you look in that uniform, an SS lieutenant colonel riding in a military transport truck arouses suspicion, and sadly, Anton's little Audi only seats two."

Ryan almost smiled. "You intend to leave me here."

"We've really little choice, and I'm sure you see the logic. Your face is plastered at every border checkpoint, thanks to your recent Reichsbank caper, and everyone witnessed your leadership in this morning's heist. Once that cat's out of the bag, I'm sure the Gestapo will credit the Reichsbank robber with pulling off an even greater score."

"Exactly as we'd planned."

"Yes, exactly as planned. But I'm sorry to say you've now become a bit of a liability. My superiors will connect the dots when they find Anton and me missing along with those millions in counterfeit notes. That makes assigning you the blame moot, does it not?"

"Indeed it does."

"Before the alarm spreads, however, we'll be off to the good life in Franco's Spain, thanks to the government's open arms to anything that profits *El Generalissimo*."

"Well played, Inspector. I'm sure you'll both be very happy together."

"And equally satisfying for me personally, Karl reunites with his lovely Isabel, setting right that nasty business I started a decade ago."

Karl had remained quiet, accustomed to holding his tongue by years in prison. Now he interrupted forcefully: "Ryan and I can easily manage the remaining hours in the back of the truck."

"Afraid not, Karl. We've a good stretch ahead and the men can't run that risk. The Potsdam checkpoint worked because Anton called in markers, but we can't be certain about any surprise controls ahead. Our papers protect only five men. An SS corporal in the cargo bed makes sense, but a lieutenant colonel would be a definite red flag. I'm sorry, but we must say 'auf Wiedersehen' to Herr Lemmon."

"You're forgetting I owe this man my rescue! Without his role-playing I'd still be a prisoner."

Ryan interceded, knowing the discussion would go nowhere. "Listen, Karl, thanks for your efforts, but you and Isabel have suffered for too long. Go find your wife. I'm resourceful, and for the moment," he tapped his pocket, "Hallinger's papers should serve me well."

"What if I insist on staying with you? The two of us can figure this out on our own." Karl gave Brandt a challenging look.

Kessler tossed his cigar in the snow and finally turned to face them. "Whether you realize it or not, Herr Wittenberg, this entire escapade puts you in my debt. Lemmon here was only an accessory. Should you fail to get back in the truck, and alone, my men will restrain you for the duration. You have been bought and paid for with your release, and your counterfeiting talents will be my asset when we set up shop in Madrid." He approached with subtle menace. "Consider me your new boss," he pointed to his henchmen leaning against the truck as they eavesdropped, "and feel free to ask those two how I handle insubordination from my men." He dusted snow from his trouser cuffs. "Now get back in the truck and do as I say."

"I agree with Herr Kessler," Ryan said. "You have to move on, and now." He gave Karl a reassuring smile. "I'm sure we'll meet again." He turned back to Brandt. "Can you at least drop me at the nearest rail station? I'd hate to slog any distance on foot, and I must get back to Berlin."

"Consider it done, Herr Lemmon." He smoothed his mustache. "Now back to the truck, but only as far as the nearest depot, you understand."

Ryan was already considering his next move.

CHAPTER EIGHTEEN

Lustenau, Austria

December 1941

The inn on the edge of town faced a snowy field fronting the Rhine. Across the river the Swiss village of Au twinkled beneath a starlit sky. Just a few steps from the inn lay a short approach to the Reich border station, where key personnel facilitated Anton Kessler's illicit shipments, whether material or human. The Berlin gangster greased additional palms on the Swiss end of the truss bridge, rendering the border irrelevant.

The Gasthaus zum Zoll was known for its homespun cuisine. With six small but impeccable rooms, Frau Weberli's inn on the Dammgasse also suited the needs of the smugglers. Here was the ideal spot for Kessler's caravan to take a break before crossing into neutral Switzerland. The vehicles could lose military tags and markings under cover of darkness and the men trade out SS uniforms for civilian wear. With both tasks now accomplished, Kessler and Brandt relaxed in the warmth of the dining room, filling up on hearty Austrian fare and dark beer.

The Boss himself had never before shown his face in Lustenau, and Widow Weberli felt honored to have such a notable guest praising her *Schweinebraten* with parsley potatoes. Advised that very morning to expect her special visitor, Frau Weberli had posted a hand-written "closed due to illness" sign on the front door. Word had spread quickly among the locals that the inn-keeper, beloved for her culinary skills, was down with the flu, and they begrudgingly sought out an alternate locale in town.

After a brief introduction to the famous Herr Kess-ler, the innkeeper was happy to remain in her kitchen until further summoned. The widow of a successful smuggler in his own right, she understood that hush-hush matters were under discussion. Kessler and Brandt sat in the far corner near a ceramic-tiled stove spreading heat into a nearly empty dining room. They had chosen the *Stammtisch* normally reserved for select regulars. Heinz sat apart near the swinging door to the kitchen, beyond range for eavesdropping but ready to relay orders.

With stomachs rapidly filling but thirst not yet quenched, Brandt and Kessler settled into the easy sort of conversation so common between old friends. After the strenuous drive they would have preferred over-nighting upstairs before crossing the border in the morning, but such a delay might give rise to new prob-lems. They reviewed the day's events and spoke of the next steps in getting the booty to Spain. The discussion came around again to the successful gutting of the print shop.

"All things considered, I do regret turning the tables on poor Lemmon," Brandt conceded. "A capable sort, really, and he did perform as hoped."

"The man will do fine on his own. He may be pissed for now, but he'll move on." Kessler took another bite of pork roast. Out of character for such a fastidious dresser, he released the lower buttons of his vest and exhaled in satisfaction. "Lemmon would have been in our way, and we couldn't have him blowing the whistle to the Brits, right?" He took more bread to sop up gravy from his plate. "Without evidence to pass along, his handlers will deem him a fool and the Bank of England will remain none the wiser." He stuck the dredged bite in his mouth and talked as he chewed. "And look at the bright side—you, my old friend, are now fabulously wealthy."

"I suppose you're right. I do need to readjust my thinking now that I've joined your side of the business, and my retirement looks rosy indeed." He sat back, shaking his head in disbelief. "I only wish dear Gisela could have lived long enough to enjoy it all with me." He pulled the tucked napkin from his collar, calling it quits on the meal and reaching for his glass.

Kessler laughed. "She would never have agreed to all this. Your wife was such a stickler for 'law and order,' she never did appreciate our close ties. Gisela— bless her heart— held me for some sort of dangerous criminal rather than an industrious entrepreneur, and she always let me know it."

"But she surely would have approved of reuniting Karl and Isabel. Of that I can be proud, especially after the hell I put them through." He sighed and took a long draw on his beer. "Our only challenge now is convincing her to join him in Spain where we'll print an even greater fortune."

"Consider it covered, my friend, so no worries. She'll follow her man, and he's not going anywhere without us." He signaled Heinz, whose full plate still sat before him. He was riding high on the meth and had little appetite. "Tell the woman to bring us more beer. Better yet, have the young one do it. I like her look." Frau Weberli's daughter Anna had served their meals and delivered supper to the men waiting out in the truck cab. The twenty-year-old, gifted physically if not mentally, was popular with border officials and smugglers alike. Heinz jumped to his feet and disappeared through the swinging door to the kitchen.

Outside in the cab, Gerhardt guarded their precious cargo and captive. A regular on this route, he had occasionally enjoyed Anna's charms. Tonight he was forced to decline with regret when she brought sandwiches and beer and suggested he join her upstairs for a quick tumble. His orders were to keep an eye on Karl, just in case he thought of making a run across the border on his own. The Boss had been displeased with the attempted mutiny in the woods. The counterfeiter was clearly as valuable to the enterprise as the stock of stolen banknotes, so Gerhardt would receive special compensation both for guard duty and for missing out on a warm meal. The anticipation of coming good fortune kept him on his toes and alert. The little white pills didn't hurt.

A solitary figure appeared in the driver-side mirror and Gerhardt recognized a possible threat. The man in the dark overcoat had already passed the small Audi and now neared their truck at a brisk pace. He used a furled umbrella as a walking stick despite the clear night sky. "Well now, what have we here?" Gerhardt rested his hand on the pistol at his belt as he observed the newcomer's approach.

"What is it?" Karl hastily checked his own mirror. "There's nothing over on this side."

Gerhardt shifted his body toward the door. "Perhaps nothing, perhaps something." The stranger was alongside the truck now, observing the cab but appearing at ease. When he knew he had Gerhardt's eye, the stranger tapped on the glass with his umbrella handle. Gerhardt, pistol hidden but now in his hand, rolled down the window with his left. "What do you need, mister?"

"Sorry to trouble you, sir." The accent was off but the smile friendly enough. "I'm looking for Lustenau-erstrasse."

"You're almost there, mister." Gerhardt glanced forward. "Continue straight on."

"Oh, sorry to be a bother." He touched the brim of his hat and turned to leave. "A most pleasant evening to both you gentlemen."

Gerhardt reached for the window crank. In that moment the umbrella handle seized his neck and slammed him into the cab frame. Karl immediately delivered three solid rights to the chin, then wrestled the pistol from the stunned man's grip. The stranger gave another solid yank on the umbrella, bashing then pinning Gerhardt's head, and he slumped, his fight over.

The door on the far side swung open and Karl greeted Ryan with a smile. "Not a bad sort, really—just misguided."

"Then it's time we guided him on a proper course, straight into the tool shed out behind the inn." Ryan holstered his pistol and handed Karl some cord filched at the train station. "By the way, the gentleman so adept with the umbrella is my brother Edward."

Karl stuck the confiscated Walther into his belt and they shook hands across Gerhardt's inert body. "Pleased to meet you, Edward."

"The pleasure's all mine. We'll get acquainted under more favorable circumstances soon, but for now, let's hurry."

Ed helped Karl ease the lolling Gerhardt down to the sidewalk where they bound and gagged him. While they were busy stashing the captive, Ryan found a gap in the drapes and peered inside, spotting Kessler and Brandt nursing a bottle of schnapps. Heinz was chatting at a far table with the young woman who had visited the truck earlier.

Ryan gave his returning partners the thumbs-up as he hurried up the street to get Ed's Buick sedan. Returning moments later with lights off, he stopped beside the truck and left the engine running. While Karl deflated the Audi's tires, the brothers climbed up into the cargo hold. Once Karl was ready, they handed down the heavy satchels of notes and plates to stash behind the seat of the sedan. That task complete, Karl climbed into the trunk of Buick and Ed shut him in for the duration of the border crossing. Ryan took to the rear seat. In case of trouble, his pistol would have a broader field of fire, plus the darkness would obscure his face. It might be recognized from that damned flyer.

Ed slid behind the wheel and accelerated, the powerful sedan quickly covering the fifty meters before making a tight right onto the Zollstrasse. The checkpoint fronted the bridge straight ahead. Two border policemen beneath the streetlamp observed their approach. One raised a red-and-white paddle demanding they stop. He had a holstered pistol at his waist and a carbine on his shoulder. The other casually held a rifle in his hands.

"And you do this for a living?" Ed's throaty chuckle couldn't mask his nervousness as they approached the reception committee.

"Easy now," Ryan said. "This doesn't necessarily mean trouble."

Ryan's doubts had surfaced at the previous morning's meeting in Kessler's townhouse. The gangster had refused to engage with him on any personal level. Ryan knew full well that team efforts relied on rapport to further a common goal. Kessler kept his distance, and Ryan suspected the man might deem him expendable once the heist was done. Would a notorious mob boss underwrite such a caper solely to please an old buddy seeking absolution from past sins? Certainly not when millions of pounds sterling were up for grabs. This Kessler didn't strike Ryan as either selfless or magnanimous. The final straw had come that evening at the stables while awaiting Isabel's arrival, when he overheard Gerhardt remark to his buddy: "The colonel in there will buy us all castles in Spain!" Ryan knew he should follow Klara's advice and watch his back.

After the morning meeting he'd returned to the Emmengasse for a quick nap in anticipation of a sleepless night. After retrieving his hidden funds and pocketing minimal possessions, he sought out Frau

324 | PATRICK W. O'BRYON

Küpfermann to say his good-byes. A gift of two hundred marks brought tears of gratitude and a motherly embrace. He suggested she sell the clothing he'd left in the room. For better or worse, his cover was now blown. He would seek new lodging once back in Berlin. Finally, he'd stopped at the post office to place a call to Ed's landlady in Geneva, asking her to relay an extremely important message: "Imperative meet tomorrow 18:00 Bregenz station ticket booth. Bring auto, old ID, clothing." The landlady read it back to him. He then wired the identical message to Ed at the consulate. In the final minutes of the heist, when back in the shop ostensibly to get blankets and flashlight, Ryan placed a quick call to Geneva for confirmation from the landlady that Ed had received the message.

Once underway in the rear of the truck he'd advised Karl that their circumstances might change on a moment's notice. "Whatever you hear and see in the next hours, don't make waves. One way or another, I'll find you when this truck reaches Lustenau." Grateful beyond words for his sudden release from bondage, Karl agreed to follow Ryan's further lead. During that final short stretch in the back of the truck, Ryan had shared the specifics of his plan with Karl.

Brandt and Kessler had left him at a station on the main rail line just north of Leipzig, where his SS field officer's uniform won a salute from the sentry and quick service from the ticket seller. No problems arose on his long express ride via Nürnberg and Ulm into the

Ostmark and he caught up on sleep for much of the way. His train, even with the delay of a transfer, was sure to beat Kessler's caravan by at least an hour. The Opel Blitz and little Audi cabriolet would find slow going on winter roads.

Ed needed only five hours or so to reach the Bregenz station. They met at the *Bahnhof* shortly before seven. Ryan had secretly observed his brother for several minutes before making contact, just to be certain that no one had tailed him from Geneva. He was pleased with the '39 Buick Ed had borrowed from the consular car pool, a Swiss-built sedan with powerful engine and a baggage compartment roomy enough to stash Karl for the brief crossing into Switzerland. Ed reported his diplomatic plates had proved to be an open sesame at the border.

Ryan suggested waiting until underway to discuss his plan, since time was precious. While Ed fetched beer and sandwiches, Ryan switched to the civilian wear his brother had brought and ditched the SS uniform in a waste bin. He kept Hallinger's identity papers since COI could make good use of them. Returning with the food, Ed handed his brother his old State Department passport and they got underway.

Ryan quickly recapped the events of his last few days, and Ed listened intently as his brother recounted the morning's caper and his plan for the rest of the evening. Once Ryan had finished, Ed broached a matter of his own. "So what's Berlin's stand on the war?"

"The Wehrmacht is sure to take Moscow in weeks if not days."

"I meant Pearl Harbor. Will Hitler jump in now?"

Ryan looked puzzled. "You mean Hawaii, right? Home of the Pacific Fleet? What on earth are you talking about?"

Ed shook his head in amazement. "Hold on to your hat, brother—I can't believe you haven't heard!" He took his eyes from the road to glance at Ryan, trying to tell if his brother was joking. "Japan's navy attacked us on Sunday! No advance warning, no declaration of war, no nothing! Many of our guys dead or wounded, our fleet at the bottom of the harbor. A crippling blow! By God, we're at war with Japan and you haven't even heard of it!"

Stunned, Ryan tried to grasp the ramifications for America, for the world, for him personally. "Incredible!" he finally muttered. "I've been so wrapped up in this Isabel business..." He tried to clear his mind of pressing personal issues. "So Hirohito's forced our hand."

"Will Hitler follow suit?"

Ryan thought for a moment. "He's certainly not obligated. The Axis agreement calls for mutual support only if a fellow pact member is attacked, but we can't bank on anything. Hitler sure doesn't give a damn about agreements—just ask Stalin. But declare war on us while still dealing with the Russians? Doesn't seem likely."

"Glad I could fill you in. It is pretty momentous." Ed lit a Chesterfield and just as quickly put it out, too worked up to drive and smoke simultaneously. "But we knew America wouldn't sit this out forever."

"How are they taking it at home?"

"The country's getting on board. Roosevelt gave a damned fine speech declaring a state of war with Japan."

They had driven on quietly for a few minutes, each considering where things would head next. Ryan finally broke the silence: "Tonight's task is far less 'momentous' but demands immediate attention. Best we solve my little problem before we take on the world's big one." He glanced at the dashboard clock. "I reckon their caravan will show in less than an hour and I know exactly where they'll take a break."

Neither had touched the food and beer.

Entering the Reich hours earlier had been a breeze. Ed had shown his passport and the diplomatic plates did the rest at both ends of the Rhine bridge. Something had clearly changed in the meantime. The same Reich officers who had waved him through now blocked the approach to the lowered barrier gate, and the unshouldered weapon meant business. "I hope you're right about this being no problem," Ed said.

Ryan handed his passport up to Ed, then took his pistol off safety and set it at his side, well out of sight. "First we see what they want."

"We have a choice?" Ed was no longer joking. They rolled to a stop and he lowered the window.

"*Papiere, bitte.*" The border policeman squinted into the rear seat. "For both." Ed handed over their passports and the guard glanced at their covers. "Americans, yes*?*"

"Yes, on a diplomatic mission. You passed me through a couple of hours back, remember?"

"Yes, I remember you, but alone, *nicht wahr?*" He flipped through the two passports. "And now you drive a passenger who shares your surname?"

"My brother is also with the Foreign Service. He was handling a delicate negotiation in Bregenz."

"And you make him ride in back?"

"He's exhausted. Plans to nap as I drive."

"You both have been very busy today, I assume."

"Yes, a full day. We're looking to reach Zürich before midnight. We both need rest."

The sentry grinned. "Well, I can guarantee your rest for the next few days and likely very much longer."

Ed glanced back at Ryan before responding. "I'm afraid I don't understand. My German is only adequate.

What exactly are you saying?" The free hand of the man with their passports rested on his holster flap.

"With such a full day you surely missed an interesting development in Berlin."

Ed's knuckles showed pale as they tightened on the steering wheel. "And what would that be?"

The officer looked over to his comrade, now standing on the passenger side of the car, and his grin stretched into a smile. "You should pay more attention to the latest news, my American friends. Our Führer made an important announcement before the Reichstag today." He bent over to look directly into Ed's eyes. "You see, Germany has declared war on the United States, and we have just received orders to detain any American attempting to leave the Reich."

"My God..." Ed appeared stunned.

Ryan leaned forward and whispered in English: "Uncle Virgil's farm—those kids who locked us in the barn. Remember how we got out of that scrape?"

The border guard gave Ryan a quizzical look. "I must ask you both to exit the vehicle, and now! *Sofort!*"

Ed remembered. "The tractor?" Ryan met his eyes in the rearview mirror and nodded once.

The guard suddenly turned toward Frau Weberli's inn where a rising column of fire and smoke pierced the darkness. "What the devil?" he muttered. His comrade also watched intently as flames consumed the canvas cover of the Kessler's truck and spit scorched fragments skyward. One moment the blaze engulfed only the cargo hold, then the entire truck exploded in a cataclysmic shudder as the fuel tank ignited. Ed's fuse of smoldering cigarettes and the many liters of flammable solvent Ryan took from the print shop had done their trick. Kessler and Brandt would not be celebrating their good fortune any longer.

Ryan's pistol was already in his hand. "Let's get this tractor moving!"

Ed released the clutch and floored it. The Buick lurched, tires smoking as he aimed toward the gate arm blocking the bridge head. The startled guards leapt back in surprise, shouting "halt!" and raising their rifles. The sedan made quick work of the fifty meters to the barrier as Ryan and Ed braced for a collision and bullets shattered the rear window. The car shuddered and bucked on impact. The long metal arm tore free and twisted sideways, slamming into the front grill and dragging the Buick to a standstill.

"Again!" Ryan shouted over the crack of the rifles, and Ed threw it into reverse, dragging a piece of the arm with them. Ryan's hat took a hit before the same slug webbed the front windshield. They backed fast toward the unrelenting gunfire, then Ed changed gears and stomped down as steam erupted from beneath the hood. Ryan fired repeatedly through the gap left by the missing rear window. The border police dropped to the roadbed and more rounds raked the rear of the car.

Ryan feared for the gas tank. "Oh my God," he shouted to Ed in sudden realization, "Karl's getting hammered back there!"

Ed aimed for the left lane of the deck. Despite the twisted metal extending into their path, the route along the guardrail appeared their best and only bet. The car tore past the downed barrier, peeling a front tire from its rim. The exposed wheel scraped on the roadway but the car kept rolling. Incoming rounds shattered what little remained of the split-front windshield and a ricocheting bullet grazed Ed's shoulder. "God damn but that stings!" was all he could say, too intent on reaching the midpoint of the bridge to even look. Ryan fired until he came up empty. The guards took shelter behind the bridge parapets but their barrage rapidly faded out.

As the Buick growled and scraped into Switzerland in a cloud of radiator steam, the gunfire finally ceased and Ed cried out: "Look! They have the gate up for us!" The car limped to a halt. Without waiting for the Swiss sentries to reach them, they raced around to the pockmarked trunk. One round had damaged the mechanism of the handle. Ryan yanked at the grip while pulling with all his might until the lid finally surrendered and swung up.

With only moonlight as a guide, they peered into the luggage compartment. Karl lay on his side, legs drawn up, his body facing outward. He appeared not to have moved since the first bullets struck. Blood streaked down his face, purple rivulets pooling beneath his tucked head. His glasses were splattered, his eyes closed. He wasn't breathing. Ryan slipped a hand beneath the bloodied jaw in search of a pulse. Words failed him. Isabel's misery would continue to haunt her.

Karl opened his eyes and grinned. Ryan and Ed howled in relief as they clapped each other on the back, much to the surprise of the approaching Swiss police. Karl stretched his legs and joined in the laughter. "As I told Isabel long ago—when the battle appears lost, just play dead. But now, if you'll help me out of this hell-hole, I need to clean up a bit." Removing his glasses, he gingerly touched his scalp. "Can't count the times I hit that damned lid! If it's all the same to you, I'll ride up front from now on."

AFTERWORD

The horrifying treatment of inmates in prisons and concentration camps of the Third Reich is described in many first-person accounts and historical treatises. This fictional story takes place in the earliest years of Nazi extermination camps, but the means of targeted mass murder as portrayed in the Gusen camp are factual, including the so-called Death Baths. These *Todbadeaktionen* were discontinued in early 1942.

I am indebted to Howard F. Cohn of Connecticut for sharing his monograph detailing the bravery and suffering of his late father August Cohn. Mr. Cohn spent twelve years leading resistance efforts in a number of camps before his liberation. The experiences of my fictional Karl Wittenberg were inspired by August Cohn's honor and courage in the face of great adversity, though I chose to make my character a counterfeiter as well as a political dissident for the purposes of the plot.

Admiral Wilhelm Canaris, a complex man of apparent honor and humanity, held a position of immense power in the Reich. A confirmed anti-Nazi, he worked covertly and diligently to undermine Hitler while protecting both his country and his position as head of German Military Intelligence, the Abwehr. To more fully appreciate this complex figure, I suggest Richard Bassett's fine study, *Hitler's Spy Chief*.

The German Reichsbank colluded with top American and British corporations and industries in support of Hitler's war. Ryan Lemmon's bank caper is described in *Fulcrum of Malice*. The interested reader is invited to consult Charles Higham's *Trading with the Enemy; The Nazi-American Money Plot 1933-1949.* This complicity continued even after Germany's declaration of war on the United States in December 1941.

"Wild Bill" Donovan consolidated American intelligence-gathering operations in 1941 with the Coordinator of Information Office (COI). After the United States entered the war late that year, Donovan established the Office of Strategic Services (OSS), forerunner of the Central Intelligence Agency. A good resource is Douglas Waller's *Wild Bill Donovan; The Spymaster Who Created the OSS and Modern American Espionage.*

"Operation Andreas," the plan to undermine the pound sterling, was also very real. Ryan was undoubtedly disappointed to learn that the existence of the counterfeiting scheme was already uncovered by the British as early as 1939. In 1942 the mismanaged project was moved inside the Sachsenhausen concentration camp to use solely prisoner labor. Readers with further interest might enjoy *Krueger's Men* by Lawrence Malkin.

Special thanks, as always, to my wife Dani. Her dedication to the demanding task of editing and her attentive eye on pace and plot are invaluable in bringing these stories to life. And I must mention again the man whose courage, brilliance and inquisitive spirit inspired these stories, my late father, Leonard L. O'Bryon, Sr.

Patrick W. O'Bryon

Patrick W. O'Bryon travels to Europe as frequently as possible to research his stories. He shares life's adventures with his wife Dani, his family, and several very demanding cats.

DISCOVER THESE OTHER RYAN LEMMON
ESPIONAGE ADVENTURES
By Patrick W. O'Bryon

Corridor of Darkness—Dashing Ryan Lemmon, a young and naïve reporter, loses himself in the decadent underbelly of 1930's Berlin. As the country falls prey to Hitler, Lemmon earns the hatred of a powerful Nazi whose brutality and cunning haunt him when he returns to the Third Reich as an American spy.

Beacon of Vengeance—Intent on helping friends facing death in a French concentration camp, reluctant American agent Ryan Lemmon becomes lost in a maze of deception in Nazi-occupied France. Hidden deep in the shadows, a ruthless enemy plays an evil game of cruelty and subterfuge.

Fulcrum of Malice—Ryan Lemmon conspires with a powerful German spymaster to subvert Hitler's state, all the while working to save the life of a loving friend held captive by the Gestapo. Threading his way through the menacing wartime streets of Berlin, he wears a target on his back as he prepares to give his all for both goals.